Also by
MARIE ESTORGE
(penned under Marie Etienne)

Storkbites: A Memoir

*Confessions of a Bi-Polar
Mardi Gras Queen*

in
the
middle
of
otherwise

a novel

marie estorge

Alluvium Books

FIRST EDITION

Designed by David Provolo

Library of Congress Cataloging-in-Publication Data has been applied for.

ISBN 978-0-9748474-2-9

For Avery and Burgess Stratford

2009

ON A TYPICAL Saturday morning on your average, oak-lined suburban
street forty-five minutes' drive east of San Francisco, birds chirp over the
piercing rev of the neighbor's leaf blower. The aroma of freshly ground,
organic coffee beans lingers in the air. Unwashed bowls with traces of oat-
meal are stacked unapologetically in the sink. Beds are left unmade—one
sticky and rumpled after a quick, but fervent love-making. Jenny is running late for a yoga class while her husband, Jerrod, sits in the other room
at his grand piano, his fingers dancing up and down the ivory and black
keys, coaxing, she believes, the most exquisite music from the instrument.

Jenny leans against the edge of the sofa and hurriedly braids her long,
curly blond hair. Daniel, her three-year-old son, bounces on the plush down
cushions in riotous laughter at the ongoing war between Wile E. Coyote
and the Road Runner. After securing her hair tie, Jenny unscrews the cap
on the bottle of Amoxicillin she has tucked in the pocket of her hoodie.

"Daniel, look at mommy," she says, hoping he'll cooperate.

When he sees the dropper filled with the chalky medicine, he scoots
to the edge of the sofa and grabs his Spiderman action figure to protect
himself. His Spiderman jammies have crusty, pink smears and drips across
the sleeves and shoulders from him having pulled his head away in her
repeated attempts over the week to get him to sit still for his medicine.

"I know, right?" she says, crossing her eyes and sticking out her
tongue. "This stuff is the absolute worst." She pretends to gag, and he
giggles. "But look," she says, holding up the bottle. "It's almost empty.
Home stretch, sweetie pie."

He covers his mouth with his dirty sleeve and shakes his head. She
moves to block his view of the television.

"You don't want your ear to start hurting again, do you?" she asks.
"On the count of three?" On the count of two he opens his mouth. "Good,

sweetie. Now go to the bathroom at the commercial break. Otherwise, you might have another accident."

Daniel's eyes fix again on Wile E. Coyote as the cartoon character sets up another catapult. Bam! Smashed under another boulder, only his feet stick out from the red rock.

"Earth to Daniel. Do you copy?" she asks over her son's uproarious laughter. He wipes a drip of antibiotic on his sleeve and nods as he bounces up and down. She grabs the end of her thick braid and tickles his nose with it. He squirms and giggles. She tickles his ears until he nudges her hand away. Jenny smiles and plants a kiss on his head. "I love you, you little whippersnapper."

He looks at her, points to his chest, crosses his arms, and then points to Jenny. *I love you.* One of his preschool teachers had taught the students a few words and phrases. Jenny signs *I love you* and blows him a kiss.

Now, standing at the piano bench, a rolled yoga mat under her arms, Jenny waits for Jerrod to sense her presence. She always hesitates to leave Daniel in his father's care when he is playing the piano. The moment Jerrod sits down, he tunes out the entire world. It practically takes a magnitude 7.5 earthquake to break his concentration when he is working on a new piece. But Daniel is finally feeling better. Jenny needs, and truthfully, has earned a couple of hours' freedom. Surely somewhere in the definitive parenting rule book, it states that after a week confined to a house with a cranky, feverish child (while also answering a barrage of work emails) a parent is allowed some personal reset time. She isn't like Jerrod. He seems to manage the constant demands and lack of sleep as if it is a perfectly natural state of being. She tickles his neck with nails she'd let Daniel paint hot pink. Jerrod startles and traps her lingering fingers between his shoulder and stubbly chin.

"Gotcha!" he says. His warm green eyes always devastate her.

"I'm heading out," she says, leaning against him. "Will you try to get Daniel to drink something to keep him hydrated? I gave him his meds."

"Will do." He pulls her in for a lingering kiss, a kiss that says he's still, and will always be, fervently in love with her. As her body responds, she pulls away.

"Hold that thought, my dear. I'm late." She starts to turn away and says, "Please keep Daniel inside. I think it's going to be a scorcher today. I don't want him to overheat, or else he might relapse."

"Yeah, yeah. I've got this." He glances at the sheet music and grabs a black pen bearing the name of his law office. She watches as he draws a circle around a tight cluster of musical notes. The page is dotted with marks. To her untrained eye, all of the markings—the dots, dashes, bars, numbers, notes, and lines—look like gobbledygook. She is forever amazed that her husband creates such incredible sounds out of these meaningless marks.

"Really, keep an eye on him," she says. "You know how you get when you're in the *zone*."

"Go, already," he says and taps the pen against his lips. "We'll be fine. I promise."

Jenny wavers at the garage door. She listens to Daniel's giggles over the loud television and the piano. That rascal has turned up the volume again. She pauses, nagged by the feeling that she has forgotten something or that something is just not right. *Quit worrying*, she tells herself. *Make a break for it while you have the chance.* She hesitates a moment longer before pressing the automatic garage opener. The large illuminated button, white when installed, is now stained with Daniel's fingerprints. "Lift me, Mommy, so I can press the button," he always asks, even if her arms are filled with bags.

As the garage door opens, she is immediately assaulted by the piercing sound of a leaf blower. She jogs unnoticed, hopefully, to the edge of the driveway to pick up their newspaper. On the curb near her mailbox, there is something square and brown. A wallet. She picks it up and starts to call out to her neighbor to ask if he has dropped it. His back is facing her as he blows the dried, fallen needles of a towering redwood into a pile. *Whatever happened to using a simple rake?* Last week she signed the petition that was circulating around town to ban those noxious, annoying blowers. The cause was gaining momentum. She smiles, feeling hopeful. She glances at the California drivers license photo. She doesn't recognize the man as her neighbor. She jogs back to her car. She will deal with the wallet after her yoga class.

The clock on the Volvo's dashboard is set five minutes ahead. Even so, she knows yoga starts in ten minutes. Saturday morning classes are always full. Most people are usually nice enough to make room for a latecomer, but some act as if sliding their mat over a foot or two is the greatest imposition in the world.

She quickly snaps in her seat buckle, puts the car into reverse, and remembers the Wine and Art Festival. *Damn.* Locust Street will be closed. Parking and traffic will be impossible. She figures that if she detours down Main Street, parks on Second, then sprints, she will just make her class. She lifts her foot off the brake and presses on the gas. Her back tires hit something and she slams on the brakes. *Shit!* She prays she hasn't just run over the neighbor's cat who is always prowling the neighborhood. Hopefully, it is just a ball—one of the neighbor's soccer balls that are constantly finding their way into her yard or driveway. She pulls forward, shifts the car into park, and unbuckles her seatbelt, praying she hadn't blown a tire.

As she steps out of the car and approaches the rear bumper, Jenny looks for a flattened ball. No cat, please, she says to herself. She stops. Gasps. "Oh, no, no, no," she screams. Daniel is splayed out on his back, his head turned to the left, eyes wide open as if staring at something curious in the neighbor's yard. His foot is pinned underneath the back tire. There is no movement. No crying or whimpering. Her screams reach decibels greater than the leaf-blower and the piano. The neighbor, his wife and their three children, and, finally, Jerrod come running over to find Jenny on her knees, trying in vain to pull her son out from underneath the tire.

"What's going on?" Jerrod says. He is panting as he comes around to the rear bumper. He looks down, the panic on his face suddenly mirroring Jenny's. "Oh, fuck! Someone call 911." He doesn't notice that their neighbor is already on her cell phone describing the situation for the dispatcher while also trying to shush her young daughter who keeps asking if the boy is still alive.

Jerrod grabs Jenny's arm. "Stop tugging on him. Don't move him." He pushes her out of the way; all of the tenderness from earlier is gone.

She crawls back a few feet and stares into her son's unblinking eyes, his pupils fully dilated. "Wake up, sweetie," she coos, helplessly. "Daddy's going to pull you out. You'll be fine." *Blink, Daniel. Let Mommy know you can hear me.* She stretches her fingers to reach his soft, sticky hand that is still clutching Spiderman. Her eyes blur with tears.

In a haze, she hears Jerrod yell, "Has someone called fucking 911 yet?" His voice is off-kilter. Strange. "I can't dislodge him," he says. "What should I do?"

jenny
2011

IN A SEALED BOX at the back of her closet are the grief counseling books that were recommended to Jerrod and her by their son's pediatrician two years ago. There are books from her mother-in-law Rhonda that promised to help grieving parents and children find their way from loss to healing. The shared experiences and wisdom held no balm for Jenny's pain. She couldn't, it seemed, find her way to forgiveness, healing, inner peace, and certainly not joy. There were gleams of hope now and then, but only fleeting sparks. They passed as quickly as a shooting star, and once gone, it was as if they had never existed.

Jenny towel-dried her hair and teased out the curls around her temples and ears. She looked away from the mirror, and quickly turned back to check her reflection. Each time, she'd startle and smile at this stranger with a Meg Ryan bob. If she'd known how giddy—however fleeting—she'd feel once freed from the weight and bother of her mid-waist curls, she would have lopped them off years ago. She rolled her shoulders and shivered at the unfamiliar sensation of burdens lifted.

Today was the day. What a relief it would be.

She stole a glimpse of her husband in the reflection of the bathroom mirror as he flipped through the tie rack that hung in their closet next to the tuxedo he'd rented for their upcoming Alaskan cruise. He stopped on a solid teal tie, ran his thumb over the silk fabric, then moved to the next. Two ties slipped off the rack and fell to the carpet. As he bent down to retrieve them, she shook her head. *Just pick a damn tie, any tie*, she wanted to say. *It's not as if it's the most important decision of your life.* She sighed, ashamed of the resentment that had consumed her these last two years.

He held up a gold and blue tie—one Jenny had given him when they were still exchanging gifts—but then flipped through several more. She held her breath. He went back to the teal one. Finally, he threw a striped one in the overnight bag on their bed. Next came a belabored decision on a shirt. Then the suit. There was a time he would have solicited her help in assembling a deposition ensemble. A time she would have stood before him in her lacy panties and bra, or perhaps naked and rosy from her shower, and together they would have considered several ties—testing each against his suit and exquisite, angular features. But now, she checked her watch. If he didn't leave soon, it would be too late to call her mother-in-law *and* see Brodie before he took his daughter to school. She applied foundation to conceal the circles under her eyes. Jerrod joined her in the bathroom to collect his toothbrush and toiletries.

"What time is your flight?" she asked as he flipped and closed the plastic lids of various brand and off-brand dental floss containers in the top drawer. He inspected each spool. He had to find the container with an adequate supply of floss for an overnight trip. *God forbid he go one night without flossing.*

"Nine."

He snapped the lid shut on the fourth package of dental floss—the winner—and grabbed his travel-size tube of toothpaste and mouthwash. She removed one of the recycled sandwich bags from under the sink.

Meeting her eyes, briefly, he said, "Thanks. I always forget." She waited for him to add, "By the way, happy anniversary. Sorry I won't be in town, but we can celebrate on the cruise." He nodded at their reflections in the mirror, two strangers now, and said, "Well, I think I've got every-thing." No. He hadn't remembered. She went to the separate bathroom, shut the door, and stayed there until she heard him clear his throat and say, "See you tomorrow night."

Not likely, she thought as she covered her mouth to stifle a cry. She exited the bathroom and listened for the opening of the garage door and the rev of the car engine. When he was gone, she hurried to her nightstand and removed the letter she'd stashed between the marked-up pages of *One Hundred Years of Solitude*. She set the letter next to her purse and the bulking yellow envelope addressed to Locks of Love. Her fingers traced the smile on her son's face in the framed photograph that stood on her nightstand as she did every morning and evening. She sat on the unmade bed and reached for her cell phone. Her mother-in-law picked up on the first ring.

In a chirping voice, Rhonda said, "Good morning, lovey." Dogs barked in the background.

"I hear those rascals. Tell them it's their favorite aunt calling," she said, trying to sound cheerful.

"Let's see how much you love them after I ship them all to you."

They both laughed. "Are Mickey and his pack misbehaving?"

"That devil Mickey chewed up another one of my patio cushions. He's about to earn himself an extended stay at the doggy day care." Since Rhonda's second husband died six years ago, she'd adopted a handful of strays and closed off the second and third floors of her Pacific Heights home.

"You know you'd miss the little rat. What would the others do without their ringleader?"

"That's certainly true." Rhonda let out a succession of loud, phlegmy coughs, purportedly the dregs of a nasty winter cold. "I hear someone is sporting a new haircut," she said, once her coughing had subsided. "You had such beautiful curly hair."

Jerrod had tattled. Jenny looked at the two envelopes beside her. On the larger envelope, she'd applied eight *Forever* stamps and drawn a sunflower next to her name. It pleased her to think of children running around a playground wearing a wig made out of her curly hair and fit to their small heads. A gang of Shirley Temples.

"Well, it's still curly," she said, "just shorter, which will be easier in summer. You know what they say . . . it always grows back." She cringed. It wasn't like her to take such a sarcastic tone with her mother-in-law.

"You're absolutely right," Rhonda said, light heartedly.

Jenny sat through another round of coughing and checked her watch, conflicted about whether to rush off the call or enjoy it, as it was most likely their last.

"It was funny, though," Jenny said after Rhonda quieted. "The braid was so thick, I couldn't cut through it. Not even with my sewing scissors. I had to ask Jerrod to help, which initially he refused to do."

"There is something about men and long hair," Rhonda said. "Rapunzel, Rapunzel, let down your hair."

Jenny laughed. "I told him, 'Look, I've already cut a third the way through the braid. It's too late to stop now.' He finally sawed it off with one of those fancy Wüsthoff knives you gave us as a wedding gift." Jenny told her how he'd handed her the braid and returned to his piano without a word. She'd gone to the bathroom and done her best, snipping here and there to shape the ends into a flattering pixie. Later, she stood at his piano and asked, "So what do you think?" He cocked his head, waited a beat, and said, "It's cute on you. You know I prefer long hair. But if you like it—" She'd waited for him to finish his sentence, but he simply turned back to his music.

"I'm sure you look adorable," Rhonda said, and clapped her hands, yelling at Lucy to get her paws off the coffee table. "Are you excited about Sunday?"

"Sunday . . . oh, yes. I can't wait for the cruise and to see Alaska," Jenny said. The lie caused a spasm of unease in her stomach. "Jerrod's tux is hanging in our closet and I'm going to do some last-minute shopping tomorrow. I'm sure you've already packed."

"Yes, ma'am. All done. Though I'm not looking forward to saying goodbye to my little critters."

Jenny's shoulders sank. As much as she loved Rhonda, she was thankful she wouldn't be stuck on a ship for nine days listening to Rhonda's endless stories about her beloved dogs.

"Well, I'd better head off to work."

"Yes, well, one second lovey. You know the last thing I want to do is butt in, but . . ."

Jenny held her breath.

"I was thinking this vacation might be the chance for you and Jerrod to try again. It's not too late. Just think of it, a Valentine's baby. Otherwise, you both might regret not—"

The second half of the sentence came out in such a rush that Jenny had to replay it in her head to make sure she'd heard correctly. *Not giving it another chance.* She bit her bottom lip as she slowly exhaled.

"Don't mind me," Rhonda said, "I shouldn't interfere, but I worry about you."

"I know you mean well. Maybe the sea gods will work their magic. I love you."

"Love you, too. Call me tomorrow."

"Will do."

Jenny closed her eyes and imagined for a moment that first flutter deep inside your belly when you know it's really happening, then months later the kicking and movements, and finally the warm, pink, and beautiful bundle placed in your arms. She couldn't let her mind venture any further. Besides, getting pregnant required sex, or at least some transfer of semen, and that bodily fluid hadn't come within yards of her since the accident. Knowing how Jerrod felt about her, he'd no doubt booked a room with bunk beds. Problem solved. She was surprised that he'd even agreed to Rhonda's offer to take them on a cruise. But then again, it was his mom. Jenny grabbed her purse and headed to the garage.

She hurried across town, slowing down only on streets marked as a school zone. Soon the painted wooden sign to Brodie's subdivision came into view. As she turned onto Magnolia Lane, her mood improved. She had loved this neighborhood even before realizing it was Brodie's. The utility poles had been removed and the cables buried underground. There were sidewalks, which her street lacked, and a trail head to Mt. Diablo's open space—where several cars were already parked. Three mountain bikers were traversing the highest ridge, a dog leading their pack. This state park with its miles of crisscrossing trails made the abutting properties very desirable to home buyers. It was more than she and Jerrod could afford when they'd first moved forty miles east of San Francisco to Hidden Oaks. They'd turned down Rhonda's offer to help them with the down payment for something larger, something a little further from the BART tracks. While she never admitted it, she did grimace the first time a train zoomed by as they stood on the lawn, watching Daniel kick a ball around.

Spotting the BMW in the driveway of the rancher, she relaxed her shoulders. Her eyes scanned the windows as she drove slowly past Brodie's house, hoping to catch a glimpse of him.

She had nothing to offer this man. It was not that she needed or expected something tangible or physical from Brodie. Writing these anonymous letters had felt as if she were writing to a pen pal, someone on the other side of the world. The thought of him taking the time to open and read her letters, if indeed he did, made her feel as if she mattered. Maybe he even looked forward to receiving her envelopes and spotting his name in that familiar, school-girl cursive. Or maybe she was simply the kooky woman who'd found and returned his wallet—someone whom he and his wife laughed about, or pitied. Regardless, she wanted to feel a connection to a man, a man strong and present. Someone not acutely absent, not mechanical or cold like Jerrod. It didn't matter that this fleeting connection was problematic. That he knew her only through her letters. Or that she knew of him only what she'd spied from her car or by stalking him on the internet. He was a man, who by all appearances, seemed kind and even-tempered. Alive. A husband (but not her husband), a father (but not her son's father), a man grounded in the present, she assumed—not in memories or regrets or resentments. A man you could count on to do the right thing. Be there when needed.

She made a U-turn at the next intersection and parked opposite Brodie's house under the lush, green canopy of the saucer magnolias lining the street. Cracking her window, she breathed in the fragrance of the honeysuckle climbing and threading a nearby scalloped fence. The scent reminded her of childhood: another school year ending, and more importantly, another summer vacation beginning. The sweet nectar of freedom.

She fingered the orange silk scarf laying on the passenger seat. A gift from Rhonda who had brought it back from Thailand a year ago and presented it to Jenny on her last birthday. The combination of the orange and silk was believed to help mend a broken heart. She rolled her eyes, thinking, *if only this were true, I wouldn't be parked outside this house like some pathetic wackadoodle.*

She should simply drive away now, she knew. Give this man and his family their privacy. She meant no harm. Surely, he sensed that from her letters. As she was thinking this, a fly buzzed by her ear. She swiped at her neck—her skin still feeling naked without the shield of hair. Her eyes tracked the buzzing until she spotted the fly hovering near the hatchback window next to her son's fading stickers: trucks, dragons, dinosaurs, cars, and action figures. Someone had written "Wash me" on the dusty windshield. She rolled down the rear windows, hoping the annoying fly would be lured away by the sweet honeysuckle.

The garage door opened. She ducked slightly and watched Brodie. Usually, he alone took his daughter to school, but today his wife also climbed into the sedan with the daughter trudging behind. With their fiery red hair and petite figures, they looked like sisters rather than mother and daughter. Jenny felt envy inflate in her chest. Brodie backed out of the driveway. His car rolled parallel to Jenny's. Their eyes met. She cringed, hoping he wouldn't roll down the window to ask if she needed help. Really . . . where would she begin?

brodie

BRACING HIMSELF for the five AM bitter chill, Brodie zipped up his hoodie and slipped on his headlamp. Ginger, the family's yellow Labrador, nudged his legs. As soon as the kitchen slider door opened, Ginger shot past him. Brodie stepped onto the redwood deck. A circle of light from his headlamp illuminated the back lawn—peppered with a fresh crop of gopher mounds.

Ginger barked with impatience as Brodie shoved the redwood gate at the top where the wood always caught. The gate opened with a splintering groan, and the dog darted past the trail marker leading to the fossil-lined ridge of Mt. Diablo, golden-brown now in late May. Brodie lost sight of her in the darkness and hoped she wouldn't venture beyond his call.

A few windmills and stretches to loosen his stiff back. He checked his watch. Less than nineteen hours to sell the last five life insurance policies to make his annual quota. Otherwise, it was adios to his ten-thousand-dollar bonus. Goodbye to the last of his pride. He'd be forced to admit to Karen that he'd depleted Sasha's college fund and missed the deadline for the dorm deposit. And even after pilfering her savings, he still might not be able to keep his agency afloat and their house out of foreclosure. He adjusted the headlamp and tried to clear his head. He needed to strategize his day and figure out a solution to their financial problems. Instead, his thoughts circled around the same cul-de-sac. *Why are you such a fuck up? You've somehow managed to do two things right and you're about to lose those. What's the end goal here, Brodie? Are you trying to screw up your life completely?*

He started to jog, watching the trail for rocks and tree roots so, God forbid, he didn't twist his ankle again. Ginger barked in the distance. Picking up his pace, he called out for her and whistled loud enough to stir every creature within miles of the oak-studded hills, including a full

19

contingent of crickets. Finally, he spotted the top of Ginger's golden head as she ripped through the tall grass.

"Stay close, girl. No skunks today." He patted her back and felt the burrs and stickers that would end up in his boxers, no matter how often he'd asked Karen not to throw his shorts in the wash with the towels she used on the dog.

Picking up speed, he thought about yesterday's call with the banker. He had been flipping through past due notices and junk mail as he slumped over his desk when he stopped on one of those No Closing Cost Mortgage refinance flyers. An opportunity, possibly, to stave off creditors since it was unlikely he'd earn his bonus this year. He'd allowed his hopes to run amok. He'd let himself imagine the bank might even consolidate their credit card debt into the new loan and permit Brodie and his wife to cash out for another ten or fifteen thousand. He had closed his office door and dialed the toll-free number. Initially, the banker had been so friendly, so eager, until he ran Brodie's credit report. "Sixty thousand in credit card debt." He sucked in a breath and loudly exhaled. Apparently, he was hoping for a quick commission. "At least your home isn't underwater . . . assuming the property is actually worth eight-fifty. Going to be tricky. Let's see if we can get a preapproval."

Brodie had sat at his desk and doodled on a past-due water notice, his hope fading with each passing minute.

"Yeah, no, the preapproval was denied," he said. "We can still complete the application and hope underwriting will approve it. But I'd hate to see you waste—"

"Don't bother." He closed his eyes and massaged his forehead. He knew he should give Karen a true read on their financial situation. The thought of telling his wife the truth and the inevitable marriage-ending fight made him want to cry like a coward.

This was all my doing, he thought. He had waited until the last minute to start calling clients, stuffing the increasingly threatening letters from their mortgage company into his desk drawer. He had deluded himself that his brother would come through for him today. Despite Keith's assurances on Monday, Brodie knew he wouldn't get around to buying the last five life insurance policies. Keith always meant well, but he was flaky. Presumably his offer at the time was sincere. It was always, "Yes, don't worry. I will—" and then "Damn, I forgot." Forgot. . . like the twenty grand Brodie lent him two years ago that he conveniently *forgot* to repay even though he'd asked him about it numerous times. Granted, not recently. Being put in the humiliating position of having to ask him again to repay the loan infuriated Brodie. He couldn't bring himself to do it. What if he needed it more than me? Brodie thought. Although that hardly seemed likely as Brodie was pretty desperate. But he could hear his brother say, "I'll get it to you. You worry too much. Things always work out." Yet, whenever life pushed Keith off the cliff, he managed to grab hold of a tree limb to break his fall. He simply dusted himself off and charged toward the next adventure. Brodie? Not so lucky. Not so brave. Whereas Keith obviously enjoyed taking risks, Brodie had made it his profession to insure against risks. Maybe if life had handed him a second, third, fourth chance as it had with his brother, he would have felt more comfortable taking chances. But life hadn't.

His jog turned into a hard run as if he were trying to outpace his worries. His chest pounded. He hadn't even hit the first respectable hill. He turned right at the century-old oak tree that was slowly being reabsorbed into the earth. An owl gave out an out eerie shriek, somewhere unseen among the branches. Ginger brushed against his sweats. "Watch out, girl." He hugged the edge of the path to avoid tripping over her. She bounded off, and in the beam of Brodie's headlamp, he saw where she was headed. Fifty feet to the right of the trail sat a stagnant pond of muddy water. "Ginger! No!"

She stopped and looked back at him as if deciding how much trouble she'd be in if she defied him. Undeterred, she bounded straight ahead for the pond. Brodie held no sway over the women in his life. She would never think to patently disobey Karen. *Karen.* He pictured his wife, lying naked in their warm bed, her beautiful face buried in the pillow. He imagined pulling the comforter over their heads, snuggling against her warm curves. "Who's your friend?" she'd ask in a sleepy, sing-song voice as he pressed against her body.

Ginger caught up with Brodie and shook foul-smelling water all over his sweats. In his attempt to avoid the spray, he didn't notice a branch until his forehead collided with the limb.

Splayed out on the trail like a six-foot-seven Gumby, he opened his eyes and blinked, unsure for a moment of where he was. The silver sliver of a moon, barely visible from behind the clouds, hung above him. He felt around: dirt, leaves, twigs, roots, and a sharp piece of glass or plastic. *Damn it.* He had broken the lens of his headlamp, a gift from Sasha for his fortieth birthday. He sat up, greeted by a sharp pain in his lower back.

Ginger prodded him as if to say, Get up. Let's go.

"Hold on, girl."

Brodie's head throbbed with the sudden movement. He touched the tender peak of a bump on his forehead. Yes, the branch. The collision. As his eyes slowly adjusted to the darkness, Ginger nudged his shoulder again. He sighed and lay back in the dirt. He had no idea what he was going to do if their financial situation didn't improve. Everything, his life, specifically, felt so unrelentingly grim. He stared up at the sky, at the faint stars. Pebbles and twigs bit at his back. The dog, damp and stinking, settled beside him, her heavy breathing lending its sound to those of the night: trees rustling in concert with the damp breeze, mosquitoes buzzing at his face, crickets drumming for mates. He heard something approach. A deer, he prayed. He lay still. There had been recent mountain lion sightings in the vicinity, reports of missing pets. He grabbed Ginger's collar, squeezed his eyes shut and hoped their scents wouldn't betray them.

Whatever it was came incrementally closer. Taking shallow breaths, Brodie listened to the crunching of dried leaves. Ginger tried to stand, but he pulled on her collar.

"Shush, girl. Sit still."

She let out a long growl, warding off, he hoped, whatever lurked in the darkness. Her growl turned into a bark. He pulled her closer and said sternly, "Stay" as she fought his hold. She listened, a rare feat. The animal took off, and Ginger settled down. Brodie's shoulders relaxed, and he drew a deep breath.

Now that it seemed the danger had passed, he envisioned Ginger and himself being mauled by a mountain lion. He imagined Karen answering the door, a park ranger holding what was left of his running shoes and headlamp and Ginger's collar. Karen, falling hysterically into the ranger's arms. Who among their divorced friends would be the first to swoop in? The thought of her dating, or worse, sleeping with another, man made Brodie want to puke. The upside to getting devoured, limb by limb, would be that Karen and Sasha's financial circumstances would improve exponentially, thanks to his life insurance. It wouldn't matter anymore whether or not Keith would come through for him today or whether he earned his ten-thousand-dollar bonus.

Hey, mountain lion, he thought. Breakfast is served. Disemboweled by a hundred-pound animal wasn't really what he wanted. But neither did he want to divide the contents of their home, twenty years of memories, into three separate U-Hauls and find himself unemployed and alone, sitting in a crappy apartment in Concord scanning the jobs ads while eating Top Ramen.

He touched his tender forehead and shifted his weight to dislodge the pebbles and twigs biting through his clothes into his skin. He thought about the banker's advice yesterday, "If you pay off your credit cards and don't charge on them for a couple of months, it'll improve your credit score and you can reapply." Right, buddy. And where in hell was he supposed to get sixty grand?

"What happened to you?" Karen asked, sitting up in bed and stretching. She had crazy bedhead, her hair a fiery explosion of red curls, but his wife was still the prettiest and, admittedly, the only woman Brodie had ever had the pleasure of seeing naked, other than women in movies or magazines.

He shook his head and grimaced from the pain.

"Ginger. And a damn tree."

"We're meeting with Sasha's principal this morning."

He moaned, slid out of his clothes, and grabbed his phone. He trudged past the stack of Zig Ziglar books he had bought last Christmas.

Another failed New Year's resolution. In five months, he'd only glanced at the table of contents of the sales guru's "See You at the Top," yet he was up to date on the latest Stephen King title. In the bathroom, he leaned against the marble vanity and checked his phone. Still no response from Keith. He skimmed through his long list of unread emails and opened one from the company. The subject line: "Unblemished and Blue Just for You." *Oh, how poetic.* A photo of a secluded beach with quiet blue water appeared. The text below the smooth white sand said, "This is what you'll see from your window." Yesterday, the teaser had given the temperature: "A balmy eighty-two degrees." If he made his sales quotas plus ten additional policies, Karen, Sasha, and Brodie would be flown to some undisclosed, obviously tropical, all-expense-paid vacation. He hadn't made the quota plus ten in three years, and he would have been grateful to simply make the quota. He grabbed the canister of shaving gel. It dispensed one speck of blue gel. He bent to check the lower cabinet and felt a wrench in his side. It felt as if an invisible hand were stabbing a serrated knife into his ribs. He dropped to his knees, his eyes squinting in pain. When the pain subsided, he gently opened the bathroom door.

"Karen," he called out. "Did you buy more shaving gel?"

No answer. He hobbled into the shower with his razor. He just wanted to have this quick meeting with the principal and listen to her praise Sasha for her Stanford dive scholarship. Then arrive at the office to find Andrea had canceled his morning appointments because Keith was stopping by to complete the five life insurance applications and to give him a check. That was exactly how he wanted this day to go.

jenny

WHEN THE TAILLIGHTS of Brodie's BMW had disappeared around the corner, Jenny got out of the car and picked a dewy flower from the honeysuckle shrub. She held it to her nose and inhaled its scent deeply. On a morning much like this one, she'd introduced her son to the magic of the honeysuckle. She'd knelt down and showed him how to snip the green end and gently pulled the thread until a drop of nectar appeared. He'd been skeptical initially. Crinkled his adorable nose and shook his head as if she were playing a trick on him. To prove it wasn't a prank, she licked the drop and murmured *mmm*. After she'd demonstrated the process twice more, curiosity won him over. The surprise and joy on his sweet face was painful to recall. Enthralled, he would have denuded the entire bush had she let him. She now held the spent flower in her palm, and wondered, *why does the universe create something so beautiful if it's not meant to last?* The flower slid from her hand as she climbed into her car.

Traffic was light as she drove across town. She had plenty of time. She'd arrive first at his office and drop off the letter. When he got to work, her final letter would be waiting for him. She tried to ignore the guilt of burdening this man with her despair. The empty parking lot was enjoying a restorative silence before the businesses opened. Jenny slipped on her sunglasses and searched her purse for the letter. She checked under and between the seats, thinking it had slipped out of her purse. She struck the steering wheel. The letter must be sitting on the bed with the other envelope, forgotten in haste. She'd had it in her hands, then set it down to call Rhonda. Checking her watch, she knew she'd be cutting it close, but she put the car in reverse and drove back home.

Before she reached her front door, the neighbor—Emily, or was it

Emma? Emma, she decided, came power-walking down her driveway and cut across Jenny's lawn.

"Excuse me," Emma called out, waving eagerly. "Excuse me! Do you have a second?"

"No, sorry," Jenny said, shaking her head as the neighbor continued jogging toward her. "I'm in a hurry." Jenny's hands trembled as she fumbled with the keys.

"Please wait a sec."

Emma reached the step as Jenny opened the door and started to step inside. The woman's shoe caught on a brick and she tumbled. Instinctively, Jenny reached out to break her fall. They both stumbled, grabbing ahold of each other for balance. When they found their footing, Emma—reeking of cigarette smoke—unclutched Jenny and said, "Sorry about that. I've turned into a bit of a klutz." She laughed nervously and tugged on her tight navy slacks.

Jenny discreetly brushed her wrist against her nose and tried not to make a judgment about the fact that her neighbor smelled as if she'd already smoked a carton of cigarettes and it was barely 8:00 AM. She stepped over the threshold.

"I only came back to grab something. I'm late—"

"It's just that Keith and I are wondering," the neighbor said, peeking around Jenny into the house. She pointed at the piano in the living room. "We hear your husband playing and it's kind of—"

"I really can't talk about this right now. I don't mean to be rude, but you've caught me at a bad time."

The neighbor fiddled with a silver, heart-shaped pendant around her neck and nodded. "I'm sorry. Another time then," she said, turning away as Jenny shut the door. After grabbing the two letters, Jenny checked the peephole and living room window to make sure Emma hadn't changed her mind and returned, waiting at the door to discuss Jerrod's obnoxiously loud and late-into-the evenings piano playing.

Jenny pulled into the parking lot of Brodie's office complex for the second time this morning. Beside the old RV in the rear lot that she had noticed on other occasions, there were two cars parked out back, but neither was Brodie's as far as she could tell. She climbed out of her car and looked at his name and company logo on the front window of his office. She stared at the name. *Brodie Marshall* was painted in large red and blue letters. *Brodie*, an uncommon first name. The shades on the window and glass door were still down. She heard a baby wailing as she approached the building. A woman was yelling into the phone. Jenny froze and hid the letter behind her back. Her skin prickled as she listened to the baby's crying over the tirade of the woman. Did they need help? There were no other detectible voices or sounds. She stepped closer, pressed her ear to the door, hoping her silhouette wasn't visible through the shade.

All babies cried inconsolably at times, she told herself, trying not to panic. She had never believed those parents who swore otherwise. Her son had wailed at least once a day in infancy. So much so that at times when Jerrod was away on business, she'd fantasized about locking herself in the bathroom and sliding under a tub of water to block out the noise. But how long had this baby been crying? She didn't want to be one of those judgmental bystanders who made mothers more nervous and upset under scrutiny than they already felt. She started to drop the letter in the mail slot, but then knelt and looked through the opening under the metal faceplate.

A dark-haired woman—very young, early-twenties or possibly late teens—was sitting at a desk, bouncing an infant in one arm while holding a cellphone in the other hand. The woman shifted in her chair, cooing at the baby between blasts of angry words. Afraid she'd startle the woman or get caught eavesdropping, Jenny carefully lowered the metal plate and started to back away from the door.

"Excuse me. May I help you?"

Jenny spun around. Towering over her stood Brodie. She hid the envelope behind her back as he said, "My apologies. I didn't mean to startle you." She noticed a red bump in the center of his forehead. Unable to think of a reasonable excuse for peeping through his mail slot, she stood there petrified.

"I'm Brodie Marshall," he said, extending his hand, which she quickly shook. "Are you looking for someone?"

She discretely folded the envelope into quarters. "I'm, I'm not, I didn't mean to . . . I'm dropping off my boss's premium," she stammered. "But I'm late for work." She handed him the crumpled envelope and ran to her car. As she jammed her key into the ignition, she heard him call out, "Wait. Are you—"

The engine revved and just as she threw it into reverse and was about to press on the gas, she stopped herself. Her breath suspended. If she backed out without looking and he'd chased after her, she might very well run him over. She looked in the mirror, afraid she was going to see him coming up behind her car. But he stood at the office door—a safe distance away. She expected to see him holding a phone. Surely, he'd call the police or snap a photo of her license plate. But he just stood there looking dumbfounded with his arms by his side, the crumpled envelope in one hand.

She drove two blocks before turning onto a side street. She pulled the car over. Her chest pounding. What possible excuse was there for sitting in front of this man's house this morning and for dozens of other mornings? For the letters? For stalking him like some morbidly obsessed woman? And more importantly, she could have accidentally killed him in his parking lot moments ago. She had nearly failed, once again, to look behind the car to check that it was safe to back up.

brodie

BRODIE, KAREN, AND SASHA arrived at the high school at seven-forty-five, according to his Timex. He had sold his Rolex last month to pay the property taxes, and told Karen that it had felt too pretentious, especially in this post-Enron economy. It was a lie, like others growing between them.

Parked in a space reserved for visitors, he watched two maintenance workers hop the red curb in their battered golf cart. The driver swerved to the right, while the passenger leaned over to scoop up an empty soda can and shot for a nearby trash barrel. They were crowing and talking as if they were two old friends heading to the first tee, and he found himself envious of their uncomplicated jobs, their easy camaraderie. Since his earliest memory, Brodie had considered Keith his best friend. Lately, though, Keith didn't seem to understand or appreciate how important a role he played in Brodie's life. It was always, "Can't talk. Gotta go. No time, bro." Sometimes Brodie feared Keith was drinking again, and that was why his brother had pulled away. Yet, Keith had sworn after the last humiliating fall off the wagon, right after they'd confirmed Emma's third and last pregnancy, that he was done. To save his marriage and family, his sobriety was non-negotiable.

Brodie reached for his phone and that slight motion caused a sharp pain in his back. His head still hurt despite four Advil. He took shallow breaths to keep from groaning. Karen was seated beside him and Sasha sat in the back next to his briefcase. He was scraping his right thumbnail against what remained of his left thumbnail, completely unaware until Karen, who was singing along with Adele, reached over to quiet his hands with a gentle squeeze. Sasha smacked her gum, blasting the car with its winter freshness while her nails (black, this week) tapped on her phone. Brodie glanced in the rearview mirror and caught her eyes. She pulled her ponytail taut across her eyebrows so that her green eyes were canopied by a thick orange-red unibrow.

She yanked out her earbuds. "Why'd we have to get here so early?"" Because my day is jammed with appointments," Brodie said. "And I've got to meet with your uncle to sign the life insurance policies."

Her eyes rolled north and she dropped her ponytail. As her mother sang along to the radio, she leaned over her seat and changed the station.

"Your mother was listening to that song," he said, switching the station back to Adele. A sneer spread across her freckle-splattered face. Stanford's fall semester couldn't come soon enough.

Karen turned toward the mural painted on the wall outside of the library. The scene depicted a family of early California settlers panning for gold on the Sacramento River. Last year, a senior had been suspended after altering the painting. The kid got nailed after posting photos on Facebook. Though the bearded man's pants were now zipped and everything tucked into place—thanks to the leadership committee—if Brodie squinted, he could detect the faint outline of the man's junk. "Junk," he mumbled to himself with amusement.

Karen glanced at him. "What are you smiling about?"

"Later." He tapped the sloping tip of her nose. "It's time."

He grabbed the keys and hobbled out of the car, holding his back like a ninety-year-old man. Sasha looked at him and rolled her eyes.

"Why do you have to wear your pants pulled so high?" Sasha whispered, as they approached the front office. "You look like Pee-Wee Herman, and you need a haircut."

Brodie's black curls, greying rapidly like a second-term U.S. president, were weeks past due for a trim and tickled the back of his neck.

"Give me a break."

The scrutiny of a teenager was tough. When she looked away, he pushed down his belt to lower his pants half an inch and combed his fingers through his hair. Sasha tugged on the strap of her backpack, so jammed with binders, phone, swimsuit, towel, Gatorade, and an iPad that the zipper's teeth refused to engage, threatening to spill the contents at the office door's welcome mat. Brodie reached over and shoved the

Gatorade bottle and her iPad deeper into the pack.

"What are you doing?" She twisted away from him.

"If you lose your iPad, I can't afford to buy you another one."

"Right," she said, even though he was certain she had a better sense than Karen that he wasn't bullshitting. For some reason, he was more apt to complain to Sasha about their family's spending, the financial pressures he felt at the office, or the costs of her dive club tuition and travel for the out-of-state meets than he was to Karen. He supposed, honestly speaking, he was less concerned about disappointing or worrying his daughter than his wife.

Karen greeted the attendance secretary, a humorless woman who had ruled over decades of high school kids. She'd been the one to pull Brodie and his brother out of their classes to inform them that their mother had died. Now, she glanced up at his bruised forehead, offered no reaction, and said they were expected. Brodie, Karen, and Sasha followed in single file as she escorted them down the hall to the principal's office.

The principal stood waiting at the door. She extended her hand, a surprisingly knuckle-crunching handshake for such a petite woman.

"Mr. Marshall. Mrs. Marshall, it's a pleasure to meet you both." Her Texan accent was unexpected, given her South Asian ethnicity. Brodie smiled and noticed she didn't gape immediately at his height. She didn't say something dumb like, "Wow, you must have played basketball!"

They followed her past her office to a small conference room. Framed artwork—pen drawings, watercolors, collages, black and white photographs—presumably from some very talented students—adorned the walls. There were none of those mass-produced, sappy, inspirational posters with cute animals like the popular one from his childhood: *Hang in There Baby*. Once seated, Brodie noticed a thin folder labeled with Sasha's full name resting in the center of the table. He got a sudden feeling that Karen and he might have misconstrued the purpose of this meeting. The principal congratulated them on Sasha's admission to Stanford and her dive scholarship. Sasha reached into her backpack and dug out her phone. She wanted it understood that this was, no doubt, *Way Too Boring*. Brodie shook his head.

"I keep thinking there's a catch," he said, keeping his guilt over the unpaid housing deposit to himself. He'd find some way to pay it next week. At least that was his prayer.

Karen raked her tongue over her teeth, a habit that exposed her nervousness. "I just didn't realize time could pass so quickly." She petted Sasha's arm and to Brodie's disbelief, Sasha didn't brush away her hand.

"All right then." The principal secured a few stray strands of black hair behind her ears. "Sasha's AP French teacher says she saw your daughter signing your name, Mr. Marshall, on a school form." The principal removed a form printed on a light blue sheet from the folder. The signature scribbled on the last line did, in fact, resemble his. He didn't recall, however, signing any school forms recently, although his memory had been shit lately. Reading from the top, he saw it was a permission slip for students who had turned eighteen to verify their own absences for appointments or illness. Brodie started to deny having ever seen this form but felt Karen's hand touch his thigh, felt her fingers squeeze his leg.

"Yes, I saw Sasha give the form to my husband to sign," Karen said. "Maybe the teacher simply thought she saw Sasha signing here." Karen pointed to Brodie's name. "But she was actually signing here." She pointed to the student's signature box. He leaned back in his chair. His wife, he realized, could also lie with ease.

"Is that correct, Mr. Marshall?" The principal arched an eyebrow.

Brodie faked a cough and pain reverberated through him. A salty piece of bacon from breakfast wedged between molars, dislodged and traveled just past the reach of his tongue. He began coughing in earnest. "Pardon me," he managed to whisper, wiping his watering eyes and clenching his fist from the severe pain between his shoulder blades. The coughing ensued; every time he thought he was done, he started hacking again. Remembering the Gatorade bottle, he said, nearly inaudibly, to Sasha, "Pass me your bottle."

"What?"

He made a drinking gesture with his hand, pointed to her backpack.

"Gatorade," he squeaked out.

She shook her head and moved her backpack away.

"Give it to me."

She shook her head again.

"Give it to him," Karen said.

Defiance squatted in Sasha's wide eyes. She refused to budge.

"Now!" Karen said.

"No, Mom."

"Sasha," said the principal. "Is there a problem?"

"I don't know," Sasha mumbled.

The principal checked her watch. She walked over to a wall phone. "Natalie, will you—"

"No. Here . . ."

Sasha shoved the blue energy drink into her father's hand without looking up. He took a huge swig and gagged, nearly spraying a fruity vodka cocktail all over the principal's conference table. A stronger coughing fit ensued, accompanied by what felt like ten angry monkeys biting him in the back.

"Excuse me," he said, wiping his face. He took the bottle and his coughing into the hallway. What the hell, he thought, holding his side and looking around for a water fountain. Sweating ingloriously, he was in full-blown panic mode.

Kids were starting to arrive. A line of SUVs, sports cars, and sedans idled in the red zone all the way past the gym. Students yanked their backpacks and sports gear from trunks and hatchbacks while lifted Ford trucks, 4x4s, and crappy hand-me-down compacts driven by juniors and seniors bypassed the idling line to park in their unofficial, yet self-designated spots. Scanning these kids' young faces, Brodie wondered why it was his daughter who decided to sneak vodka into school today. Maybe she wasn't alone, but that wasn't his worry.

He walked up the hallway, oscillating between coughing and groaning, in search of a water fountain or bathroom. There were always rumors of incidents involving drugs, sex, and alcohol, and suspensions right before prom or graduation, but he never figured this would have been something Karen and he would face. The arriving students moved out of his path, giving this red-faced, hacking man a wide berth. He asked one kid, "Water fountain?"

The boy pointed toward the library. Under a framed poster of *Catcher in the Rye* was a water fountain covered in skateboarding stickers. He'd received a blast of emails from the school superintendent reminding students and parents that skateboards and BMX bikes were not allowed on campus. His coughing finally subsided. He started to pour the vodka-spiked Gatorade down the drain, but then figured what the fuck. He took a huge swig. The cocktail felt like heaven sliding down his throat. He poured out the rest and gargled with the warm fountain water before popping a mint from the tin he always carried.

"My apologies," he said to the principal upon his return. Sasha gambled a glance in his direction, but her attention quickly retreated to the safety of the floor. Karen took Brodie's hand in what might have looked like concern for his health, but judging by the vice grip of her fingers, it was a warning.

"Regarding this form," said the principal. "Is this your signature?"

If he said *no*, goodbye Stanford. But, *yes,* would mean depriving another kid, perhaps one more deserving, a spot among some of the top young minds in the country. *No*, might mean no sex for the next twenty years. *Yes*, would prove he had no more integrity than his wife and daughter. *No*, would deny Sasha the one Get Out of Jail Free card that was within his means to deal her. "Yes," he said, without looking at either his wife or daughter.

"Just so I'm clear," the principal said, "this is your signature. You read and signed this form."

"That's my name." The principal started to say something, but stopped and instead played with her simple gold wedding band.

"Good enough." She slid the form into the folder. "I'd hate to see your daughter throw away an incredible opportunity. There are thousands of students who would jump at the chance to attend Stanford. Sasha, I'm sure you've seen their new aquatic facility. "

Before Sasha could respond, the principal stood and walked to the door. The meeting was over. "I'll see you at the meet today," she said.

As the door closed, Sasha smiled and mumbled, "That'll be a first."

"Sasha," Karen said. "Zip it."

"I've been diving here for four years, and she's never once come to a meet. Bet she's never missed a football game."

"I suspect that's the least of your worries," Brodie snapped.

A janitor approached—the guy riding shotgun earlier was now driving the golf cart alone. Brodie wanted to ask if he'd give him a lift back to his car because he wasn't sure he could walk the distance. He motioned for Sasha and Karen to stand aside. When the guy was out of range, Brodie whispered, "Want to tell your mom what was in your Gatorade?" Sasha turned away from him. He grabbed her arm.

"God, Dad. You're such a moron."

"Yes, that may very well be, but my back feels as if it's being twisted to the point of snapping, and I'd say the same goes for my patience."

"Calm down." Karen smiled innocently at two Goths who looked their way.

"I don't give a damn who hears me. Let me see your backpack."

"NO." She hugged the backpack to her chest. He yanked it out of her hands and nearly collapsed from the roar of pain.

"Brodie, what's your problem," Karen whispered.

"Her Gatorade bottle was filled with vodka. I need to know if there's anything else in here."

"Hey, Sasha," said one of her fellow divers as he walked past with a group of friends.

There were tears in Sasha's eyes. She swiped them away with the back of her hand, ignoring her teammate. "Can we do this in the car? Please, Dad."

Brodie opened the backpack and spilled the contents onto the sidewalk. He checked every pocket, every orifice, ran his hand along the seams, pocketed two energy gel packets that contained caffeine and empty calories, primarily, and had no place in any teenager's diet.

"Satisfied?" she asked.

"Hardly," he said and repacked the bag, taking shallow breaths. "Do you have any idea how angry and disappointed I am? I just lied to your principal when I should have let you face the consequences of forgery." He narrowed his eyes.

"Let's talk about this tonight." Karen grabbed the backpack and handed it to Sasha. "Head to class. We'll see you at the pool this afternoon."

"No . . . no way. No dive today," he said.

"What?" Sasha said. Her chin began a theatrical wobble.

"Brodie. It's the last meet before NCS."

He looked at his wife. "You're not going to back me up here?"

"Please, Daddy," Sasha said. She hadn't called him Daddy in years, except for the occasional "Hey, Daddy-o." Did she think he was so clueless he wouldn't know he was being played? "Pleeeaaase." She scrunched up her face into an exaggerated gum and tooth smile, pleading.

Brodie's shoulders fell forward. God damn it. "Go ahead. But we're going to sit down tonight to talk, come hell or high water."

He and Karen approached the car. The lot was nearly full. A brand-new Jeep Wrangler was parked over the yellow line leaving inches between their vehicles. No way, Brodie thought. This spoiled kid needed to learn how to park. As he approached the truck, he could feel the vibrations from the bass of the hip-hop music blasting on the radio. He rapped on the window. The kid startled and turned toward Brodie. The kid's tortured face was alight in new and healing zits. It was painful to look anywhere but at his intense blues eyes. Unlike Keith, Brodie knew the embarrassment and discomfort of acne. The experts claimed that stress and food didn't cause breakouts. They peddled bullshit theories and blamed hereditary and environmental factors. Now, according to some doctors, backpacks and bike helmets were the enemies of preteen and teen complexions.

In high school, Keith could, and often did, smoke weed for days on end and eat an entire bucket of Halloween candy without getting a single whitehead, yet if Brodie took a bite of a chocolate bar or drank one soda, a furious crop of zits would erupt within minutes. When their mom died, his skin went berserk. He had zits in his ears, inside his nose, and up and down his arms. It was as if all of the sadness and fear of becoming orphaned, living with strangers, and feeling Keith pull away as he steered toward the cooler crowd, was forcing its way through Brodie's teenage skin. When he met Karen in high school, she was the first person who could look at him without the slightest recoil. The first girl he trusted to let down his guard and show an interest in. The first, and only girl, he'd ever kissed, and later, allowed to see him undressed—who didn't, thankfully, wince at the scars. The kid rolled down the window, and Brodie smiled to let him know he wasn't another asshole grownup.

"Hey," he said. "My back is messed up right now. Mind re-parking?"

"No problem, dude."

"Thanks."

"Wait," he said. "Mr. Marshall, right. Sasha's dad?"

He nodded. He remembered the kid. In elementary school, he'd taken ballet classes with Sasha before she switched to gymnastics.

"Do you still dance?" Brodie asked.

The kid beamed. "Yes. I'm attending Barnard in the fall. They have an excellent dance program." After a beat, he added, "Much to my dad's chagrin."

Screw your dad, Brodie wanted to say. He'd have bet his last dollar (which he may have already spent) that this kid was not packing vodka or forging his parents' signatures. So what if he wanted to leap around a stage in ball-hugging tights. It has worked out pretty well for Baryshnikov. There were worse ways to spend one's life. Selling insurance, for one. "Well . . . if I were your dad, I'd be immensely proud of you. I wish you the best."

"Thanks. Tell Sasha congrats on Stanford."

"You bet." Once Brodie had finally settled into his seat, he checked his phone, hoping for a message from his brother.

"Keith hasn't called?" Karen buckled her seatbelt.

He rolled his shoulders in cautious circles. It felt as if someone had beaten him with a sack of golf balls. "Maybe I should just call in sick," he said. "Crawl into bed and hide under the blankets."

"Sorry, babe, but I know your schedule is full."

"Do you think we need a family shrink?"

Karen shrugged. "You really tasted vodka?"

The slight buzz from the alcohol was proof. Cradling his head, he nodded. He swallowed two more Advil from a bottle he kept in the glove box and leaned his elbows on the steering wheel. This day was rapidly declining. It wasn't just the collision with the tree, or the forged school form, or the vodka, or his messed up back. He couldn't believe his brother was blowing him off. He knew Brodie wanted this bonus pretty badly. He'd told Keith that besides the money, meeting his quota would have gotten Stan and the district office off his back for a few months. He didn't mention that the ten thousand would have paid the student housing deposit and the minimum due on his credit cards. Hell, Brodie wasn't asking Keith and Emma to buy five whole life million dollar policies. What about five modest term policies for themselves and the kids? He could have canceled the damn policies the next month if he didn't want the coverage. Though Emma did work, and presumably brought home a nice paycheck, she still would have been screwed if something happened to Keith. Managing three kids and a mortgage on her salary alone would be tough. Yes, he peddled life insurance to make money, but he truly believed that having adequate coverage was an essential and prudent part of financial planning. Even he followed his own advice on this count.

Surely Keith could pay back the twenty grand he owed Brodie without him having to beg. Based on a visit last week, it looked as if Keith's company was starting to turn the corner. When Brodie picked him up for lunch, two newly hired programmers were unpacking a truckload of Dell equipment from his Subaru.

Karen ruffled her husband's hair and nudged him. "Come on. Look at me."

Her Tahoe blue eyes penetrated, full-bore, his heart. He'd adored her since their freshman year in high school when the varsity tennis coach paired them for a match. It wasn't simply her farm-girl beauty, her petite figure or her toned legs and white, knee-high socks. It was her unapologetic killer serve on the ad court. It was watching her trip and fall on her butt yet still return the ball for the point. It was her dust-off-your-bum-and-get-back-in-your-ready-position attitude that made him feel safe. And her refusal to accept that he managed an A-plus in Honors

Geometry but could not conjugate verbs, or earn, at the least, a C-minus in Spanish. Her unwavering belief that he could do better, her insistence that he try harder, her willingness to sit shoulder to shoulder with him in McDonald's, going through flashcards.

He kissed her lips, aware there were students walking past. He knew Sasha would *simply die* if one of her friends told her that she spotted her parents making out in the parking lot. The payback was enticing.

"Just for the record," he said, "I'm the luckiest man in the world."

Her lips curled into her famous smile, just the slightest bit off-kilter. Soon they arrived back at the house and before Karen slid out of her seat, he asked, "Why do you think she forged that form?"

"I don't know." She took his hand and pressed it between hers. The warmth of her hands felt comforting. "She hasn't missed school once this year. Perhaps she's trying to exert her independence."

"Independence?" He chuckled. "As in getting your driver's license or a job? How many seniors refuse to get a license?"

"If I figure it out, you'll be the first I tell." She dropped his hands and stretched her arms above her head until her shoulders made that unpleasant popping sound. "But as it stands now, I'm clueless."

"That's a first." He tugged on her earlobe. "Now get out of here. I've got five life insurance policies to sell."

"Go get 'em. See you at the meet."

She blew him a kiss as she walked up the sidewalk. Ginger was standing at the window next to the front door, her nose pressed against the glass. The second Karen opened the door, she was pounced on by Ginger. Brodie started to back out of the driveway while reaching for his phone. He knew he would have heard the ping if a text had been received, but he couldn't help himself. It was the twentieth of the month. They had less than forty dollars in their checking account to last them until the first.

"Brodie," Karen yelled.

He braked and looked up. She was pointing at the road. In the rear view mirror, he saw the white tail of a deer darting across the road, then up the hill toward the browning crest of the hiking trail. A fawn stood in the neighbor's rose garden, looking unsure whether to eat the fresh bud that dangled at her nose or bolt after her mother. The flower, despite the thorns, despite the danger, was too enticing. She went for it.

Tossing the phone into the console, Brodie waved goodbye to Karen and thought about the elderly couple he had met with last week at their condo in The Oaks. They'd been driving up Highway 1 in the early morning fog, swerved to miss a deer and hit a tree instead. Four thousand dollars' worth of damage plus some nasty bruising from the airbags. The wife was wearing a sling from dislocating her shoulder. The husband, sitting in his stained, frayed recliner, was irate when Brodie told them they'd have to pay a five-hundred-dollar deductible, and the collision with the tree would likely increase their rates at renewal. He explained that if they'd hit the deer rather than the tree, the claim would fall under comprehensive coverage, therefore no deductible, no points against the insured.

"That's ridiculous," the man said. "What was I supposed to do, run over the goddamn deer? You insurance companies are all despicable."

It was a shitty situation, he agreed. He wished the rules and the companies themselves were different. He wished they governed less by a motivation for profit and more by their decency toward people in need. Truly, he did. He also understood the couple's frustration. They lived on a fixed income, lived in a cheaply constructed apartment that must have felt like a way-station between living and dying, and judging by the assorted vials of pills on the kitchen counter, they were plagued with ailments. Undoubtedly, they faced hopelessness daily. A few days after their meeting, the couple's son-in-law called to say they were changing insurance. They'd apparently found a less despicable company, and he couldn't blame them.

jenny

"HAPPY FRIDAY," Jenny said to her colleagues at the front desk as she dropped the Locks for Love envelope in the outgoing mail bin. Her nerves felt twisted and frayed by the unexpected encounter with Brodie.

"Love the new hairdo," said the receptionist as she opened a file cabinet drawer. Jenny thanked her, feeling self-conscious. She wasn't sure if the woman was being polite or if the new style really did flatter her. At this late stage, it didn't matter, she figured, as she walked through the common area. A resident was napping in his wheelchair by the window. His blanket had slid to the floor. Jenny picked it up and carefully set it across his lap so as not to wake him. By the picture window, Herman— one of Creekside's two resident cats (the less friendly one)—basked in the morning sun. With a huge belly of orange and white fur, he looked as if he'd swallowed Garfield plus a cousin. Jenny reached down to pet him and he meowed, preemptively biting her fingers.

"Grumpy Pants," she whispered, touching his ear to annoy him. He didn't bite this time. Instead, he sniffed her hand and looked up at her. "See, I mean no harm," she said. He followed her down the hall to her office. Jenny turned on her computer and Herman settled on the floor by her feet. Soon he was snoring. The important items on today's agenda were to purge old emails, private ones, in particular, delete her browsing history, and clean out her desk and file cabinet. At the top of her inbox was the daily email from her son's former preschool.

Dear Parents:

Please check the lost and found shelves by the office for your belongings. After today, whatever is left behind will be donated or discarded. Have a wonderful weekend.

Rosewood Preschool

She read the email twice, pausing on: *After today, what is left behind will be donated or discarded.* For the past two years, she had continued to receive these emails. It would have taken seconds, she knew, to scroll down to the *Unsubscribe* hyperlink, but until today, she hadn't been able to encourage herself to do so. These daily reminders, oddly enough, provided a familiar, exquisite burst of pain, not so unlike running hot water over a blistering patch of poison oak. Before she could change her mind, she clicked on *Unsubscribe* and then *Yes* to confirm she was sure.

She glanced beyond the wall of glass that separated her small office from the common room and watched Mrs. Martin walk proudly, if somewhat slowly, toward one of the attendants. From her desk, Jenny couldn't hear what the resident was saying, but she knew the script: "I'd like to go home. Can you call my son to pick me up?" Then "Today's Friday, Mrs. Martin. Your daughter-in-law will be here shortly. I know how much you enjoy having your hair done and visiting with your granddaughters." Then "I don't like her. My son could have done better than to marry a divorced woman with such a troubled child. You know my son is a doctor. He graduated first in his class at Harvard." The attendant, "You must be very proud. Would you like to sit by the window? You can watch the hummingbirds while I prepare a cup of tea." Then "I need to go home. I'm baking fig cookies today for my son. They're his favorite. You know my son is a doctor." And finally, "So I've heard."

Jenny opened the schedule of June activities. Except for the recurring Monday and Wednesday morning bingos, the schedule was blank. Creekside's director, MaryAnn, had noted in their Monday one-to-one meeting that there seemed more white space on the schedule than usual.

"*We* might want to introduce some new activities to help engage and stimulate the residents," MaryAnn had said. "*We* want to ensure they get their money's worth. Some of our residents, and even a few family members, have inquired about the downturn in activities." Her obviously prepared statement was punctuated, as always, by a moronic, toothy smile and head bob. This fake smile always made Jenny want to punch her in the throat, or at a minimum, roll her eyes and tell her to let Jenny do her job.

"Which residents, exactly, commented on *the downturn in activities*?" Jenny had asked.

"Well, I don't remember exactly. But it has been a while since we've held an off-site. What about a visit to the Oakland Museum? Something to give the residents something to look forward to. Perhaps you could get Randy and two of the other attendants to help you with the logistics."

"You know how I feel about Randy," Jenny had said, before excusing herself for a nonexistent meeting.

Randy hadn't spoken to her since she told MaryAnn he handled the residents too roughly. She'd seen bruises and heard complaints. She watched him interact with the residents. He should have been fired eons ago, at least after the recent third complaint of abuse—substantiated or not, the maximum an employee could receive before termination. Even the former Marine, Mr. Kilpatrick, with his framed Medal of Honor hanging in his tidy room, had flinched the first time Randy *helped* him out of his wheelchair. *Yanked* was more precise. Randy was one of only two male attendants who could lift and turn the heavier residents, so much was overlooked where he was concerned. It was simply deemed unfortunate that he dropped a resident from time to time. Jenny had shaken with anger when she heard him tell another attendant, who, unlike Randy, was liked by the staff and residents: *If they weren't so damn fat, then we wouldn't be scraping them up off the floor!*

Apparently, MaryAnn had shared Jenny's concern with Randy. Maybe she didn't mention Jenny by name, but he seemed to know that it was she who had complained and that it was because of her he'd been called down to the director's office for a reprimand. Although she didn't have any desire to be Randy's best friend, his cold stares scared her. She would never boldly, purposely, cross him. For the last two months since she'd reported him to MaryAnn, whenever she cordially said hello, he glared at her, his dark eyes confronting her with untold threats of physical violence.

The staff knew MaryAnn hated any hint of conflict. Instead, she kept trying to ease the tension by exuberantly praising Randy for anything he did. She handed him a hundred-dollar bonus at the last all-hands staff meeting. Despite the pitiful economy, she'd started doling out spot bonuses to improve morale and halt the high employee turnover. In front of both his cronies and detractors, Randy had accepted the check, his face showcasing a huge smirk. He had to have known he didn't earn it. Even he knew it was a bribe to inspire better behavior, behavior that precluded hurting the residents. Jenny and the nutritionist had a running joke. At their staff meetings, the agenda moved along a familiar path: housekeeping items, pending arrivals and departures, a review of the weekly menu and any new dietary constraints, and finally, to praising Randy ("I'd like to recognize Randy today. Under his care, Mr. Rosen's bruises are healing nicely after his unfortunate fall off the bed during bath time."). MaryAnn would open the meeting to questions or comments. Jenny's hand would shoot up. She'd suggest the group acknowledge, say the nutritionist for always making sure the residents had plenty of wholesome food and for not accidentally poisoning any of the residents or their families. She'd say this without a trace of sarcasm. The first time, MaryAnn clapped like an imbecile while the new ops manager snickered. The next time Jenny volunteered a similar inane compliment, MaryAnn nodded in agreement, while the ops manager just scratched his nose looking baffled. It was immature, Jenny knew. But sometimes that was how one got through the day.

A thought occurred to her. She could do something that would make it impossible for MaryAnn to continue looking the other way. After today, Jenny wouldn't need to worry about retaliation against her. She typed *Contra Costa County Elder Abuse* into her browser and searched, unsuccessfully, for an email address on the website. She wanted to file the complaint about Randy without having to speak to someone directly, but the site made that difficult. A letter should carry the same weight, she thought, as she copied the physical address listed and pasted it into a blank document.

To Whom It May Concern, she typed, feeling elated by taking action and doing the right thing for the residents and their families. As she wrote the letter, providing as many specific details as she could remember, she thought about how she'd never end up in a facility such as this. As nice as this expensive assisted living facility was, despite Randy and the fact that most of the residents appeared happy, or at least not unhappy, it still felt like a jail—no matter how many arts and crafts Jenny planned, no matter how many bingo games, yoga, karaoke, and movie events filled the white space on the calendar, the residents were still biding time. This would be someone else's job soon enough, she thought. Let them enjoy corralling a dozen or so elderly men and women, with all their equipment, on and off a bus, through ticketing, through "WHAT'S HE SAYING? THIS LOOKS LIKE SOMETHING MY GRANDSON PAINTED!" guided tours, through endless trips to the bathroom, through "EIGHT DOLLARS FOR A SLICE OF PIE!" and crowded café lines. Now, to spite MaryAnn, Jenny began filling in the month of June, and hell, why not July while she was at it: basket weaving, tap dancing lessons, nature walks, candle-making, a badminton tournament. She deleted badminton, knowing that that was going too far. She didn't want to injure the residents. Instead, she typed: San Francisco Ballet, and added more: De Young Museum, Napa Valley wine train, Walt Disney Family Museum.

Meow. Jenny startled. She'd forgotten about Herman napping at her feet and tuned out his snoring. She pinched off a piece of the lemon poppy muffin she'd found in the staff kitchen—residents' families were always bringing the staff treats. Herman sniffed the morsel and turned his nose, settling back down, his head resting on his outstretched paws.

"How can you be so picky and yet so fat? And why are you suddenly my new best friend?"

Before today, he'd hardly given Jenny a second glance. *Was he here keeping vigil?* she wondered. Was it possible that this cat could sense something amiss—smell or feel an impending death, even self-inflicted? Did humans give off an odor, a vibe, some detectible current of energy?

A few weeks back, shortly before Hospice was called for Mr. Gottlieb in apartment 209, Herman had sat vigil for days. Just as he'd done for Mrs. Junor and several others residents over the years. He was known among the Creekside staff as the grim reaper. Coaxed out of his otherwise aloofness, he had wandered into Gottlieb's room and settled at the end of the bed. He hardly left the man's room, stirring and meowing only when an attendant or family member entered the room. Jenny cocked her head and wondered if he sensed what she was going to do tonight. She rolled her eyes, then thought, why not? Stranger things have happened. Maybe he could sense how much she longed for her son. Thank you, she whispered, as if he'd confirmed by his vigil that she was making the right choice.

brodie

IT WAS A HABIT NOW—craning his head to peer over the guard rail as he moved to the right lane to prepare for the exit. What thoughts went through Scott Zabat's mind right before he stopped his car, left the ignition running, and leapt over the guard rail into the path of on-coming traffic? *And buck naked!* That was the strangest part. The part Brodie didn't get. He supposed the client never considered the emotional damage he'd inflict on the unfortunate driver who was just minding his own business when a naked body fell from the sky. Suddenly there was some guy's junk smashed all over the hood of his Toyota Corolla. Was the leap to his death a cowardly act? It was certainly desperate. Sacrifice your life so that at least your wife and kids would be relieved of the burden you bring to the table every night. Brodie wondered if he would be able to do something so bold, so permanent. He didn't believe he had the courage. But as he glanced over the rail, he thought, for the second time today, that it would certainly solve some of their problems.

Abandoning this depressing musing, he thought about the emails waiting in his inbox. He needed to check in with Zabat's widow, although he'd rather trade a colonoscopy for that call. He hoped he could get through the urgent messages before Andrea and Maria arrived. The tickle returned to his throat, and he started coughing again. A sharp pain reasserted itself between his shoulder blades. He fumbled around in his glove box, hoping to find some bubble gum that Sasha had left behind. A car honked. He had nearly sideswiped the Smart Car in the next lane. The middle-aged driver shot him a well-deserved *what's your problem, asshole* sneer.

When Brodie pulled into the visitor's parking lot of the office complex, he was grateful to see the welcome mat hadn't been set out and the front window shade was still drawn. Like many of the old motels on

North Main Street, his complex was built in the '60s, but twenty years ago it was gutted. The former two-story strip of baby blue stucco motel units now resembled a row of quaint shops you'd find in Carmel, thanks to shake shingles, craftsman windows, and redwoods planted to soften the sharp edges. Where the property once boasted a kidney-shaped pool, there now lay a kidney-shaped island of colorful flowers and birch trees.

Driving around to the back lot, he saw the old, dented RV decorated with license plates from around the world. The RV hadn't left its spot in months. It belonged to the grown son of the old man who managed the adjacent Easy Storage complex. Andrea heard from one of the other office managers that the son was thrown off the property after inadvertently setting fire to the restroom. Every morning now, the son sat on the steps of his RV, a horn pressed to his lips, greeting tenants with snippets of a limited repertoire of patriotic songs. He sat and played, pausing to suck down a cigarette, then continued till noon when he walked next door to eat sandwiches and share a game of Scrabble with his father.

Sometimes Brodie watched them from his office window. He'd think about his own father, a drinker and womanizer whom he remembered only faintly. He and Keith were young when their mom kicked him out for the final time. The two men didn't talk much. He never heard one raised voice. What little he did remember about his own father was that he seemed always to be yelling, whether he was saying hello or for the boys to get their goddamn feet off of the goddamn sofa. This father and son, however, would lean over the board, wordlessly studying the letters that had been played as they considered their next move, taking turns picking tiles from a blue-striped gym sock. The son never smoked on the Extra Storage property. Brodie supposed they had come to some sort of agreement. He marveled at how content they appeared. He couldn't imagine either of them stressing about whether they'd make their annual bonus. This economy must be a boon for the storage business. The potential problem was that they must have a large number of customers who quit paying rent, who simply walked away from their possessions. Who needs an entire living room set when you've moved back into your mom's sewing room?

Brodie sighed in relief when he saw that Andrea's dented Corolla wasn't parked in her usual spot. Yes! A few quiet minutes alone in the office. As he walked around the corner of the building, he saw a woman standing at his door and peering through the mail slot. He approached.

"Excuse me. May I help you?"

She spun around, holding an envelope behind her back. There was something familiar about her face. A mom from Sasha's school or dive team? He couldn't quite place her.

"My apologizes," Brodie said. "I didn't mean to startle you." She took a step back as if he was an ogre. "I'm Brodie Marshall. Are you looking for something?"

She shook her head and wordlessly folded the envelope in her hand into quarters. "I'm, I'm not," she stammered. "I didn't mean to . . . I'm just dropping off my boss's premium, but I'm late for work."

She gave him the folded envelope and hurried to her car. As she opened the door, he saw the assortment of faded children's stickers. Was this the same car sitting outside his house earlier this morning? He started to grab his phone to type in the license plate but realized he'd left it in the car.

"Hey, wait," he said to the slamming of the car door. He unfolded the envelope in his hand. "Brodie Marshall" was written in that familiar and perfect cursive across the envelope. He called out again, but it was too late. She nicked the curb while speeding out of the parking lot.

jenny

FROM HER OFFICE, Jenny watched as the younger Mrs. Martin entered the common area and looked around for her mother-in-law and imagined the dread coursing through her. She looked like someone approaching a waiting alligator, her posture as straight as a dancer's, a black and white checkered handbag clutched against her chest as if it were a shield.

The younger Mrs. Martin was beautiful, exotic-looking with almond-shaped eyes and glossy black hair—a cross between Cher and Cleopatra. You couldn't help but notice her when she entered a room. Her identical twin daughters, who must have been approaching school age, would one day be as stunning as their mother. She bent over and quickly kissed the elder Mrs. Martin on the proffered cheek, then brought her hand to her nose. Mrs. Martin was notorious for stinking of over-applied, expensive perfume. Subtlety wasn't her forte. Jenny had once overheard one of the girls asking her mother why grandma smelled so bad.

Conversely, Jenny's own mother-in-law was generally the model of subtlety. Why then today during their morning call had Rhonda ventured into unfriendly waters? "It's not too late for you and Jerrod to have another baby." *Where did that come from?* "Otherwise, you might both regret not giving it another chance."

She guiltily imagined Rhonda's reaction to the news tomorrow or when Jerrod discovered her body. *Her body. Her body that had once contained her precious son.* Certainly, there would be shock and sadness. Betrayal. Anger. Sympathy for Jerrod. Jenny felt guilty that they'd probably cancel their cruise trip. Rhonda had been talking about sailing through Glacier Bay for years. She'd bought a new camera to take photos of frolicking whales and dolphins advertised in the brochures. Jenny inhaled deeply. The time had come, or else she might never have the courage to do it.

She began deleting all of her personal files. Her Skype account pinged and she paused. It was Beth, who sat two offices down from Jenny.

"Tell me something interesting. Any gossip?" read Beth's message.

"Shouldn't the newly promoted Floor Manager have more important things to do than gossip with her colleagues?"

"Don't be a hater! Tell me something good. I'm bored out of my mind."

"MA stopped by to tell me how to do my job," Jenny typed. "Think she'd fire me if I told her to f*** off?"

"Haha. Just left Mr. All Hands' room. He told me that even though I'm fat, he'd still have sex with me."

"Don't flatter yourself too much," Jenny typed. "Last week he cornered me by the salad bar and told me that even though I wasn't his type, I could tickle his dick if I wanted."

Jenny heard Beth's cackle from two offices away.

"Ewww," Beth typed, adding a frowning emoticon. "TMI!!!"

TMI from the Queen of Oversharing, Jenny thought. She typed, "The man definitely needs some new pickup lines. He's been trying to get the new resident in 402 to join him for dinner. So far, no luck."

"Maybe the word is out on him."

"One can hope." Jenny added their favorite pelvic-thrusting, dancing monkey emoji. "We need to warn the residents that he probably has every STD under the sun. I walked by his room yesterday, and he was reading a *Playboy*. When he saw me looking his way, he gave me a disgusting, lewd smile."

"He should have his dick cut off," Beth wrote. "Shall we draw straws?"

Herman shifted positions at her feet. Suddenly she thought how wasteful to spend her last day being so catty. "If something were to happen," she typed, "like if I can't stop myself from telling MA to F. Off and she fires me, would you keep an eye on the new girl, Ana?"

"Sure. Why? Are you okay?"

"I'm fine. I've just seen some of the attendants are giving her a hard time. I heard one tell her that she was making the rest of them look bad by working so hard. I don't want her to become discouraged. The residents love her."

"Are you really worried about being fired? Or something else? Things must be better with Jerrod if you two are going on the cruise. Oops, here comes MA. Wanna do lunch?"

"Can't, but thanks." Jenny added a smiley face and hit send.

Beth replied with a dancing monkey. Any other day and Jenny would raise the monkey with another one of their favorites—maybe the ninja. Instead, she located the privacy setting on Skype and cleared her history. She looked around the office and tried to see the space from Jerrod's or one of her colleague's perspective. It looked as if she'd just moved in. Bare white walls. A few holes where tacks had once held her son's scribbles and drawings. The only personal item on her desk was a Waterford clock that Rhonda had given her one birthday. Later, before Jenny walked out of Creekside for the last time, she'd leave the clock on Beth's desk for her to find tomorrow—a small token of the affection she'd felt for her colleague and friend. Along with the crystal clock, there would be little evidence of *her* except for a scattering of fingerprints, some DNA, and her signature and doodles on various forms and documents.

After the accident, she'd removed her personal photos, her son's art-work, and the few toys she had kept in her bottom drawer for those rare times he'd accompanied her to work. She knew that the other managers, in the upcoming days, after a respectable period of grieving, would lobby for her office. Someone would call Jerrod to pick up her belongings, since it wouldn't occur to him to do so. The staff wouldn't realize until he started opening and closing drawers, and finding nothing that looked personal, that she hadn't left anything of consequence behind. Most certainly, Beth would be pissed off. She'd refuse to have any part of helping Jerrod locate any of her non-existent personal effects. She would, likely, boycott the office just out of anger no matter who took up residency, and Jenny loved her for that loyalty.

brodie

MARIA'S WAILS and Andrea's angry voice could be heard the moment he opened the front office door. His shoulders fell. She must have gotten a ride to the office. Andrea glanced up and frowned in apology as she bounced a flailing Maria in one arm while holding a cell phone to her multi-pierced ear. He dropped his briefcase on the floor by Andrea's desk and gestured for her to hand over the baby.

"Thank you," she mouthed as he took the red-faced baby from her. "I won't be long."

"We're all just having a bad morning, aren't we," he said, drawing Maria closer. The baby's neck felt sticky and damp. She smelled as if she were days past a good bath. Andrea was wearing her softball jersey for the Hit Squad. He looked at her feet. That she was still wearing the cleats she'd changed into yesterday before her game wasn't a good sign.

She avoided eye contact, but Brodie noticed dark circles beneath her thick black lashes. What were these kids thinking, having babies at nineteen and twenty? He carried Maria into his office, shut the door with his foot (slamming louder than he'd intended), and tossed the folded envelope on his desk. He hated to side with Andrea's father, but the man might have been justified in being enraged by the choices his daughter had made, the opportunities she squandered. He listened to Andrea's rant in the outer office and figured she was talking to Ron, the loser father of this adorable and, at the moment, fidgety and smelly baby. He was tempted to grab the phone and tell the guy he didn't deserve either Andrea or Maria. But only a fool with a death wish would have crossed that tattooed punk from Bay Point. Brodie tried to imagine Sasha dropping out of Stanford to live in a one-bedroom apartment with a baby and some creep like Ron. The image made him want to hurl.

Softly bouncing Maria on his knee, he watched her squeal. She resembled her mother with her flat nose and large, dark eyes. Andrea had come to the Marshalls as an exchange student. Her father, a big shot textile guy from Northern Spain, had sent her to California to study economics at Berkeley. At a dinner Karen cooked in his family's honor during his first and only visit, he'd explained he didn't want his oldest daughter—purportedly the smartest, yet most willful of his three girls—to live in the dorms or rent a room on campus with so many young men thinking they were free to do as they pleased. He complained in a boastful way about paying nearly six figures to get his daughter into Berkeley. He wasn't about to waste one penny of his investment.

"Knock some sense into her before she even thinks about misbehaving," he said. "I expect my daughter returned to me in the condition she arrived here today."

His much younger wife, who from the time they exchanged greetings, had yet to say anything more than hello, mumbled, "Are you sure you can let go of something so precious?"

"Ma," Andrea said, shaking her head. "Don't do that. I'm fine."

"Just saying," she continued, yet a little louder. "Some things you can't replace. Some things you can't control."

"Dessert?" Karen asked, derailing what could have become an awkward family drama. As Brodie helped her clear the plates and tried to ignore the ugly looks exchanged between Andrea's parents, he noticed that Andrea didn't have any detectible body piercings—not even her ears. There were no maroon or butterscotch highlights in her dark black hair, and certainly, no tattoos that some of the kids around town were starting to acquire. He would have loved to counter with a sarcastic remark. "Well, so far, we've kept our dear Sasha here off crack and she hasn't turned up barefoot and pregnant." But Brodie was no fool. Even back then they needed the money this overbearing father was paying for his daughter's room and board.

"Who's a happy girl?" he cooed now. Maria gurgled and kicked her feet. He remembered how this adorable baby's grandfather had reached over the dinner table that first night and grabbed his daughter's chin. "Behave like a lady. Understand?"

The first morning after she'd said goodbye to her parents, Andrea had surprised Karen with an enormous hug. From then on, she had felt like part of the family. Despite three years difference in age, the two girls got along well. Andrea accompanied Karen to Sasha's dive meets, hung out at The Village Plaza with Sasha and her friends on weekends. She attended her classes, sharing funny anecdotes at dinner about her classmates and professors. She was always eager to hop on BART to get to campus to see what student group had gathered in the quad. She read their signs, listened to their impassioned speeches, and watched their demonstrations. Karen used to tease her that if she wasn't careful, she was going to end up in law school.

As that first Christmas approached, Andrea had begun dodging her father's calls. He bought her a first-class ticket, expecting her to spend the holidays with her family. She spent hours on the phone begging her mother to convince her father to let her stay in California, claiming the classes were more difficult than she'd imagined and she wanted to get a head start on her readings for the upcoming semester. Her father finally relented. Sasha went to Austin for a dive camp at the University of Texas, and Andrea helped Karen with her volunteer work at a women and children's shelter in Bay Point.

Two things happened that holiday, permanently shifting Andrea's course. She came home one day from the mall with silver studs in her ears. Brodie thought about her father's reaction and nearly dragged her to a doctor to stitch up the holes. Then, at the annual Secret Santa party at the shelter, she met Ron—who crashed the event with his friends. This was the moment, he supposed, looking back now, that he failed to do as her father instructed: knock some sense into his daughter. In late spring, her second semester underway, she started missing classes and skipping family dinners. Mornings, he could hear Karen rapping on her door, reminding her of the time. He learned that by May, she'd quit attending class and instead took BART in the opposite direction—to Bay Point to meet up with Ron and his friends.

In early June, on academic probation, she made three announcements. One, she was taking the next year off from college to work. Two, she was moving into an apartment with Ron. And three, she was pregnant. Brodie's head nearly crashed to the floor. Not only had he failed at his charge to preserve her pristine condition, but her father was likely pacing the aisles of his rented jet, eager to inflict some serious physical pain on both his daughter and him.

It turned out that Brodie's worries were in vain. The father simply wrote her off as if she were just another failed business venture. Took the loss, held his chin high, and moved on. As upset as Brodie was at what felt like losing a daughter, Karen was devastated. She pleaded with Andrea not to move out. She offered to help with the baby. She explained to Andrea how difficult it was to go back to school once you've dropped out. She knew firsthand.

As it happened, Brodie's office manager had quit without proper notice—only a text saying she'd mail in the key. She'd been out nearly a week with an alleged case of stomach flu, yet when he did a little sleuthing via Facebook, he found pictures of her partying at the Biltmore in Phoenix with her scrapbooking club. When he called and asked her to bring in a doctor's note upon her return, she hung up on him. He'd already written her up numerous times for hanging up on calls with foreign-speaking clients whom she complained should learn to speak English if they were going to live in this country. It was the perfect opportunity to give the job to Andrea.

Now, it was one thing to let Andrea care for a newborn who, until recently, slept most of the day between feedings, but these tirades with Ron and now her camping out in the office had to stop. Brodie's office door opened, and he turned to see Stan from the district office. Of course, he didn't knock or ask if Brodie was in the middle of something. That would have required manners or some understanding of boundaries. He was dressed in a suit and tie. Brodie couldn't recall when Stan White had last worn anything other than a Polo shirt and khakis. He approached the conference table shaking his head so that the fat under his chin jiggled.

"For Pete's sake, Brodie. You running a daycare? It stinks in here." He stuffed his hands in the pockets of his immaculately pressed slacks, the black belt weighted down by an overflowing belly. The door opened wider. He glared at Andrea as she entered, and she glared right back at him. Brodie smirked. *You go, girl!*

"I'm so sorry," she said, reaching for Maria.

"Do I need to remind you what today is?" Stan asked him, his eyes following Andrea's breasts.

"Five to go," Brodie said. Stan managed to pry his eyes off Andrea and gazed down at the folder on Brodie's desk marked CANCELLATIONS. "I'm just waiting on a call to meet my client with the paperwork."

Despite a steady decline in revenue from core product lines, he had always managed to write just enough life insurance policies to earn the annual bonus—even when the country had suffered the worst financial meltdown since the thirties. But this year, when he desperately needed the money, he had ignored Stan's advice to get an early start, given the depressed economy. When clients all over the Bay Area were facing the choice of paying their mortgage or feeding their families, they were largely uninterested in the abstract notion of life insurance. The thought of telling Karen the credit cards were maxed out, that they had just enough money in the bank to celebrate Mother's Day at Pizza Hut, and even better, she needed to find a job ASAP, completely depressed Brodie.

He wouldn't give Stan the satisfaction of hearing him admit that unless his brother came through and bought policies for Emma, the kids, and himself, there was no way he'd make the quota this year. How Keith would likely continue ignoring his calls until the deadline passed. He wanted to tell Stan that he hated this whole thankless business, and some days, like today, he'd rather clean high school bathrooms than endure another day of selling insurance or defending the company's greed and unfair decisions.

"Any reason for your visit?" Brodie asked, sitting on the edge of his desk to block Stan's view of the CANCELLATION folder.

"Just checking in on an old friend," Stan said. He started to add something else but grabbed Brodie's shoulder and gave him a hard squeeze. "See you at the meeting," he said and offered one of his insincere smiles. Before leaving, he added, "Your numbers are down. And check your emails." A wink and he was out the door.

Alone again, Brodie felt like an egg boiled to a hardened mass. He closed his eyes and shook his head. He folded envelope and tossed into the top drawer of his desk. He couldn't read her letter, not now, not until he was at least in sight of selling the last five policies. His curiosity would have to wait.

jenny

JENNY LEANED AGAINST the staff kitchen counter as she waited for the kettle of water to boil. Randy rushed past for the unisex bathroom that she avoided for its reek of urine and thin walls. In seconds, it sounded like a quarter horse was taking its first piss in days.

Come on, she said to the kettle. Boil already.

"Hey, mom," she heard him say. "Are the boys alright?"

Nice, she thought, *talking to your mother while you take a piss.*

"Son of a bitch," he shouted.

Something hard struck the wall and Jenny flinched. The instant after the kettle clicked off, she filled her mug and left the kitchen. She closed her office door. After today, she would never again see Randy. This fact brought her immense satisfaction and relief. She thought about the vials of prescription drugs she'd accumulated over the past two years, one hundred and fifty pills, give or take, waiting in her nightstand. Prozac and Ambien prescribed after her son's death. Percocet and Horizant prescribed after her fibroid surgery. Zofran prescribed to combat vomiting during a nasty flu. The nausea pills, she hoped, would help prevent her body from throwing up the narcotics. She needed to be certain that her stash was enough to do the job. She could always raid Jerrod's bathroom drawers hoping for more supplies or perhaps swipe a handful from the residents— something she would never do even though it seemed as if the majority of the Creekside residents hadn't a clear understanding of which of their pills combatted which of their ailments.

The idea of a failed suicide attempt worried her. She didn't want to wake up in a psychiatric hospital with her body irreversibly damaged from the drugs. She didn't want to face Jerrod or Rhonda or any of her work colleagues. She'd chosen pills because one, they were handy, and two, overdosing seemed less painful and less frightening than other methods, jumping off the Golden Gate Bridge, for example. Given that pills might not be foolproof, she wondered if she should wash the pills down with vodka, then just as she started feeling drowsy, tie a rope around her neck? She searched on her browser, *How to die by strangulation* and clicked on the first result. *In hanging, death may occur from (1) cerebral congestion (2) asphyxia (3) coma (4) shock (5) injury to the spinal cord and (6) any combination of the above. If your neck breaks, you will immediately become unconscious and you will die within a few minutes.* That sounded horrible.

What if these sites are monitored, she thought. What if simply clicking on one of these censored links, and they, whoever *they* were, were able to track her down? She imagined a mob of concerned white coats barging into her office. Surely we haven't advanced to that stage of Big Brother, she thought, as she read further.

She took a swallow of tea, trying not to imagine the sound of a neck snapping. *If the blood circulation to the brain is cut off, the brain can die in four to six minutes.* She looked at her crystal clock. Six minutes. Someone added an anonymous comment that the person might just end up in a vegetative state. "Is that any better than what you're currently going through?" he or she had asked. In the rectangular box, it said, "Add your answer." There were no other responses.

Jenny typed, "Maybe?" but deleted her comment. Herman stirred in his spot under the desk and scooted his body against her ankle. She gently nudged him away. He settled a few inches over. She knew her situation wasn't unique; millions of people across the world suffered loss daily.

She bent down and grabbed Herman. He meowed in displeasure. Held prisoner in her lap, he kept pawing at her to release him, yet she cooed, "Don't be such a hater, Herman. It's always on your terms, you rascal."

She finished the tea in a succession of gulps, felt the mint infusion burn down her throat, and in her mind, she was standing at the piano. Weeks earlier, she had entered her living room unnoticed, and stood by her husband as he hunched over the piano. His hands moved back and forth as if possessed by a demonic puppeteer. He glanced up, his glasses having slipped to the edge of his nose, and he startled as if she were a ghost. The puppeteer's hands stilled, and the music stopped. Before her husband could ask if everything was alright, she told him she was meeting her girlfriends for brunch.

He smiled broadly, obviously pleased that she had finally reconnected with her friends. He was so easily deceived, or simply eager to have the house to himself for the day. He had removed the pen pressed between his perfect teeth. His green eyes scanned the marked-up sheet music and he made a meaningless notation on one of the bars. She watched him stand and stretch his arms above his shoulders, cracking each vertebra, one by one. "You might want to grab a jacket," he said. He didn't see that she was, in fact, wearing her blue pea coat.

In truth, she was not meeting friends for brunch. Her only plan was to put some distance between her and her husband's relentless piano playing. After driving around different neighborhoods in the East Bay, looking for clues as to how other families, *normal* families, were spending their Saturday, she found herself at the entrance to the cemetery where her son was buried. It was starting to drizzle. She parked under a massive redwood and left the car running to stay warm. A small group of mourners dispersed from a nearby gravesite service. One of the guests trailed behind, allowing greater and greater distance between him and the others. The rain picked up with a sudden ferocity. The group rushed to their cars under the protection of their umbrellas, yet the man seemed unable, or unwilling, to keep pace. By the time he reached his car, his hair was slick against his head and his dark suit jacket was, presumably, soaked. Watching him had reminded her of Jerrod after Daniel's funeral. Beth and Rhonda had reached the car first. Moments later, after hugging and thanking the last of the guests, she had turned to ask Jerrod if he was ready to leave. She did a full pivot and spotted him wandering through the gravesites as if lost in a labyrinth.

brodie

THERE WERE FORTY-SIX new emails since eleven last night. One marked *Urgent* was sent at 6:00 AM. by Stan, no doubt another reminder that the deadline was looming like the Grim Reaper.

He clicked on his agency dashboard to scan the company News Bulletin. Uncontained fires in the greater Pasadena area. No new home policies in the following counties . . . until further notice. Basically, the company pulled up stakes at the time of greatest demand for their products. A company-wide auto call-a-thon was scheduled for June 3rd. Like hell he was wasting another Friday night pestering people at home with some bogus claim to lower their premiums. The last list of warm leads some jackass at corporate had given the agents was *accidentally* distributed to the entire district. By the tenth call, Brodie had been hung up on twice, warned that they were calling the Better Business Bureau about this repeated harassment, gotten three answering machines, yelled at in Chinese by one woman, and told by another with a strong British accent to piss-off.

He picked up the green and white Porta-Potty foam toy that adorned his desk and squeezed it between his fingers. Across the toy's green door, it read, *Too much crap? Call Keith at We Haul It All.* His brother and his crass marketing giveaways. The garbage hauling business was his third venture. Karen and Brodie thought it was his second to worst idea to date. They'd warned him that there were probably a million illegal immigrants willing to haul people's crap away for next to nothing. All you needed was a truck, a pitchfork, and some gloves. Keith had shrugged off the naysayers and borrowed money from his in-laws for the down payment on two dump trucks. Within a year, he added two more trucks and paid off his in-laws. His waiting list grew to three days. He hand-picked a dependable crew and paid them a dollar an hour more than his competitors plus pizza on Fridays. When 1-800-Got-Junk offered him three hundred thousand,

Brodie and Karen told him he was crazy to sell his cash cow. But he'd grinned and reminded them of their initial skepticism. He was ready to move on, and he'd already begun researching some internet cloud idea.

Brodie thought about how he had always taken the safe, boring route. He had taught tennis lessons at the local high school courts because he was a good player and he had patience, while Keith and his buddies rented a big house in Brentwood and set up a pot farm—filling each room with plants and whatever other equipment one needed to grow weed. He'd never seen his brother's operation. He was afraid of being swept up in an inevitable raid. After college, Brodie accepted the first job offer, and now for the past two decades, he'd sold insurance, while Keith switched from selling marijuana to licensing rock band T-shirts, posters, iron-on patches, and all the other must-have merchandise found at concerts. This was his least successful venture, but still he came away with his entrepreneurial spirit intact. He strutted right up to the next big opportunity and introduced himself.

Brodie's Sent folder listed three messages to Keith yesterday and two the day before. He had even forwarded two monk jokes he knew Keith would love, hoping for a response. Despite not wanting to look at the numbers, Brodie glanced at his agency statistics on his dashboard. The down-facing red arrows always seemed brighter than the up-facing green arrows. Auto policies: 550 Down four. Home policies: 600 Down two. Life policies: 125 No change. Umbrella policies: 97 Up one. Flood, Earthquake, Health, General Liability, Workers Comp and Flood weren't included in the agency's daily snapshot, but if they were, it'd mean more down-facing red arrows. There was an Excel spreadsheet somewhere on his computer that he had used to chart his policy count. It showed an all-time high of 2,100 policies, including two Homeowners Associations that made up nearly ten percent of his annual commissions. But thanks to the implosion of the housing and stock market, his agency's growth had stalled, then reversed direction. He looked at the CANCELLATION folder sitting on his desk and wondered if Andrea even bothered to update it, knowing as he was sure she did, that he never looked at it, and if he did, he never took any action.

His phone rang. Andrea said, "David Knight is on the line. Says he'll only talk to you."

Brodie pulled up the client's information on the computer. Renters and auto policies. No life. He scribbled LIFE on a Post It.

"How are you, David?"

"Not so good, I'm afraid." The man sounded tired and old. Brodie looked at his date of birth and was surprised to see he was born in 1954, which made him fifty-seven. He sounded more like eighty-seven.

"Fire at the house two nights ago. I lost everything."

"Anyone hurt?" Brodie asked while clicking on the renter's policy.

"No, my cats and I got out. Fire department took their sweet time."

"Well, it looks as if you've got twenty-five thousand in personal property and you're covered for loss of use. A two-fifty deductible. That's good. Standard loss of use coverage. So you'll—"

"What about the house. *You're* going to fix my house, right?"

The emphasis on *you're* prickled Brodie's neck.

"David, please hold one second." He shook his head. The man is a renter, not a homeowner. Totally different coverages. "I need to grab your file."

In his file, Brodie found a PG&E 24-Hour Notice of Nonpayment on which Lisbeth, his previous Office Manager, had scribbled: *No lender. Closes 11/29/06. 500/100. 500 deductible. First-time homeowner.*

Brodie read again, *First-time homeowner.* Fuck! They'd written the wrong type of policy. How could they have missed this? And how in the hell did the title company miss this?

"Hey David, thank you for holding. It looks as if you bought the house in 2006, right. But you must have been renting it before?"

"Yes. The house was left to me when my mother passed away."

"Oh shit," he mumbled.

"Pardon?"

"Hang on." Brodie opened his planner and searched for an hour slot. Client meetings all morning. District office at noon, appointments all afternoon. He had blocked out five to seven to attend Sasha's dive meet, which started at four-thirty. He was counting on their typical late start, followed by a quick family dinner before filling out insurance applications with Keith, assuming he called Brodie back.

"You're probably too busy today," he said, "but we could meet tomorrow—"

"I'll come by your office now."

"Uh, no. That is . . . I've got a client here already and we might be a while." Brodie picked up a glass paperweight, tossed it up and down, and imagined hurling it at the idyllic Currier & Ives porcelain cottage that sat on the conference table next to the "Cover Your Assets" brochures.

"How about four-thirty in my office?" He crumpled the Post-It note on which he had optimistically scribbled LIFE.

"Four-thirty then."

Slumping in his chair, Brodie closed his eyes and bit his lower lip, wanting to press hard enough to taste blood.

Andrea tapped on the door and peeked in. Brodie glanced up and saw that she had pinned up her hair and applied lip gloss. She'd buttoned a pink sweater over her softball jersey but apparently didn't have a change of shoes.

"Your nine o'clock is here." She handed him the file folder for Victoria Martin.

"Give me a minute."

He picked at his cuticles while trying to figure out what to do about David Knight and his home loss. He couldn't really blame Lisbeth even though he wanted to. Sure she was sloppy. A lot of details slipped past her in her indifference to her job and their clients. He should have checked her work more closely. They were his clients. It was he who was supposed to have protected their assets.

jenny

HERMAN HAD MOVED from the floor to the top of Jenny's desk. He cleaned himself as she deleted emails from various subfolders.

"Holy shit, what did you do to your hair?"

Jenny looked up. Beth stood at her door, arms akimbo and head cocked.

"Thanks a lot." She touched her naked neck. "Does it look bad?"

"No. It's just . . . I'm surprised. It's short, but it looks nice on you." Beth sat on the edge of the desk and scrutinized her. "You okay?" she asked, reaching over to pet Herman. He hissed and jumped to the floor, returning to his spot near Jenny's foot.

"Not a big fan of yours," Jenny teased.

"It's mutual. But seriously, how are you?"

"I'm fine. Just trying to wrap things up before my vacation."

"Take me with you on your cruise. This place is driving me nuts."

Jenny thought about the two-day conference they'd attended in San Francisco a few years back. Even though the meetings were long, often repetitive, and she hated being away from Daniel and Jerrod for even one night, she and Beth had had fun. They'd bonded over room service, two bottles of wine, and back-to-back chick flicks. They gave each other pedicures, and before falling asleep in their queen-sized beds, they shared their first-time sex stories.

"Even though we'd definitely have more fun," she said, "I'm going to have to pass."

"I'll carry your bags, massage your feet, babysit Rhonda, and even entertain you and Jerrod with my recent Match.com escapades."

"Sorry, as great as all of that sounds."

Jenny felt uncomfortable lying to her friend. She wished she could confide in Beth, but she knew her friend would call Jerrod. She would enlist everyone and everything in her power to thwart Jenny's plans. She knew that when Beth recalled this conversation in the coming weeks, she'd realize Jenny had lied to her, betrayed their friendship. That she'd never had any intention of boarding the ship or giving Beth the opportunity to say or do something to dissuade her from her decision.

"Party pooper," Beth teased.

"Freak," Jenny replied half-heartedly. She wasn't in the mood for their silly banter today. She wanted to hug Beth. She wanted to tell her how much their friendship meant to her. Express her gratitude for the days after Daniel's death when Beth had literally pulled Jenny out of bed. Insisted she eat something. Talk to someone about Daniel and the accident. Reminding her, over and over, that it was an accident, just a horrible, horrible accident.

"I'm behind on my monthly reports," Jenny said, fearing an onslaught of tears. "I was just about to start them."

Beth slid off the desk. "My offer stands if you change your mind."

A few minutes later, Jenny's Skype pinged with a message. "Warning," Beth wrote. "MA is on her way."

"Jenny," MaryAnn said, standing at the door. "Quick word?"

"Sure. Have a seat." In her mind, she was thinking, after today, I won't ever have to deal with you again.

"I'll stand. I've been sitting all morning. I like your hair." She bent down to pet Herman. He let out an angry meow. "I know Randy isn't one of your favorite people."

Jenny started to explain, once again, her valid reasons for disliking the guy, but MaryAnn held up her hand to hush Jenny. She leaned against the file cabinet. "Here's the thing. Our vacancy rate is nearly twenty percent. There's no way we can raise our prices again. And we can't afford to operate at anything less than ninety percent occupancy."

"Yes, it's a bummer that the residents have a tendency to die."

"Even so," MaryAnn said, either ignoring or not getting the sarcasm, "we've got to do something to bring up our numbers. I sure as hell don't want to start looking for a new job at my age." Jenny nodded. She had seen how the Board treated her boss during their last visit.

"How would Randy, of all people, help improve our numbers?" Jenny asked. "You know that guy is bad news. One day he's going to really hurt one of the residents, then the Board will shut down this place in a millisecond. One lawsuit—"

"Humor me . . . okay? What if you, Beth, and I meet next week to brainstorm about a low-cost marketing campaign? If we hired a couple more guys like Randy who are capable of lifting and bathing the obese residents, then we could differentiate ourselves . . ."

"Bring us your fat loved ones, and we'll get them to the toilet without dropping them."

"Perhaps a little less crass than that. But . . . yes."

Jenny chuckled. "Is there really such a niche?"

MaryAnn shrugged.

"We could start by getting rid of the aides who don't do their fair share of the work and find others like that new girl."

"Ana . . . yes, she's a gem."

"I've overheard families gushing with thanks, saying their parents have never had such good care. They bring her gifts. I think if we start improving the lives of those who are here now, our reputation will soon speak for itself."

"I don't know if we have the time."

"Are things that bad?" Jenny looked at MaryAnn's face. She had aged years in the last few months.

"I've got five years before retirement. I don't want to go back out there and compete against a bunch of thirty-year-olds."

It took tremendous effort for Jenny not to roll her eyes, and say, Yes, well, we all have our challenges. Instead, she said, "Send me an Outlook invite for next week, and I'm happy to brainstorm with you and Beth."

On her way out, MaryAnn nodded to Jenny's hair. "Looks good on you. You and Jerrod ready for the big cruise?"

"As ready as I'll ever be." The clock on her desk read 11:30. "I need to skip out early today, though, if you don't mind."

"Fine. Don't forget your out-of-office email."

Alone again in her office, Jenny thought about her run-in with Brodie earlier that morning. She thanked the universe that he hadn't insisted on opening the letter while she stood by. The potential humiliation. It was difficult to believe that two years had passed since she had found Brodie's wallet at the edge of her driveway. Two years since the accident. His wallet had sat in her car for weeks before she carried it inside and sat at the table in her kitchen. Jerrod was playing the piano in the next room. She had fallen in love with her husband, in part, because of his ability to mesmerize her with his beautiful music. He was so talented. Now all she felt when he played was resentment and grief. She had emptied the content of the found wallet onto the table. Three tickets to an upcoming Giant's game. A California driver's license: Brodie F. Marshall. Six feet seven inches. Two hundred and five pounds. Green eyes. A pink dot denoting donor. There was a school picture of a pretty redheaded girl. Another photo of the girl in a swimsuit showing off a gold medal and hugging a woman—presumably her mother and Brodie's wife. There were credit cards, medical cards, business cards . . . the usual. She remembered sniffing the wallet and that it had smelled like Tide and leather. She had pressed it against her face, illogically hoping it still held some of the man's warmth. After gathering a notepad and pen from the kitchen junk drawer, she wrote her first letter:

Dear Brodie,
I found your wallet in the street. I kept one of your business cards in case we ever need to switch agents.
Regards,
J.M.

She didn't sign her full name nor include a return address on the note. She wanted to be a bit mysterious and to imagine his curiosity about who had found it: *Who was J.M.?* A week after returning the wallet, she'd been feeling depressed, more than usual, and decided to write him another anonymous letter. This time she asked about the redheaded girl with the medal in one of the photos she'd found in his wallet. The fact that he couldn't reply didn't matter. She imagined him sitting down and reading her letter, pulling out the photos to see which one J.M. was referring to.

Since then, she'd written a dozen more letters. A couple of them she didn't mail, couldn't mail for they revealed too much—in essence, confessions of her darkest thoughts as though he were a priest. Twice she had slipped the letters into his office mail slot, perhaps subconsciously hoping she'd get caught.

Jenny heard a tap on her office door. If she kept her head down, refused to look up, would whoever it was, eventually go away?

"Jenny?"

She looked up and saw Ana, the new attendant, holding a Tupperware container, fork, and napkin. Surely the kid wasn't hoping to lunch together.

"I don't mean to bother you," said Ana, "but my mom made an enormous batch of German potato salad. I was wondering if you'd like some. It seems like you're always working through lunch and I brought you—"

She held a single-serving container with a fork and napkin. She looked so sweet that Jenny didn't want to hurt her feelings. She said, "I'd love to try some." She was indeed hungry, and she knew that the sooner she accepted the food, the sooner Ana would leave her alone. After the accident, people were always trying to force food on Jerrod and her. It had gotten to the point that the sight of someone standing at her front door with a pie or a casserole made Jenny wanted to scream "Get the fuck off my porch!" at these well-intentioned friends and neighbors.

Ana stood at the desk, twisting the hem of her smock around her fingers as Jenny opened the container. Petite purple and gold potatoes glistened with a fragrant vinegar and Dijon mustard dressing. Herman meowed and came out from under the desk. He stood like a beggar by Jenny's chair. "Hungry?" she asked, bringing the container close to his nose to watch him sniff it. Which he did, briefly. His curiosity satisfied, he arranged himself into a semicircle and closed his eyes.

"It's got capers," Ana said. "I hope you like those. And, um, your haircut looks pretty. I've been thinking about cutting mine for eons. Just haven't the courage yet."

Jenny looked at Ana's black hair. It reached past the edge of her

69

smock. The ends were healthy. "Absolutely not! Your hair is stunning," she said. "This smells delicious. I'll just take a few."

"No, they're all for you. I brought some for myself."

"Oh. Thanks. Would you like to sit?" Please say no.

An enormous smile overtook Ana's face. She sat down, smoothed her uniform, and fiddled with the crystal clock as Jenny speared a potato.

"How are things going?" Jenny took a bite. The vinegar made her mouth water.

"You know." The girl shrugged and started twirling her hem again.

Jenny knew. The other girls hadn't warmed up to her and probably never would unless Ana's work ethic sunk to their level.

"This is really good." Jenny thought about how Jerrod would enjoy this salad with grilled Ahi. The old Jenny, the Jenny before the accident, would have asked for the recipe and surprised him with dinner that evening.

"Did you hear that I dropped iced tea on one of the residents?"

Was that the real purpose of her visit, Jenny wondered, looking at the girl's slumped posture and praying she wasn't here for a pep talk. Jenny just didn't have it in her today.

"We all have accidents. Well, I appreciate the salad, but I've got—"

"The thing is, I kinda did it on purpose."

"What do you mean by *kinda*?" Jenny set the potato salad and fork down. She glanced toward the living room. The sofas and chairs were nearly filled for the afternoon reading. Last week, they'd started *Pride and Prejudice*, and the novel had drawn an enthusiastic crowd. Every school year, especially toward late spring, Creekside was approached by desperate high school seniors who needed to earn volunteer credits to graduate. They usually didn't last more than a few weeks. But the latest kid tore into the parking lot in his topless jeep, tires screeching and music blaring, and seemed to enjoy being around the residents. He had stuck it out past his required hours.

"I'm sorry," Jenny said. "What were you saying?"

"You know that group of women who always play bridge together?"

"Lottie and her clan?" The Almighty Foursome that all the other residence and staff regarded with equal parts fear and loathing.

marie estorge

Ana nodded. "And you know that new resident? Mrs. Ferris, in 312. Yesterday Lottie and her friends were playing cards, except one of the ladies was sick, so they were short a player. I was helping another resident, so I didn't notice at first what was happening, but I guess Mrs. Ferris went over and asked if she could sit in as a substitute. When I saw Mrs. Ferris at their table, I was so happy, thinking that she was making some friends. But as I watched, I saw them completely ignore her. They didn't even look up as she stood at their table and spoke directly to them. Then Mrs. Ferris just kept trying until it must have dawned on her that they were ignoring her. I watched her walked away. I kinda felt humiliated for her. And you know what they did?"

Jenny shook her head. She watched a high-school volunteer help one of the wheelchair-bound residents open a bag of pretzels. The teenager made a straining face as if it required a Herculean effort to tear open the bag. The resident laughed. She held out the bag to offer him some. He shook his head and patted her shoulder.

Jenny sighed. "What did they do?"

"They started giggling like a bunch of middle schoolers. I kept imagining my grandma being treated that way."

Jenny watched Ana rub her nose. The girl's eyes were moist, but she held back the tears.

Ana sniffled. "What would it hurt to act a little nicer?"

"Apparently, despite their puffed-out chests, they have very fragile egos." Jenny wondered how Rhonda would have handled the rejection. She figured her mother-in-law would have told Lottie and her gang where they could shove their cards and let each of her dogs discretely poop in the ladies' handbags.

"I asked her if she wanted to join me on the patio to enjoy some sun, but she said she was going to take a nap. It just sucks."

"Yeah. Sometimes things just suck. I know it's frustrating. There have been times I've wanted to dump a pitcher or two on some of the residents or their abrasive families. I completely understand your empathy for Mrs. Ferris." Jenny pierced another potato. "But Ana, you can't go around spilling tea on residents every time they act like a jerk."

71

"I know. I got a similar lecture from the director." Ana stood and started to leave.

"Hang on. If it makes you feel any better, these women are so horrible that even their children rarely visit them anymore. I think that's why they behave so badly. They're lonely and miserable, and it makes them feel better when others are also lonely and miserable."

Ana nodded. Jenny knew she sounded like a schoolmarm. To show she wasn't so stuffy, she said, "The funny thing is . . . Mr. All Hands in 406 hasn't ever made a pass at any of them. And he's not too discriminating."

They both grinned. "He's probably afraid they'll take him up on it!" Ana covered her mouth and giggled at her comment.

"Perhaps. I've seen them watch him. Especially when he starts courting the new residents. Sure they snicker at him. Nudge each other and probably call him a fool. But they watch him like a hawk. And you just wait . . . the next time Mr. Farley comes to play the piano. The minute Mr. All Hands gets up to ask someone to dance, these crotchety old women are sitting up and practically holding their breath in hopes he'll choose them. But he never does. He's got them figured out."

Ana pulled a loose thread from her sleeve. "He asked me the other day if I was of *age to consent*." Her face turned pink. "I wasn't sure what he meant. I mean, he couldn't mean what I thought he meant, so I asked him, 'Consent to what?'" She laughed. "He pointed to his crotch and did this thrusting motion."

Jenny and Ana started giggling. "Ew. Did you warn him to settle down before he broke his hip?" Ana giggled so hard she let out a little snort, which caused a further eruption by both women.

"I lied and told him I was sixteen and that my father was a judge. And we were Mormons."

"Good recovery."

"Well, I'll let you finish lunch and get back to work. Thank you."

"Thank you for what?" Jenny asked. "You brought me lunch."

"For being nice to me."

"The others will come around." Jenny hoped this was true. "They're a bit standoffish at first. And Beth's door is always open. She is always looking for someone to talk to, especially if you've got any good dating advice."

As Jenny watched Ana leave, she was thinking about how tomorrow, and in the upcoming weeks and months, Beth, Ana, and the others whom Jenny had interacted casually with before her suicide, would be left searching their memories, replaying snippets of conversations for clues. *She seemed a little distracted*, they might whisper to one another, *but not depressed. Certainly not suicidal. Even considering what she's been through.* Her suicide would likely be perceived as selfish, but to Jenny, it was also an act of selflessness. Jerrod could move on without her presence to continually remind him of what they'd lost. Friends could stop feeling guilty about procrastinating in calling her to check in. Beth and her coworkers would find someone to fill the office, and soon Jenny would become an anecdote: *Remember that woman who ran over her young son?*

brodie

VICTORIA MARTIN WAS waiting outside Brodie's office, and he knew he should have been preparing for their meeting. Instead, he closed his eyes and exhaled loudly. The metallic taste of the Gatorade and vodka from earlier was still detectible. He popped a mint and wondered if the vodka was meant for the meet. Sasha didn't weigh more than a hundred pounds. Holy shit. He pictured her starting her hurdle on the diving board, drunk, losing her balance, then splitting her head open on the hard metal. He shuddered and wondered which of her friends would have raided their parent's liquor cabinet on Sasha's behalf? Karen and Brodie drank wine, nothing fancy or expensive, so he knew the vodka hadn't come from them. He couldn't recall when she last slept over at a friend's house. Weeks, at least, maybe months. Was it Lake Tahoe in January? No, that was her junior year. It must have been Santa Cruz after Thanksgiving. Did she get the vodka from that Brad kid? Perfect, Marshall, blame it on the sophomore who was dumb enough to brag about his weed to the entire lacrosse team. More than likely, she had a fake I.D., as they all did at her age, and could buy her own damn liquor.

In the Martins' folder, there were printouts of email exchanges between Dr. Martin and Brodie, a couple from Victoria to Andrea, and several back-and-forths with the underwriter who refused to reinstate the Martins' four million dollar Umbrella Liability Policy after it lapsed due to non-payment. Given the fact that many people had lost their dental coverage along with their jobs, it was not difficult to believe that many of his patients weren't scheduling their semi-annual cleanings or expensive dental repairs. Plus, there was that short-lived scandal about an elderly woman claiming he'd molested her when she was under sedation. It took a half dozen attempts to sell Dr. Martin on the umbrella policy, to convince him that with his various exposures—the dental practice, the boat and jet skis, two homes, two rentals, a trampoline and swimming pool, the unproven accusations of his propensity to fondle blue-haired patients, and a teen driver with a terrible driving record—that he and his family needed as much liability coverage as they could afford. Yet each time Brodie had broached the subject, the dentist pushed the brochure back across the table and said the umbrella business was just a big scam. Four million dollars in protection for less than two grand a year? How is that possible?

Now, after his stepson racked up two reckless speeding tickets, including one that resulted in personal injury to his passenger, and a DUI, Dr. Martin claimed he never received any emails or calls reminding him that his umbrella premium was past due and his policy in jeopardy of cancellation. Who was he kidding? Of course, the email records still existed. Brodie was sure the man was no better than he in cleaning out his email folders. Yet he'd insisted it was Brodie's fault his policy lapsed, and now the dentist didn't have four million dollars' worth of legal defense in his back pocket. He reminded Brodie of a whiny kid on Sasha's team her freshman year, always blaming the slightest noise for her failed dive and insisting on a do-over. Sometimes, in life, there were no do-overs. That certainly had been his experience.

A thought struck him. Sasha had been grumpier than usual in the mornings. Yesterday, all he'd asked on the drive to school was how her reverse one-and-a-half somersault was coming along and she said, "Could you not talk?" in a voice so flat he hardly recognized it.

"Sure, I could do that. And how about you walk the rest of the way."

She'd been irritable and aggressive for months. Non-stop. Parents with whom he commiserated at dive meets, particularly those with older children, had assured Brodie that soon he and Karen would witness a positive shift in their teenager as she approached nineteen, and definitely by twenty. The anger, the moodiness, the disrespect would slowly shed to allow new growth; underneath would be a shiny young adult that they'd want to spend time with again. Of course, there were the outliers, but they assured Brodie that that wouldn't be the case with Sasha. He prayed they were right.

He read the first email Andrea sent to the Martins in January advising them that their umbrella policy would cancel February tenth unless Brodie received a check. The next document was a formal, company-generated letter saying that their policy had been canceled and to contact their agent immediately if they wanted to reinstate. Last week, four months after the last email, Victoria brought in a check and told Brodie that her son had had an accident. His license was revoked. Although this wasn't stated outright, this insurance matter had now taken priority, and they somehow found the funds to pay their bill. But reinstatement was denied. The underwriter, a by-the-book, nasally man disliked by all the agents in the district, said the DMV's revocation of the teenager's license made the Martin's policy ineligible for reinstatement.

Brodie had unsuccessfully tried talking him into offering them one million in coverage, hoping to get something in place while shopping around for more appropriate coverage. Yesterday, however, he had proposed a solution, which received a lukewarm reception from the underwriter. The hitch . . . convincing Victoria and Dr. Martin that it was their only option at the moment. Maybe they'd be so grateful that they'd buy five Life policies today, thereby allowing him to collect his bonus and let Keith off the hook.

Huddled around Maria's playpen were Victoria's twin kindergarten-aged daughters, who shared their mother's exotic, Egyptian cat-like eyes. They had thick, dark eyebrows like their mother, who looked like a young Elizabeth Taylor. The girls leaned against the portable structure, watching the baby suck on a pacifier. Victoria's mother-in-law stood nearby, staring adoringly at her granddaughters as their mother warned them to step back or else they might fall on top of the baby. The elder Mrs. Martin noticed Brodie and startled. Her eyes traveled the length of his frame as she grabbed her daughter-in-law's hand and moved behind her. He smiled to assure her he meant no harm. He could smell her strong, earthy perfume from where he stood and leaned away. The girls had not budged from the playpen. Victoria touched the slightly taller twin's shoulder and lifted an eyebrow. The threat worked. The girl pulled on her sister's lace collar, and they took a half step back from the playpen.

They noticed Brodie and took another half step back. The first time he'd met them, they had asked if he was a giant. He said, "Indeed I am." That seemed to delight them.

"Victoria," he said, extending his hand. Her red-framed glasses served as a headband, revealing a pink indentation on the ridge of her sphinxlike nose where the glasses had rested previously. Three gold chains of different lengths hung from her pierced earlobes, tiny diamonds punctuating the end of each delicate chain. Her incredible beauty always made Brodie nervous. Self-conscious, somehow.

"You remember my mother-in-law, Mrs. Martin," Victoria said.

"Yes." He offered his hand, knowing she wouldn't take it.

"Who are you?" she asked in a faint voice, still using Victoria as a shield.

"Mom, you've met Mr. Marshall before."

Nothing registered on her face, but Brodie was not surprised given it had been some time since her diagnosis of Alzheimer's.

"Young ladies," he said to the girls, who were, once again, leaning against the playpen. "We've got paper and markers. You can draw in my office while your mother and I talk."

"I think they're fine here with Andrea," Victoria said, "unless, of course, you mind."

Andrea shook her head. Brodie looked at the elder Mrs. Martin, still clinging to her daughter-in-law's hand and hoped she'd stay behind with the twins. Andrea swiveled her chair around to open the credenza behind her desk where a tray of colored markers was kept with the office stationery. She produced an assortment of coloring books she had purchased from The Dollar Store, and the twins grabbed for them. Mrs. Martin followed Victoria and Brodie into his office.

"How is Michael doing?" he asked once they were seated at the conference table.

"It's been hard," Victoria said, her eyes misting. She fiddled with her diamond tennis bracelet and cleared her throat rather indelicately. She straightened her shoulders and her hands settled in her lap. He noticed how skinny her bare arms had become. Her collar bones more pronounced, her face thinner.

"There's never been much affection between Michael and Dr. Martin. It's not like . . . well, you know, it's hard when the child isn't your own—" She sighed. "I don't mean to say . . . He's tried. Anyway, so what are our options?"

"Why does that man play music in a parking lot?" the elder Mrs. Martin asked, staring out the window. She held her handbag in her lap, both veiny hands holding firm on the bamboo handle as if she worried Brodie might reach across the table to steal her wallet.

Victoria looked at him, and he explained how the RV guy had come to live behind their building.

"I spoke with the underwriter," he said now. "She said for the company to consider reinstatement, Michael would have to live out of the household. Literally."

"We were poor like him when we first started out," Mrs. Martin said, nodding to the window. "Not a dime to spare. But we worked hard. And now, my son is a doctor. Do you know Dr. Martin?"

"Yes, I've had the pleasure." He gave her time for rebuttal before he continued. "In addition to being out of the house, all financial ties with Michael would need to be severed. Otherwise, his liabilities are your liabilities. But I told the underwriter that was unlikely since he—"

"He no longer lives with us," Victoria said.

Brodie suspected she was lying, although she looked directly at him without a blink or a twitch. They had spoken yesterday afternoon, and she hadn't mentioned anything about her son leaving home.

"Pardon?"

"He's gone. There's no risk of him stealing our cars or damaging other's property."

Her android-like, cold tone made Brodie uncomfortable. He imagined the teenager buried in the backyard under the fruit trees. When Dr. Martin first invited him out to the house to review the property and provide a quote, they'd toured their half-acre garden. The swimming pool and barbecue were the doctor's domain. Victoria claimed dominion over the grove of fruit trees: figs, pears, apples, citrus, and persimmon. After admitting he'd never eaten a persimmon, Victoria asked him to pull one of the last of the season from a high branch. She insisted he taste the tomato-shaped fruit. He was skeptical at first, feeling the waxy, yellowish-orange skin. He took a bite hoping she'd look away so he could spit the fruit into the bushes if he didn't like the flavor or texture. It was crunchy like a pear with a sweet cinnamon flavor.

"Not bad," he had said, taking a larger bite.

She pulled two black figs from one of the gnarled branches of a nearby tree and offered him one. As kids, he and Keith called them "old man balls." They would hurl the fruit at each other in a game of war whenever they visited their grandmother.

"Michael's gone," Brodie repeated. "Do you have an address for him?"

"Where's Michael?" Mrs. Martin asked. "What's that boy done now?"

Victoria rested her right elbow on the table and set her chin in her palm. She stared, without blinking, at the painted window of the porcelain cottage figurine. When it was clear that Mrs. Martin had lost the thread of the conversation, Victoria whispered, "He's at county jail in Martinez. I don't know where he'll go from there, but it won't be home. Our lawyer says he'll be locked away for a while."

"Oh." Brodie swallowed, hoping he'd never have to deliver this news about Sasha. "I'm terribly sorry."

"Obviously, I spoiled him too much. Tried to make up for an absent father. Or that's what I've been told." She shot her mother-in-law a sideways glance. "Now it's out of my hands. The girls don't know. They think he's backpacking through Europe before going off to college."

"Why is Michael backpacking in Europe?" asked Mrs. Martin. "Shouldn't he be in school? That boy needs to straighten up. You spoil him too much."

Victoria scratched so aggressively at the back of her head Brodie feared she would draw blood.

"I'll need some documentation verifying his new address and situation. I'll call the underwriter to give her a heads up. Is there anything else?"

She looked at the clock on his bookshelf. "Is ten AM too early to start drowning myself in bourbon?"

"Too bad I polished off a vodka cocktail I found in my daughter's backpack this morning. I should have saved it for you." Realizing this must sound peculiar coming from one's insurance agent, he added, "Long story. Teenagers."

She nodded. "You know what his father told the judge at the custody hearing? 'His mother can have him. I want to focus on my new family.'" Her eyes fell back on the porcelain figurine, and her fragile shoulders caved in. He waited to see if she was finished. He'd learned not to probe into clients' personal matters and never to offer an unsolicited opinion. Even when solicited, the opinion should be vague enough not to warrant a recall. Unless the matter posed a potential liability, something that could be insured against by the company, he didn't care to know about it. Sounded cold? Sure. Yet it was a matter of survival in this industry. Don't get tangled in the misery of others. He wasn't like Stan and many of the other agents in this district who sought amusement in gossip.

"Pardon me, may I use your restroom?" Victoria asked.

"Certainly." He stood and indicated the door to his right.

"Where are you going?" asks Mrs. Martin.

"Mom, I'll be right back. You'll be fine with Mr. Marshall. He's a nice man."

When they were alone, Brodie tried to think of something benign to say. It was tricky with Alzheimer's. He never knew what was safe. Figuring silence was the best course, he flipped through the Martin's folder as though he were looking for a document.

"My husband and I honeymooned at this motel," she said.

"Oh, that's nice." The man outside the window was playing a soft, lazy rendition of The Battle Hymn of the Republic. Brodie wanted to close his eyes and let the music lull him to sleep.

"No, not at all," she said, emphatically. "It was a flea trap motel. Bed bugs, the whole caboodle. But it was all we could afford. We didn't have money like my son and Victoria here. Now they think they're poor because they have to sell one of their houses."

"It's a tough economy." Brodie squirmed.

"What's your name?"

"Brodie Marshall."

"Marshall. That sounds like a first name. My husband and I honeymooned here. I got my period, imagine."

Where was she going with this anecdote? Brodie wondered. He prayed Victoria would soon return.

"Boy, what a mess," she said, rubbing a cluster of age spots on her wrinkled hand as if trying to bring the skin back to its former glory. "I was mortified knowing the cleaning lady would see the sheets. My husband said I was acting childish. Refused to help me strip the—"

The doorknob turned. Thank you, God . . . Victoria was back. Her eyes were bright, her makeup smoothed over, and her lipstick reapplied.

"Where's Michael?" Mrs. Martin asked. "He's supposed to take me to the DMV. I need to renew my license." Victoria patted her mother-in-law's hand.

"He's on vacation, Mom. I'm sure he hasn't forgotten about you."

Brodie wasn't sure which was worse: worrying about scrawny, young, misguided Michael Martin locked in the Martinez County Jail, enduring who knows what, or picturing Mrs. Martin frantically stripping blood-stained sheets from a bed in some hotel room—a room that could possibly be the one he was now sitting in. He was sure about one thing: Victoria had enough on her mind without him pitching her Life insurance. Now, if he had any Get Out of Jail Free cards, those might interest her. Instead, he politely walked them to the door and slumped back into his chair. He picked up his phone. It was ten-fifteen. A final plea to Keith. He was either in, or he was out.

The call went straight to voicemail. No surprise. Brodie had told Kevin that he must stop by no later than five to sign the life insurance applications and drop off a check for the policies to count toward this year's quota. The deadline was actually midnight, but he didn't want to cut it so close. There was desperation in Brodie's voice as he added, "Or tell me where and when, and I'll meet you. I really need this." He pressed the phone against his forehead, and thought, I could always follow Sasha's example. Fill out the five applications, sign Keith and Emma's names, and then use a personal check to pay the initial premiums. What next,

Marshall? Watch the check bounce? He startled when his cell phone rang.

"Where you've been?" he asked his brother, collapsing in relief. "I've left a million messages."

"You can't imagine what's happening here. I'll fill you in later. How about I stop by after dinner? Oh, shit . . . gotta run—"

"Keith . . . wait. Keith . . ." The line went dead. "Shit! Shit! Shit!"

The office phone rang. Maybe it was Keith calling back. Maybe he'd dialed Brodie's office rather than his cell. He picked up and was about to say hello when he heard Andrea's greeting.

"Brodie Marshall's office, Andrea speaking. Oh, hi, Kirk. How may I help you?"

Kirk. Fuck. Brodie hung up. His head fell forward and rested on the keyboard. He was so thankful he hadn't spoken first. Mental note: Buy Andrea lunch next week. For the last two weeks, she had dealt with Kirk Boyle, the thirty-year-old, never-once-held-a-job imbecile whose widowed father paid his insurance and gas just to get his son out of the house.

Brodie typed into his phone, "Need to talk. Are u still buying 5 life policies?" A grey bubble with the three dots appeared. He picked at his thumbnail as he waited for Keith to finish drafting his response. Seconds passed. He popped a couple more mints. The text bubble and ellipses disappeared and with it his hope. He sent another text with a question mark. No response.

"He's not available right now," Andrea said from the next office. "But I—"

Half listening to her conversation and half feeling as if someone had scrambled his brains with an electric whisk, he nervously tapped his thumb against his desk. Bloody sheets. Vodka. Kevin. Kirk. Foreclosure . . . Words and names popped in and out of his head, making it nearly impossible to maintain a coherent thought. Sasha. Dive. Stan—*you snooze, you lose*. Vodka. What was she thinking? Panic rose in his gut. He opened Facebook to see if any of Sasha's recent postings would offer clues behind the forgery and vodka, the irritability.

He saw that she'd removed the moody black and white profile photo she snapped in her bathroom mirror a few weeks back after a terrible dive meet. Now her profile showed one of those white silhouettes with the gray background that appeared when you first opened an account. The only posting for the entire week was written yesterday. "End of Story. C'est la vie."

What in the hell? he thought, scanning the thirty-two responses. They were all as clueless as Brodie was. One kid responded, "RDC," which, after consulting Urban Dictionary, he learned meant Really Don't Care. Guess that was the new *Whatever*. Smartass punk. He opened her album and clicked on a picture of her doing a handstand on the three-meter board, her red ponytail over the edge, her eyes frozen wide. She stared eerily right past whoever was standing at the top of the ladder with the camera. The caption read, "Everything looks upside down from here." There were pictures from Turks and Caicos taken two summers ago. A beautiful photo of Karen and her in their matching purple polka dot bikinis, both sunburned after a day of sailing and snorkeling. Karen looked as if she could be Sasha's sister. If you softened the focus, they could pass for twins.

He couldn't find the cute picture of Sasha sitting on the diving board in her *Diving Princess* T-shirt, kicking her feet, looking so happy after winning NCS for the second year straight. Or the one of her asleep on the flight from Oregon after the Zones competition, "RIP" written across her forehead by teammates. It looked as if she had done some purging. Scanning her list of friends, Brodie noticed that so many of the teenage girls tended to gravitate to profile photos that made them look slutty with their pushup bras, softly-lit babyfaces, and duck lips. Only two girls out of the entire bunch looked wholesome enough to take on a family vacation to Disney World. It occurred to him that he hadn't seen any of the girls—classmates or dive friends—at the house in months.

"I told you before . . ." Andrea's voice sounded strained as if she was trying hard to remain polite. How she was able to show that nitwit any patience was a mystery. A hint of attitude from Kirk was all the justification Andrea's predecessor felt she needed to hang up on him. "Drop off the car at an auto service shop . . . If you don't trust that guy, pick another one. Yes, they'll help you arrange a rental car."

There were a half dozen posted messages to Sasha that had gone unanswered. One said, "We missed you last night. Why the no-show?"

"I can't call The Help Desk to demand they upgrade your rental to a Mercedes," Andrea said. "Your coverage allows twenty-five dollars a day, and a limit of three hundred dollars. No, I've never rented a Mercedes, but I'm sure it's much higher than twenty-five dollars."

Brodie thought, What a moron.

"It doesn't work like that. Please don't be so rude. I'm just trying to explain—"

Enough. He closed Facebook and headed over to Andrea's desk. When she looked up, he held a pretend pistol to his head and pulled the trigger.

"Put him on speaker."

She set down the receiver and grinned.

"Hey, Kirk, Brodie Marshall here. Sounds as if you're giving Andrea a hard time. What's up?"

"Your secretary doesn't understand that I need the rental car company to give me a Mercedes. I might have a job interview and I want to make a good impression."

"An interview, eh?" Brodie rolled his eyes at the remote possibility. "Well, heck, I wouldn't mind driving a Mercedes myself," he said. "But the thing is, there are laws prohibiting you and anyone else from profiting from an insurance loss. Let's say we were to upgrade your 95 Ford Taurus to a Mercedes SL500, then we'd be covering your loss plus giving you extra. You can see how this monetary gain doesn't work, right?"

Andrea bared her teeth like a rabid raccoon and raked her nails in the direction of the speaker.

"But . . . but I don't like the guy at that shop you sent me to. He keeps hanging up on me."

"Big surprise," he whispered to Andrea.

"Pick another one," Brodie said. "I haven't any vested interest in that shop or any other one."

"Could you tell them to pick up the Taurus from my dad's house and drop off the rental car there as well? I'm staying with him temporarily. Just until I get a job."

"You'll have to sweet-talk them yourself," he said as the front door opened. Karen entered with the healthy pink complexion of someone who just spent an hour and a half at a Pilates class. As she headed to the crib, Brodie admired her round ass accentuated by the tight black pants.

"And Kirk, take down this number. It's the company's Help Desk. You should deal directly with them in the future." Brodie motioned for Andrea to hang up. At the sound of the click, he said, "Good luck."

"Bad day?" asked Karen.

"The nitwit is the exception to the client-is-never-wrong rule," he said, kissing her soft lips.

"Andrea, do you mind if I hold her?" Karen reached for Maria before Andrea responded. She buried her face in Maria's neck as if to inhale her, cell by cell. Even now, watching Karen with a baby, a thread of jealousy wove through Brodie's heart. She had marveled endlessly over Sasha's every feature. She couldn't get enough of cuddling her, studying her, kissing her. A man should expect to sit on the bench after a birth. Maternal instincts should take precedence. But hell, he couldn't reason his way past resentment.

He nodded toward his office.

"May I steal Maria for a bit?" asked Karen.

"She's about ready for a bottle so holler if she gets cranky."

Once the door shut, Karen nuzzled the baby and said, "You look frazzled."

Brodie let out a long sigh and sat on the edge of the conference table that Karen helped him pick out when he first opened the agency after college. The table still looked as if it belonged in a dining room. The six office-style chairs couldn't disguise its intended purpose. They had bought the table on credit at Sears. He'd always hated that it reminded him of how he had struggled those first years to pay the rent on the office as well as the apartment. He could still see Stan's smirk when he saw the polished dining table.

"All you need is a warm apple pie and a doily," he had teased, "and maybe some checkered pillows."

Combing a loose strand from Karen's face, Brodie started to tell her that he felt overwhelmed and he didn't know how they were going to survive until the end of the month if he didn't get his bonus. How he was worried that this thing with Sasha was even greater than they both knew. How he was so burnt out at work and wished he could to tell the next demanding customer to go screw himself. He wanted to admit all these things, but he saw how happy she was holding the baby. He wondered, as she cooed and kissed the baby if maybe he never confided in her about his worries because he sensed she didn't want to hear them. Or maybe he was just a coward. He was too scared to pierce her happy bubble and risk losing her.

"This morning has been one shit-storm after another," he said.

Maria started to squirm. Her balled fist struck, by virtue of a mis-calculation, her cheek rather than her open mouth. She made another attempt, this time punching herself in the nose, and started to whimper.

"No Keith, then?" she asked, bouncing Maria gently in her arms.

"No. Have you spoken with Emma?"

Karen shook her head and planted a kiss on Maria's nose. "You want me to call her?"

"Thanks, but he said he'll call me later. I don't want to hound Emma. There's still time."

"Not much, though, right?"

"Right, my lovely lady," he said, pulling her toward him. "Coming in here looking hot. Distracting me from my work. It's time for you to go. Otherwise, I might devour you."

Karen pulled away and said to Maria, "Men, my little princess, have one primal goal. And after, it's 'Don't let the door hit you on the way out.'"

"Yep, we just chew you up and spit you out." Brodie shook his head and pointed at the door. "Out of here."

jenny

JENNY WATCHED MARYANN pace outside of the building. Her boss walked up and down the sidewalk that faced the parking lot, checking her phone every couple of minutes. Sweat had soaked through the light fabric of her jacket leaving, grey patches under her arms. A car pulled into the lot. MaryAnn stepped off the sidewalk, then shook her head. Obviously, she had hoped it was Randy. He was going to face hell when he returned to work.

Jenny pulled out her bulging, red leather wallet to purge. She emptied each compartment onto her desk, and created two piles: keep and toss. Contra Costa County Library card—toss, Fandango gift card—toss (Jerrod hated crowded theaters), bank deposit receipts—toss, Starbucks gift card—keep (Jerrod would use it), AAA card—toss (Jerrod had a copy). She flipped through the business cards, looking at the images of jewelry and art on some. Cards picked up at local crafts shows. Artists whose work she admired and had hoped one day to acquire. These cards were added to the discard pile. She had acquired everything she was ever going to acquire. When she came to a grey card with an embossed logo of a dove, her breath caught. She ran her finger gently over the raised bird.

She and Jerrod had visited only one funeral home. Jerrod usually conducted a thorough research before making any large purchase, but this time, he just picked a name from the internet, and made an appointment. When the funeral director introduced himself and held out a business card, Jerrod stared at the man's hand. It was as if he'd forgotten the protocol that he'd practiced so often in business. The proffered card was suspended in a space between two realities. For a few awkward seconds, seconds that hung in the air like minutes, neither she nor Jerrod moved. Finally, Jenny took the card. She must have tossed it into her bag. How it ended up filed along with the other business cards didn't matter now. She removed two BART tickets. They each had a $1.25 balance. She knew exactly when she had purchased them. She and Daniel had stood at the vending machine, the sound of traffic rushing past the station, and her son insisted on having his own ticket. He refused to be carried through the turnstile like a baby.

His cheeks were pink with excitement. They were taking the BART train to meet Jerrod at the San Francisco International Airport. He'd stood on the stained-cushioned seat and stared at the business traveler seated behind them.

"Hi . . . Hi . . . Hi," he said until the man looked up. "I'm going to the airport."

"Turn around," Jenny said, tugging on his corduroy jumper. "Let the gentleman read his book."

"That's okay. Is this your first time on BART?"

Daniel nodded and leaned over the seat, nearly spilling into the man's lap.

"Sit." She patted his diapered bottom and pulled his wiggly body into a tight embrace, plastering him with kisses. "You're such a rascal. Want to send a text to Daddy?"

His heart-shaped face moved up and down and side to side like a bobblehead with an extremely loose spring. He bounced in his seat as Jenny typed: *Surprise! We're meeting you at the airport. We're both eager to see you. XO.* Before she hit send, he reminded her to add a smiley face. They watched and waited for a response, but the screen turned dark. His bottom lip stuck out and his eyelids drooped into a pout.

"He's still in the air, sweetie. He can't send a text yet."

She sometimes wondered if Jerrod had affairs while away on business. When she was lonely, if he'd been away a week or longer, she'd torment herself by imaging her handsome, gregarious husband drinking in the hotel bar after taking depositions all day, striking up a conversation with a group of women. She'd play out the banter in her mind, give him clever, sexy (but not creepy or practiced) lines, some fresh script where the ultimate plot was to get one of the women in the sack. It was a sick game she played with herself. Perhaps it had helped to prepare herself for one day pulling a condom out of his suit slacks. Prepare her to finally admit to herself that she wasn't enough for him. For anyone.

Her son had settled in her lap. Jenny felt his muscles relax and soon he was as heavy and lifeless as a teddy bear stuffed with rice. The memory of Jerrod's return from that business trip was bittersweet. She'd planned some after-hours Mommy and Daddy playtime. In their bedroom that evening, Jerrod had laid naked on a Power Ranger beach towel set down to protect the bed linens. Wearing a lacy teddy she'd purchased earlier in the week, she slid a fluffed-up pillow under his head and asked, "Comfy?" He frowned as she opened the box of watercolors. She dipped the paintbrush into a glass of water, then dabbed and twirled it in a pad of blue. "Are you ready to become a great work of art?"

"Thought I was already," he said, smiling so that the dimple in his chin deepened.

"We'll just embellish nature's gift." She turned on the CD player and hit play. The Beatles "Abbey Road" album had been loaded earlier, and the loud volume startled them both. She lowered the volume. The last thing she wanted was to wake her son and ruin this time with her husband. She crawled over Jerrod's legs, singing along with "Come Together." With his legs spread apart, she sat on her heels and touched the tip of the paintbrush to his left nipple.

He shivered and tried to sit up, but she pressed down on his chest. "Shit, that's cold," he said, his stomach jiggling slightly. He'd put on some weight from all the business travel and hotel food.

She kissed the tip of his nose and told him to relax. His body shivered as she traced the outline of his left nipple. His stomach muscles tightened and his nipples instantly hardened. She dipped the brush in the water, making a swirl of blue and dabbed the brush into the black paint.

"Looks like someone's given my chest black eyes," he said as she painted the pink middle of his puckered areola. "I think your artist skills might be a bit lacking."

"I've just begun. Hush." She cleaned the brush. Next came yellow. Soon a huge sunflower with a smiley face emerged on his belly.

"Is this your Van Gogh? A sunflower?"

89

She cupped one hand over her ear and gave Jerrod a tormented look. Next, thunderous clouds overtook his belly. He tried to sit up, saying, "My turn. I feel rather vulnerable."

"Vulnerable is okay. You must trust me. Your turn will come soon enough. Now, what is it that teenage boys are always complaining about . . . blue balls? How about—"

"No way." He covered his balls with his hands. "Are these paints toxic?"

"*Now*, you ask." She grinned mischievously. "As if I'd put toxic paint on your body." He refused to let go of his balls, so she said, "May I paint your pecker then? Maybe something patriotic . . . red, white, and blue?"

To her disbelief, he relented and settled his hands at his sides. Beginning with the lower shaft, she painted blue circles, stretching the skin gently as she worked her way up. Each brush stroke summoned his blood until it looked like she'd hoisted a pole. She added red stripes. His cock moved on its own now as if reaching for the soft tip of the brush.

"Too bad I don't have a camera," she said, admiring her work. "I'm sure my Facebook friends would appreciate this work of art."

"Not going to happen. My turn."

They had switched places. He cleaned the brush and chose orange. The instant the cold, wet paint touched her skin, Jenny jumped. "I think, I think," she said, hardly able to catch her breath. "I'm way too ticklish for this. Stop, please."

"Not so quick." He bit on his lower lip as he drew curlicues all over her belly.

"One last thing . . ." She watched him paint his left hand red. He placed his hand over her heart, and when he pulled away, a perfect imprint was left. She would never take another bath, she remembered thinking. They were so in love. So optimistic and happy. They'd trusted, naively, that this was how their lives would play out. He had looked at her with such longing. God those looks had made her heart flutter.

Neither of them had said a word. He closed the paint box, dropped the brush in the murky glass of water. As he entered her slowly, tenderly, Jenny refused to worry about possible infections the watercolor paint might cause. She looked at Jerrod's face, his beautiful green eyes, and begged them to hold her in their gaze, to never release her, ever. Soon the paint that covered their bodies merged, blended, and their individual art became something of its own. They made love as hungrily as two people who believed they had suffered the acute deprivation of a week-long absence. How they took for granted the future.

Jerrod cried out first, and soon Jenny followed. They both lay still, their hands touching, their bodies spent. The air conditioner clicked back on. A chill shot up Jenny's spine. She sat up to reach for the blanket and looked at the paint covering both their bodies.

"We're a mess," she said, smiling. The towel had only provided so much protection. There was a huge red print next to her pillow. It looked like a bloody hand.

Her son had napped to the rocking of the BART train while she looked around at the eclectic collection of passengers. A cell phone rang, and her son's eyes fluttered open for a moment. A girl seated across the aisle started talking loudly on her phone. Even though Jenny tried to tune her out, wishing she'd take the call to an empty car, she found herself trying to place the girl's half of the conversation into some recognizable context. But the girl was all over the map, leaving a trail of "You know" along the erratic journey. There was a framed poster at the end of the train promoting continuing education classes at U.C. Berkeley. A decade ago, she couldn't wait to finish her degree. Ninety percent of what they were learning had seemed so pointless. She recalled a freshman speech class. The students were asked if they were given the last two spots on a lifeboat in the middle of the ocean, and they could save one other person, who would they choose: their spouse or their child?

One jock had replied, "Neither. Haven't you ever heard of the saying, every man for himself?" Some students laughed, some rolled their eyes, some sighed in annoyance, but one older lady asked, "Why would we have to choose? Why couldn't we try to save both?"

The rules were explained again.

"Are there sharks in the water?" asked a girl who always sat in the front row. The kid behind Jenny mumbled, "Idiot. It's the fucking middle of the ocean." The professor looked Jenny's way. "What would you do?"

The answer was simple. She was nineteen and had no reason to suspect she couldn't have a dozen babies if she wanted. But having a husband or even a boyfriend that lasted longer than a packet of birth control pills was something she'd dreamt about constantly. "Guess I'd save my husband. We could always have more children."

After a beat, the professor said, "You're so young."

Jenny recalled being offended by his arrogance. What did he know? She figured now, looking at her sleeping son, the professor knew more than she did back then.

Jenny tossed out the BART cards along with the other items in the discard pile. MaryAnn knocked on her door. "Have you seen Randy?"

Jenny shook her head. It wasn't her job to keep track of him. "Last time I saw, or rather heard him, he was having an argument on his phone in the bathroom."

"Well," said MaryAnn, rubbing her nose aggressively. "If you do, tell him I'm looking for him. His lunch break was over a half-hour ago and 302 had an accident and needs a shower."

Beth had sent Jenny a Skype message: "Appears Randy is still AWOL. Just saw Ana and another attendant struggling to lift 302 into the shower. I predict a Worker's Comp claim."

"Yeah, MaryAnn is about to go ballistic." Jenny slipped off a sandal and felt around under the desk for Herman until her big toe brushed against his fur. She stroked his belly, and he didn't bite her. She smiled, enjoying this hall pass that Herman was giving her. For two years, she'd craved affection, some physical comfort, so now even if it came from a four-legged creature, the feeling was nice.

"The other guy isn't around to help?" Jenny asked and Beth replied that he was taking another resident to physical therapy.

"Want to sneak out and go have margaritas? I'm buying."

Jenny shook her head. Beth was exhausting. "Can't. I'm still finishing my reports."

"Your loss."

"Probably. Raincheck."

"Now or maybe never."

Jenny's throat constricted. She let out her breath when Beth added, "I might win the Mega Millions and ditch this place."

In a text or Skype exchange, one participant eventually ends the conversation. They choose to walk away as one does at cocktail parties when spotting someone more interesting or simply tiring of the banter. These days, Jenny was usually the one to become distracted or lose interest. The one to walk away and leave the other waiting in vain for the next three dots. She grabbed her wallet and returned the items she'd chosen to keep. Shed of half its contents, the stained and scratched leather did not deflate back to its original shape, instead it maintained its engorgement, as if it still contained the ghost, the memories, the scent of its former contents. The wallet looked as deflated as she felt.

Jenny's phone pinged and she looked at the text.

"How many suitcases are you bringing?" her mother-in-law wrote. "Is four too many?"

"Bring whatever you think you'll need."

Jenny felt guilty as she set the phone face down. It was cruel playing along as if she had any real intention of going on that cruise. It would ruin Rhonda's long-held plans. She knew that Jerrod would be relieved not to have to spend a week in such close proximately to his wife. He'd never admit it, and of course, he'd play the grieving widow. Hopefully, Rhonda had thought ahead to purchase travel insurance.

Jenny rolled her neck from one shoulder to the next. She couldn't postpone her plan another day, much less another week, even if she would have liked to say goodbye to Rhonda in person. She had no idea how long it would be before Jerrod scheduled another out-of-town business trip. She drummed her fingers on the desk. Her decision was final.

brodie

ANDREA SET THE DAY'S stack of mail, sorted by urgency, in Brodie's inbox. "Sorry," she said and grimaced as if it were her fault that he had so many bills. He massaged his temples, wondering if Warren Buffett would respond to a desperate philanthropic plea.

A bill from PG&E was first in a lineup of bad news. The thin, orange-striped envelope would be his seven-day notice. For past due accounts, the utility company didn't bother with billing inserts—no glossy newsletters on how to reduce your carbon footprint or special offers on new furnace rebates. No, once a customer became delinquent, the utility company folks preferred to get right to the point with bold print: Pay before . . . or risk service interruption. That was not as impressively threatening as their 24-hour notice, where they announced that your utilities would be disconnected at noon the next day and a reactivation fee plus a deposit would be assessed to your account unless you *Act Now*. And this, he knew, was no idle threat.

Last month, Andrea had tapped on his door, apologizing to the clients, then motioned for Brodie to step out for a moment. From her worried look, he feared something had happened to Karen or Sasha.

She whispered, "There's a PG&E guy outside saying he's here to shut off the electricity."

"You're kidding me, right?"

She bit her lip and pointed to the young technician leaning against his truck in the parking lot.

"Go offer the clients coffee or something," he'd said in a panic before heading out to the technician. "Hey, I'm Brodie Marshall." They shook hands. "How are you today?" he asked, laying the niceties on thick. Treat these guys with respect, and it was likely they'd help you out if they could. Act like a dick, and they'd be more than happy to disconnect you.

"I think there's been a mix-up with my bill. Can you give me ten minutes to sort this out?"

The guy nodded without making eye contact. Sure, dude, he must have thought. Haven't heard that one before. Brodie walked to the far end of the parking lot and called the number on the back of his VISA card.

"I'm sorry, Mr. Marshall, you're past due on your payment. It looks as if you're over your limit as well. Do you want to make a payment today, and once that is applied, we can . . ."

He called the next card company. "Can't you increase my credit limit this one time? It's an emergency."

"Are you stranded somewhere?" the customer service operator asked.

"Sort of." He looked at the PG&E truck. The guy was now sitting behind the wheel, smoking a cigarette, looking Brodie's way. "Never mind," he said, as another idea occurred to him.

He waved at the PG&E guy and called out, "Just a couple of minutes." He checked Sasha's money market balance in her college fund on his phone. She had one thousand four hundred and change. He'd nearly wiped out her account. An online money transfer could take two, maybe three days. Fuck me, he thought. He didn't have time for that option. He found the bank's 800 number and explained to the representative that he needed to withdraw three hundred from Sasha's account for immediate use. Was there a way to wire funds between accounts immediately? The agent gave him the fax number to their wire department and told Brodie the required information to include on his wire request.

"There will be a wire fee of twenty-five dollars," he cautioned. "If we mailed you a check, you could avoid—"

"Yeah. No, I need it now." He headed inside and gave Andrea the information. "Please make sure the fax goes through. If the PG&E guy comes back, plead for more time," he whispered. His heart had banged around like an ice cube in a blender. He took a deep breath and walked back into his office. Gripping the back of a conference table chair, he explained that Sasha's school had called to say that she was feeling ill and wanted to be picked up.

"I hate to do this . . . since you're already here. But could we possibly reschedule?"

Luckily, they obliged. As he walked the clients to the door, he saw the PG&E guy's truck pulling out of the lot. For Christ's sake, he screamed silently. Can't I get a break? It turned out, however, the technician told Andrea he had another business down the street to shut off. He'd return in thirty minutes. It seemed the man in the sky had finally decided to show a little mercy. Before the technician returned, the money hit his personal account. He made a payment by phone and pumped his fist when assured they'd cancel the disconnect order on his account. He had sworn then that that was the last time he'd ever tap into Sasha's college account to keep his office running, even though the remaining balance of eleven hundred dollars wouldn't be enough for her dorm deposit.

Today, however, he still had a week before the thinnest PG&E envelope arrived. The other bills, he pushed aside. He didn't have the mental wherewithal to open them. The company's missives he ignored as well leaving the last group—the junk mail and magazines. He remembered the envelope the woman had slipped into the mail slot this morning and retrieved it from his desk.

Hi Brodie,

It's me again. I'm sure by now you recognize the handwriting. I hope, even as I write this, that you throw out my letters without reading them. And yet, a part of me hopes you do read them.

I had a son. I've mentioned him briefly in a few of my letters. His name was Daniel. He died two years ago, ironically, the same day I found your wallet. I know you must think I'm pathetic but writing these letters has been a life-line for me. My husband refuses to talk about our son. I can't see a way I'll ever escape this loneliness and grief. I want to be with my son. God only knows if there is anything else after this life.

The bell on the front door rang. Brodie set the letter down and swiveled around to listen.

"*Hola*, Andrea."

Thankfully, the man's voice was too jovial to be Ron's.

I haven't had the courage until now . . . He read again before being interrupted by a tap on his door. What now? This woman, J. M., could be in serious trouble. How was he at all equipped to help her? He had no idea who she was. How would he even find her? For all he knew, she could be a nut job, simply playing with him or looking for attention. But maybe she was really reaching out for help. Help . . . hell, he couldn't even find his own way out of a box.

Andrea poked her head inside his office. "My friend Carlos is here. He wants to talk to you about car insurance."

She was smiling and anxiously kicking the toe of one cleat against the heel of the other. Last year, there was a falling out between Ron and his friend. Something about the friend finding God and pestering Ron and Andrea to attend church and take Jesus Christ into their hearts. Now Ron refused to talk to him or allow him over to their apartment. Knowing how much Andrea adored him and his family, Brodie was happy to see that things had been sorted out.

He followed Andrea into the front office as he saw Carlos holding Maria and running his index finger down her tiny nose.

"How are you?" Brodie said, extending his hand and noticing that this guy had the straightest and whitest teeth outside of toothpaste ads. That and his aqua green eyes. He looked as if he was wearing a pair of those colored contacts Sasha once bought off the internet for Halloween, which gave her a nasty infection.

"Pretty good though we're not sleeping much with the new one."

"They've got four now under the age of six," Andrea explained.

"Four! You're a brave man."

"My wife and I found one a handful," he said to Carlos. In truth, Karen had wanted another baby. The minute she held Sasha in her arms, she gasped and said, "Oh, god. She's perfect. I want to have another one, and another right after that one. We should have five or six babies. They're so beautiful."

She was so drunk on love for this new creature she didn't seem to notice the panic in her husband's eyes. Within days of watching her wrap herself around her precious baby, a funk overtook Brodie. The male version of post-partum depression, he supposed. After she'd stopped breast-feeding and would get those mild cramps that coincided with her ovulation, he'd find a reason to avoid intimacy, or he'd pull out early. Finally, she quit asking if he was ready yet to have another baby, and although relieved, he always felt like such a selfish prick.

The irony was that just as she entered early menopause, and Sasha was pulling away from her parents, he realized, regretfully, that he'd gotten his way. They would, indeed, have only one child. Karen could have tricked him by saying, "Oops, well, you know what they say, the pill is ninety-nine percent effective. That darn one percent chance!" But that kind of deceit wasn't part of her DNA. Or was it? Brodie would have never imagined her lying to Sasha's principal as she had done today.

"Please, Carlos, have a seat." Brodie sat on the edge of the nearby credenza and Andrea handed him a folder. "How may I help you?"

"I just bought a truck and figured I'd transfer my policies to you. Andrea says you're a good Christian man and that you might be able to save me some money."

He couldn't look at Andrea for fear he might laugh at the Christian bit.

Carlos pulled a folded pink slip from his back pocket and handed it to Brodie. The policies were written by an agent in Concord that had nearly lost his state license for financing auto insurance premiums at obscene rates.

"You have three trucks, and now a fourth, and one insured driver?" Red flag.

"The trucks aren't always reliable," he said. Brodie donned a poker face, letting the silence sit between them to see what else he'd come up with. "Sometimes, I let my uncle use one."

"Is your uncle insured?"

Andrea and Carlos exchanged a puzzled look.

"I'm not sure. But he doesn't drive it that often. Only if one of my guys calls in sick."

"I'm assuming your employees are insured."

The Adam's apple on Carlos' neck moved up and down. Okay, so no insurance for them either.

"I'd make sure that anyone driving your trucks is insured. Even though you've given your uncle or employees permission to drive your vehicles, if they cause an accident, only the damage to your auto is covered. Worst case scenario, they total another car or kill someone—you stand to lose everything."

Carlos didn't say anything. He just nodded and bounced Maria in his muscular arms.

"Follow me," Brodie said. "Let's go write up the quote. While we're at it, have you thought about life insurance? With four kids, and a stay-at-home wife, you need to think about their financial security should something happen to you. If your wife found herself having to work outside the home, daycare alone could be a couple of grand a month."

"Things are pretty tight right now and it sounds expensive," Carlos said, sitting across from Brodie's desk with Andrea on his left.

"I feel you, but I strongly encourage you and your wife to think about it. If you want to get some coverage in place, you could start with a term policy. Those are the most affordable for the protection they offer."

"I'll definitely talk it over with my wife."

That was a no, Brodie thought. He had tried. Sometimes clients surprised him. What had seemed like, at times, a certain no had turned into maybe and even, at times, yes. Sometimes all he had to do was plant the seed, and clients would call back a few days or weeks later to get more information on whole versus term life insurance and to ask for quotes. He made a mental note to follow up with Carlos in a few months. The guy was a great candidate for life insurance. Brodie really didn't want to see the guy and his family get screwed if he suffered a disabling or fatal accident.

He entered the information on the five vehicles while Andrea and Carlos talked in Spanish. Carlos's DMV and loss history reports came out clean. He printed three quotes and recommended the third option—a five-hundred-dollar deductible versus two-fifty or a thousand, and set him up on monthly payments. Andrea processed the paperwork for Carlos's signature, printed the ID cards, then took Maria from him. He counted out three hundred and fifty-two dollars in cash from a wallet filled with bills. The roofing business must have been booming despite the drop in new construction.

Carlos shook his hand just as Brodie's cell phone rang.

"I've got to take this. Let me know if you need anything from me?"

His phone indicated a private number. Keith's number was programmed into his phone, so he figured it wasn't him.

"Brodie Marshall."

"Mr. Marshall, this is Deidre Zabat. I just received a letter from your company denying the life insurance benefits for my husband."

Shit. "Deirdre . . . I was going to call you today." He scanned his unopened emails and found the underwriter's email from yesterday morning.

"What's this business about him missing a lot of work?" Deirdre asked. "Why is that relevant? And someone from your company contacted Scott's former boss, asking her a bunch of questions about his attendance and performance. What damn concern is it of theirs? It's humiliating . . . for the kids and me."

"I'm very sorry," he said, knowing *sorry* didn't help one iota. This company, the entire industry, was run by a gang of bastards. If they had had any decency at all, they'd just pay the goddamn benefits and leave Deirdre and her family to grieve and rebuild.

"Please hold on a minute while I retrieve your file." Before he stood, the door opened, and Andrea entered with the Zabat's folder. The building's paper-thin walls must have made staying at the former hotel a rather intimate experience.

Brodie set the folder aside and opened a PDF attached to the underwriter's email. The signed letter to the client started with the typical "We want to assure you that we've given serious consideration to the above-referenced claim. Our investigation turned up facts that had not been disclosed by the insured, including the matter of Scott Zabat's prolonged absences from work."

You're shitting me, he thought. Bastards.

"We have found gaps in the application, missing information concerning the general health of the policyholder. Specifically, we discovered, the applicant had missed an excessive number of workdays due to illness prior to obtaining coverage. Therefore, per Section 8.2A of the policy, the company has determined that the life insurance had been obtained by fraud, and we must deny the claim for death benefits for Scott Zabat."

In the email sent to him as the agent of record, the underwriter had the audacity to offer the following advice: "Our research shows that the sooner an agent contacts a client after the resolution of a claim, the greater chance you have of retaining their business." Right. Fuckhead! And while we're at it, why not hit her up for a few life insurance policies for her and her kids.

When he returned to the line, he heard sniffling. "Deirdre?"

"He left us nothing but bills," she said. "He quit paying on the cars and credit cards. Our house is in foreclosure. My son was accepted to Davis, but there's no way we . . ."

Her words, incoherent now, rained down like fiery cinders. Rubbing his temples, Brodie said, "I'm so sorry. I'm very, very sorry."

Outside of his office window, the RV guy had finished playing his horn for the morning. Now he sat on the bottom step cleaning the brass mouthpiece with a tube sock—the type Keith and Brodie had worn pulled knee-high in middle school, attracting the attention of the school's worst bullies. Two scrawny geeks, wearing clothes one to two seasons behind. Thank god for growth spurts. Once he hit eighth grade, it seemed as if he grew an inch a week, and with each inch, he got picked on less and less.

While Deirdre cried, Brodie watched the man set the mouthpiece in the black case and reach into his pocket, shaking something from his hand into a metal bowl. With the toe of his boot, he slid the bowl across the asphalt a short distance, then rested the horn on his thighs to polish the metal. From the privet hedges that separated the parking lot from the storage facility, two kittens—one orange, one gray—appeared and approached the bowl cautiously. The gray one ate first while the runt sat beside him, watching and waiting, probably half-starved.

Deidre blew her nose, and he realized she had stopped crying. She said, "If there's anything you can do to help us, you'd have my eternal gratitude."

"I'll speak with the underwriter." He cringed at the thought of dealing with the prick. Most of the agents in the district despised him even more than some of the others. It was the luck of the draw when you phoned underwriting. Whenever the guy, in particular, answered, Brodie always asked a stupid question—his favorite: what's the maximum deductible available on a home policy—just to get him off the hook and cast again for someone reasonable.

"I'll need some time to read through Scott's application and file. Get a better sense of what's there and what they're claiming isn't. I'll call you tomorrow." And he would. No matter what happened today, whether he sold the last five life insurance policies or not, he would go into battle for Deidre and her family.

He watched the guy in the parking lot clap his hands and shout at the gray kitten. "Move away, greedy bastard," Brodie imagined him saying. "Give the little fellow a chance." When the gray cat refused to budge, the man prodded him with his foot. The kitten finally lifted his head and the orange runt came to the bowl.

Brodie scanned the notes he had taken a little over two years ago when Scott Zabat sat at this conference table. The man had come in specifically to talk about life insurance. Whenever that happened, which was rare, Brodie was always suspicious. He remembered the client was thorough in reviewing the policy. Often clients would make a lame joke or ask for clarification when they got to the suicide clause, the two-year waiting period. But Scott didn't say anything. In his notes, Brodie had scribbled "depression." Prozac was listed. That would help build a case. People didn't take antidepressants for the fun of it. There was nothing in the file about long absences from work. He'd need something in addition to Prozac to build a case.

jenny

JENNY LOOKED UP from her computer and saw Ana walking the man from 605 down the hall. The resident, a wanderer, clearly had no idea that he was bare assed, and that his privates were dangling below the hem of his Hanes undershirt. His legs and arms, bruised and sagging, were as thin as linguini. She watched Ana, who smiled patiently and cooed assurances as she escorted the resident back to his room. Jenny sighed, thankful once again, that she would make sure to never end up like him or any of the other residents in this way station.

Caffeine. That was what this afternoon demanded. Normally she wouldn't drink coffee so late in the day. Worse than her nightmares was lying in bed wide awake all night and alone with her thoughts. But today was a day for breaking rules. Living on the edge, she thought, smiling to herself.

Herman followed her out of the office. On her way to the break room, Jenny spotted a newspaper abandoned on one of the coffee tables in the reception area. It had been months since she'd bothered with even a quick glimpse of what was happening in her community, much less around the world. She bought a soda from the vending machine. She scanned her thumb to charge her employee account and paused at the snack vending machine. There were easily twenty dollars left on her account. She pressed the button below the M & M's. Ordinarily, she preferred the intense, bitter taste of dark chocolate, but today these candies reminded her of her son. She and Jerrod had bribed him with M & M's during those agonizing potty-training months. Eventually, Daniel got great satisfaction in watching his poop swirl and, like magic, disappear down the pipe.

She sat at a table near the window that overlooked the parking lot. Herman settled on an adjacent chair and curled himself into a ball. She watched one of the attendants, Keisha, climb out of the passenger seat of her Corolla. She walked around to each window to kiss her two young sons goodbye, then her husband. Jenny knew she should turn away and not stare at the prolonged kiss. Jenny sighed with envy. As much as Keisha might complain about the crummier aspects of her job, and for the attendants, there were many crummy aspects, she went home every evening to that family—two healthy boys and a loving husband.

The headline on the front page of the newspaper read: "Tensions rise after North Korea conducts its second nuclear test." One of these crazy dictators was going to eventually blow the world to smithereens, Jenny thought. Maybe it wasn't a bad idea to get out while the getting is good. Wasn't that the expression her dad had often used? She found the local sports section and scanned the photos submitted by parents and coaches: a lanky teenage girl dribbling past an opponent, a muscular rock climber hanging at the top of an artificial rock wall, a soccer team of young boys displaying their ribbons.

After her son's accident, she'd attended a few bereavement group meetings. Jerrod refused to join her. He'd said there was nothing anyone could say that would change the situation or change how he felt. Exactly how he felt, she wasn't sure. He wouldn't share his feelings with her. Did he blame her? Himself? She had had no clear answer. In these meetings, however, she'd heard aggrieved parents say, over and over, that they were heartbroken not only for the child they had lost but for the adult their son or daughter might have become. All the milestones yet unvisited—the bar mitzvah, the first dance, high school graduation, the wedding, grandchildren, and everything that followed.

Her grief had been too raw, too piercing at the time; she couldn't cast her line past the immediate shore to some distant point. It was the milestones already achieved that she had remembered and mourned. The first time her son sat up, the first pair of big boy underwear, the preschool photo of him holding his Bugs Bunny lunch box. Days and days spent exploring new San Francisco's neighborhoods and parks. Hours spent cuddling a limp, feverish son at the after-hours clinic. And truly too few hours of warm bubble baths and storytime. When the capacity for grief had finally expanded to make room for what might have been, then what first seemed like a finite loss expanded infinitely.

She paused on one photo: a group of adolescent boys, posed in their pristine white uniforms, all down on one knee.

"Take a knee," her son's soccer coach would call out whenever there was an injury. The first time he yelled, "Take a knee," her son, seeing a rare opportunity before him, ran over to the abandoned ball and started kicking it toward the goal. The assistant coach ruined what would have been her son's first goal by snatching up the ball. She remembered how adorable he looked in his bright green uniform. He'd felt like such a big boy in his rubber cleats.

At the height of his soccer infatuation, she'd bought an easy-to-assemble net for the back yard. The instructions were anything but easy. If Jerrod had been the parent making the purchase, he would have read a dozen reviews and studied the various packaging to find the absolute best and easiest-to-assemble net. After hearing a few mumbled curse words, her son laid his hand on her shoulder. "It's okay, mommy. Daddy can fix it when he comes home." Trouble was, by that point, Daddy was never home. Daddy was always working. A deposition here, a deposition there. Chicago. Dallas. Seattle. Portland. In the early days of their marriage and parenthood, Jerrod always came home for dinner. Compared to their friends and colleagues, they were old-fashioned that way. But his work demanded more and more of him, and he relented. Even before Daniel's accident, it had gotten to where he'd missed more family meals than he attended.

She looked at the photo of the soccer players. There was a dark, curly-haired boy that looked the age her son would have been now. She traced the boy's face with her finger and felt the fresh swell of pain. She straightened her posture and breathed deeply as MaryAnn entered the kitchen to pour herself some coffee. Probably her sixth cup of the day. How she ever slept at night was a mystery.

"Any sign of Randy?" Jenny asked, stroking Herman under his chin.

She shook her head. "I'm starting to worry. Say what you will about him, but it isn't like him to ditch work. He's got two sons to support."

Jenny scanned the next page of the newspaper. There was a photo of a diver in mid-air, her arms wrapped around her torso as she spun off the board. The caption said, *Diver Earns Gold. Sasha Marshall.* It must be Brodie's daughter. The girl that she would watch climb into Brodie's car in the mornings when she stalked him. If today wasn't the day it was, and there would indeed be a tomorrow, she might be inclined to write him another letter. She drafted the letter in her mind.

Dear Brodie,

I just wanted to say congratulations. I read in the newspaper that your daughter placed first in a recent dive competition. It said that she's headed to Stanford. Apparently, she's beautiful and athletic as well as smart. You and your wife must be very proud of her.

Regards,

J.M.

MaryAnn stood near the sink blowing on her steaming mug of coffee. Prussian blue crescents spread beneath her eyes like bruises. Her lips were cracked and dry. Jenny hadn't noticed before how unhealthy she looked and suddenly felt ashamed for judging her so harshly. Surely MaryAnn had her own demons. They'd never become quilting buddies, but would it have greatly inconvenienced Jenny to have made an effort?

"I'm sure he'll be back," Jenny said. "Maybe one of his sons needed to see a doctor and Randy forgot to mention it. It seemed like I was always taking my son in for ear infections."

MaryAnn tapped her wedding ring on the mug and cocked her head. Surprised, no doubt, by Jenny's comment. After the accident, she never talked about her son to anyone at Creekside. Beth, who considered herself a close friend, not just a colleague, had made one attempt to offer solace, and after the rebuke she received from Jenny, she stepped in line with the others who somehow knew Jenny preferred they never mentioned her son and certainly never inquire as to how she was doing.

"You're probably right. He loves those little boys. He just lights up whenever he talks about—"

"Excuse me . . ."

MaryAnn and Jenny looked up to see Ana standing at the breakroom door, her face undone with tears and panic. She was waving both hands as if she was having a seizure.

"Mr. . . um . . . I need you to come . . . 206 . . . please."

"Calm down," said MaryAnn. They followed Ana to Room 206. Herman stepped in line behind Jenny. MaryAnn's heels clicked against the linoleum as she rushed down the corridor, trying to keep up with the girl. They entered Room 206 to a monastic silence. The resident lay on his back. His jowls—slack, sagging—had already turned grey. The sheet covered his body leaving his ankles and feet exposed, including one foot with three missing toes. Diabetes.

"Call 911," MaryAnn said, turning Ana away from the body. "Then bring me his files. And where is Randy, damn it?"

"I'm here," he said, appearing at the door. "What's going—" He stopped midsentence and rubbed his forehead.

MaryAnn glared at him and pulled the bedding over the man's feet. When she noticed that Ana hadn't moved, the girl still just staring at the body, her shoulders shaking, MaryAnn gently nudged her away.

As Jenny followed Ana into the hallway, she heard Randy say, in a surprisingly contrite voice, "I'm so sorry. My mom called. My little one stepped on a nail in the park. I had to take him to get a tetanus shot. I didn't think I'd be gone so long. I didn't think . . . shit, I messed up."

"Shit is right," MaryAnn said. "You don't just walk off the job and leave your residents unattended. I'm not sure how this is going to play out."

Play out, Jenny thought. Uh, let's see . . . How about, "You're fired. You let a resident needlessly die on your watch." Jenny wanted terribly to leave this place right now.

"You'll be okay," Jenny said to Ana as they walked down the hall. "I know it's difficult."

The first time a caregiver found a resident dead in their room or on the toilet was a day they'd likely never forget. Over the years, Jenny had heard the attendants talk about it during breaks, consoling each other, sometimes laughing—not out of unkindness, rather as an awkward way of dealing with their discomfort and anxiety.

Ana buried herself in Jenny's arms.

"It will be okay," she said, emphatically while rubbing the girl's back.

No doubt, this experience, Ana's first, would now fill her with dread every time she entered a resident's room. In her mind, Jenny saw Jerrod returning home from his deposition to find her body. It was cruel to leave the mess for him. She still loved him. Yet a small part of her felt he deserved to be hurt for abandoning her. In a disturbed, selfish, vindictive way, she felt almost happy. Almost.

brodie

IT WAS NEARLY NOON, and Brodie was no closer to selling five life insurance policies than he had been at six this morning. His phone pinged. He prayed it was a text message from Keith saying, "Got an hour. Let's do it. What docs do u need?" But the text read: *Christmas is coming early this year! Get your scuba gear ready to see the amazing, colorful Christmas Tree Worms. This beautiful destination boasts 4,000 square miles of coral reef, including the Great Astrolabe Reef.* Another teaser from the company.

He searched the internet for the Great Astrolabe. It was a reef off Fiji—the world's largest living organism, a scuba diver's paradise. The thought of spending a week with Karen snorkeling, sailing, sex on a hammock, sex on the beach, sex after breakfast or lunch or dinner, or whenever the mood struck them, fruity cocktails poolside, beach football, volley ball, tennis . . . it was all enticing as hell. Less enticing was the notion of running into all the old farts with their tired insurance anecdotes and their bored spouses at the buffets—morning, noon, and night. Even so, leaving Andrea in charge of the office to deal with irate clients was infinitely more appealing than staying behind. Yes, he would have liked to fly off to Fiji if given the opportunity. He laughed. *Given the opportunity.* He had been given the opportunity. He knew half-way through the sales year that his numbers were down. How many leads had he blown off? How many district phone-a-thons had he ignored? He kept thinking, as he got closer to the deadline, that he'd find a second wind—do some cold calling on his own, take out ads in our local magazine, and attend some networking events. Instead, he had been sitting here in his office procrastinating, not even trying to catch the wind, and as a result, going nowhere, just bobbing along aimlessly.

He looked around his office. He'd rented this space for twenty of his twenty-three years as an agent. A frayed path in the carpet connected his desk to the door and circled around the conference table. His foster mom would be horrified at the floor's condition. She laid those tacky vinyl runners, the kind still sold at Wal-Mart, at every entrance and up and down the hallways, any pathway inside the house that might be spoiled by wet or muddy shoes.

To the left of his desk hung his framed agent license with the official seal of the California Department of Insurance. After his third sitting for the fire and auto exams, he watched the test administrator check off his wrong answers and wondered what he was going to do for a living if he couldn't even score a measly seventy-five percent. When the man said, "That'll be thirty-five dollars," Brodie stood there, stunned. Finally, he managed to say, "You mean I passed?"

There were display shelves covering the far wall of his office. Originally, he'd built them to showcase his growing collection of sales awards and plaques. Yet thanks to Karen's redecorating, the awards were stuffed in the hall closet and had been replaced with a miniature chair collection. A Frank Lloyd Wright Barrel chair. A folded gum wrapper chair. And dozens fashioned from twisted metal wire and cork and nearly every material, every style, every architectural period. Karen thought it made the office interesting and less "icky-insurance." He had cut her off before she brought in the balloon curtains and beaded lampshades.

For years, though, he'd displayed his awards proudly. He'd struggled so long just to cover the overhead and eke out a tiny salary. Once he hit the tipping point, once he was making some real money, he wanted to impress his friends and clients. Hey, look at me. I can take my wife and baby girl to Hawaii for the weekend. I can buy a car that doesn't require a jump every other day and that you won't hear or smell from a block away. Yes, he had stuck with the cold calling, the twenty no's for every astounding yes, the late night meeting with wishy-washy clients who always "Just need to think on it a little longer," and the irate "Please take me off your calling list" hang-ups. He had become successful. His first Topper Club 2003, he had displayed proudly, as he did the next, and the ones that followed.

Then the economy tanked. Even now, three years after the 2008 crash, clients, neighbors, business associates, and friends were still losing their homes. Unemployment had shot up to nine percent. First time home buyers, as well as long-time customers in their retirement years, were calling and emailing to ask what coverage they could eliminate or reduce to save money while still maintaining some protection. People began reading their policies and shopping around for the best rates. Loyalty and service became secondary.

Eventually, prospective clients—exhausted husbands, stressed-out wives, disillusioned young adults—would sit at his conference table, looking as if the economy had dragged them out back for a beating. They'd glance at the polished crystal awards, Toppers Club 2003, Toppers Club 2005, Toppers Club 2006, and at the photos of Karen, Sasha, and Brodie on a sailboat in the Dominican Republic. Immediately, he'd see a change in their faces. It was if they were thinking, Who is this guy? He has no clue how the rest of us live. Only a greedy narcissist would boast about sales and success while people are scraping by.

The prospective clients would draw their hands into their laps and lean away from the table. Their answers to personal questions about income, assets, lifestyle, goals, and risks became vague, mumbled approximations. Soon, he lost his footing. Confidence, gone. Warm leads from friends and clients turned cold. It seemed as if overnight, his knack for turning a No into a Yes vanished. Instead of closing a sale and collecting the premium, he was back to "Just need to think on it a little longer."

Except for a few agents in his district, Marty Clayton, for instance, whose business seemed impervious to tough economies, the rest of the agents had felt the shift in buying patterns. After Brodie had complained one night at dinner about losing another client, Karen suggested he replace the trophies and plaques in his office with a miniature chair collection. He had laughed, thinking she was kidding. But she'd gotten the idea from one of her morning home decorating shows. *Ah ha, miniature chairs. That was what Brodie needed to turn things around.* And while they were redecorating, why don't they frame some photos of modest family outings—Sasha as a toddler sitting in a red wagon filled with miniature pumpkins and gourds, Karen and Sasha in matching scarves and hats riding the merry-go-round in Tilden Park, the three of them playing put-put golf? The family photos of them sailing in the Caribbean or swinging from the trapeze at Club Med no longer seemed appropriate in this economy.

Looking around, now, Brodie wondered if she'd overdone the just-your-average-husband-father-agent theme. Sales had plummeted. More clients were walking. Miniature chairs? Really? He looked around his office and wondered, What the fuck was she thinking?

He scrolled through the list of eighty-six unread emails, scanning the subject lines for something easy to handle. A message popped up on his screen warning that his mailbox was almost full. He deleted the message. He grabbed the CANCELLATION folder, opened and closed it. His mind chased one negative thought after another until his brain was crammed with a funhouse of mangled thoughts. Part of his anger at this moment, he knew, was the fact he was too much of a coward to finish reading his stalker's letter. This is bullshit, he mumbled. Read the fucking letter.

His name was Daniel. He died two years ago, ironically, the same day I found your wallet. I know you must think I'm pathetic but writing these letters has been a life-line for me. My husband refuses to talk about our son. I can't see a way I'll ever escape this loneliness and grief. I want to be with my son. God only knows if there is anything else after this life. I haven't had the courage until now. I've never told anyone what happened.

My husband, son, and I were camping on the Eel River with two other families from our son's school. One of the husbands brought pot-laced brownies. My husband and I hadn't smoked since college, since his fraternity days. The grownups planned to meet down by the river once our children fell asleep. You're thinking, how irresponsible. Yes, it was. I knew it then, as well, but I hadn't done anything wild since becoming a mom, and I was feeling restless.

My son had always slept so soundly. He was such an easy-going baby, the envy of other parents. I'd have to wake him to nurse, and he always preferred his own bed. I never imagined he'd wake up that night and leave the tent.

We were gone . . .

"Brodie," Andrea said, knocking as she opened his door.

"One second," he said, finding his place again.

We were gone—

"You're going to be late for the district meeting."

"Hold on," he said, impatiently. He looked up and apologized. "It's not you."

He folded the letter and slipped it in his drawer.

"While I'm gone, can you do me a favor? Will you look on the Internet to see if you can find a news article or an obituary about a five-year-old boy? It would be around two years ago, a camping accident. See if you can find anything on the parents. Thanks!"

jenny

THE POLICE HAD ARRIVED at Creekside and were now gone. Jenny hovered nearby as they questioned Ana and MaryAnn. The dining room records showed the resident of Room 206 hadn't attended either breakfast or lunch. His last meal was yesterday at 5 PM. They'd collected his medicines, including, among the prescriptions, insulin. The resident's younger sister, who had been called, told the police he'd been diagnosed with diabetes ten years earlier, at sixty-two, but hadn't managed it very well.

There was no way, Jenny knew, in his condition, his body could function that long without food. It didn't take a medical degree to know that he needed to eat regularly. Otherwise, his blood sugar level would plummet. And he wasn't well enough to walk to the nearby convenience store. It was Randy's responsibility, as his attendant, to escort him to the dining room if necessary.

Jenny took the elevator to the third floor, where the more independent residents lived. No matter how often maintenance shampooed the elevator carpet, it always smelled like cough syrup. She walked by Room 311 and waved to Lottie as the woman pushed a vacuum cleaner around her sparse, one hundred and fifty square foot apartment. A cement statue of a rabbit propped open the door to the hallway. God forbid something happen outside Lottie's room and she not bear witness. She didn't allow visitors. Even the women in her clique were forbidden to enter her apartment, but for some reason she felt it vital to vacuum at least three times a day. What had her life been like, Jenny wondered, before being distilled down to gossiping, playing bridge, and vacuuming?

Jenny sat at the piano bench in the common area and watched three residents paint in watercolors. They'd created a still life on one of the coffee tables and positioned the nearby lampshade to direct the light over their subject: a large platter of fruits and a wedge of cheddar cheese, Ritz crackers, all borrowed, no doubt, from the dining room.

The steady hum of Lottie's vacuum spilled out into the hallway. Jenny's thoughts traveled back to the previous Christmas, what would have been, she figured now, her last visit to the Sierra Nevadas, specifically glorious Lake Tahoe. That holiday, they'd been short-staffed at work, so Jenny volunteered (eagerly) to cancel her vacation. When she'd told Jerrod and Rhonda the unfortunate news, they had offered to stay back, to skip—just this once—their annual white Christmas at Squaw Valley. But Jenny had been adamant they maintain the tradition.

In a previous life, she had loved to ski. Daniel had adored his grandmother from the start, so Jenny never hesitated to leave him in her care. Each day, while a marathon of gingerbread cookie baking and snowman-making got underway, Jenny and Jerrod raced down their first of many black diamond runs. But last year, after sending Jerrod and Rhonda to the mountains without her, Jenny's initial relief at having the house to herself quickly dissolved into loneliness. Sure, she had work to distract her from unwanted thoughts. But many of the residents were spending the holidays with their families. Those who had no families were, to be honest, a sad group. It was like seeing herself in forty years.

Every evening during that holiday she had returned home to a quiet house. She ate dinner alone in her PJs, she stared at a barely begun jigsaw puzzle, she watched a stream of mindless sitcoms, she fell asleep after swigging Nyquil. By New Year's Eve, she was depressed through and through. She had to find a better distraction than a jigsaw puzzle or another endless evening of television. She retrieved the vacuum. The revved-up motor gave off that musty smell like crushed moths. She started with the living room, then as her heart slowed, she headed to the dining room. This room and her son's bedroom were two areas of the house she dreaded.

Back and forth across the burnt orange carpeting, she pushed the vacuum cleaner, keeping her head down, eyes focused on the pattern she was creating. She and Jerrod had meant to replace the carpet with cork flooring. But that was before things changed. As she made her way toward the corner of the room, the vacuum marks stopped inches from the cardboard fort she had constructed with her son. She turned off the vacuum, drew in a deep breath, and lifted her head. Her son had spent more time playing in the fortress than in the Little Tikes castle now fading and cracking in the backyard. Above the arched doorway they'd created dual gumdrop-shaped dormer windows to resemble cartoonish eyes frozen in a state of amazement. Though generally not a very crafty person, she had been proud of their efforts.

The fort was Jenny and Daniel's special place after school to have snacks, read books, and play cards. He'd tell her about his day—art projects he'd worked on, a story they'd read, who the class bully had picked on at recess. He'd describe something yucky someone's mom had packed in their lunchbox. He loved details. He noticed so much.

A sneezing fit overtook her as she knelt by the arched door. She hadn't crawled inside the fortress since days before the accident. She rubbed her nose and peeked inside. A juice box, the bent straw half-chewed, an opened bag of goldfish crackers and a deck of cards lay abandoned in the corner. She had taught her son to play Slap Jack, dealing the cards slowly, saying, "Oh, look . . . a Jack." She'd wait for his young mind to catch up to the game and as he lifted his hand, she'd make a delayed overture. He'd yelp in delight as he gathered the cards in his lap and bounced on his knees. He'd gotten sly, though, sneaking a glance at each card he peeled off the top of the deck so he knew when a Jack was coming.

She crawled inside the cardboard now and picked up the deck of cards. Shuffled them. Remembering. "Nobody likes a cheater," she'd said to her son when he peeked at the next card in his hand before playing it.

"I'm not cheating," he'd insisted. He peeled three cards off the deck, and by the smile on his face, the way he leaned over the pile, she knew a Jack was coming.

"You're a rascal," she'd said, setting down her cards. "It's no fun if you don't play by the rules." She'd told herself to relax, it was just a stupid card game, when she felt a sharp kick to her shin.

"I don't like you," he said, tears falling from his tired eyes. He kicked her again and said, "I want Daddy."

Me too, she remembered thinking. It was tiring being the sole caregiver while Jerrod lunched with clients and colleagues or dined between depositions in some fancy hotel somewhere in the country. There were times when he had traveled two or three times a month that she wanted badly to put motherhood on pause for a few hours to climb into bed and finish reading the novel she'd started months ago. She wanted to make love to her husband while he was more than just half awake, half interested.

"Stop. Stop kicking Mommy," she had said sternly, grabbing and squeezing her son's feet. The strange roughness of her voice got his attention.

Sometimes, when Daniel was very young, it had felt as if motherhood had conspired with Jerrod's ambition to cheat her out of a husband, a partner, a life. Now these thoughts summoned guilt and regret. But there had been times she wondered why couldn't it be just Jerrod and her again, college students, in love, hours of unhurried loud sex, wine-fueled all-night jam sessions with his friends, the *New York Times* on Sundays sipping mug after mug of coffee?

That day in the cardboard fort, her son's legs finally settled, and his chin began to tremble. He tried to break free from her grasp, but she pulled him closer. "Today, you're stuck with Mommy. And you know what . . . Mommy loves you to the moon and beyond. What do you say we blow this joint and you help me make pancakes for dinner?"

How many long afternoons had she fantasized about going back to a time of only Jerrod and her? A time before the unrelenting demands of parenthood? How many times had she been so arrogant in testing fate?

That holiday, alone in the house, she had crawled inside the fortress and held the cool deck of cards against her face. She dipped a finger in the abandoned goldfish cracker bag to taste the crumbs. They had no flavor. That had surprised her. She picked up the juice box and put her lips on the chewed-up straw, the same straw her son's lips had touched, but she couldn't bring herself to take a sip. She didn't want to know if the juice had turned rancid.

brodie

THE RECEPTIONIST AT the district office possessed a frightening disposition. She punched in numbers on the fax machine as if she were poking out eyeballs. She was dressed in a black pencil skirt and grey pleated blouse. She always dressed in shades of mourning. Her hair, as usual, was severely twisted and clipped so not a strand dared fall out of place. The gray pearls around her neck finished off the whole throwback to the fifties look. Stan had inherited her from his predecessor. She had two sons in college. He complained she had had the gall to ask for a raise "when the company's stock and the entire economy was in the shitter." Judging by the diamond ring she wore on her left hand, Brodie figured she was still married. She was not unattractive, but her cold demeanor didn't invite one to imagine her out of these work clothes.

"Hi, Rebecca," he said, bracing himself for her rebuff.

She turned away from the fax machine toward him. Her usual scowl began to form, but then her thin lips lifted into a smile and her brown eyes widened.

"Hey, Brodie. I've got something for you," she said, and her voice trilled like a bird. She handed him a letter from her tidy desk and said, "Well done."

They're sacking me, he thought, and she could not have been more pleased. That was why Stan asked if he'd read his emails. Brodie felt like a fool. Did everyone here know he'd shown up, in person, for his dismissal? There was an odor drifting from the kitchen area, the caustic smell of burning plastic. Part of him hoped the entire district office would burn down with him in it ending his misery. No matter what he did or didn't do to deserve this sacking, he was screwed.

"Open it," she said. He figured she wanted to relish in his humiliation. His client's name, Janet B. Coulter, was printed in embossed gold lettering on the soft linen stationary. "To Whom It May Concern," she wrote in perfect cursive. He tried to recall the circumstances of her recent visit to his office. Did she leave upset? If so, why hadn't she written to him directly rather than contact the district?

"The man of the hour," Stan said, coming up from behind and slapping Brodie on the shoulder. The pain in his back that had subsided now reasserted itself.

"What'd you do, give the old lady a happy ending?"

"You're a pig," he said as Rebecca stood between them, looking bored by Stan's humor.

In her letter, Mrs. Coulter informed the company that Brodie Marshall should be recognized for his superior service in helping her with a recent home burglary claim.

"In my sixty years of dealing with insurance companies, I have never met an agent as compassionate and thorough as Mr. Marshall. He exceeded my expectations by going beyond his duties."

Now he recalled her visit. She'd insisted on picking up her settlement check in person, rather than having it mailed to her home. She squeezed his hand between her trembling, papery fingers and said that having her home burglarized while she slept had been the most traumatic event since her husband's death. Doubting she'd ever feel safe again, she'd said his weekly telephone calls had made her feel less frightened, less alone. She made such a fuss in front of Andrea and her caregiver that Brodie had felt embarrassed, unworthy. He'd simply made a few calls. Shown some concern. Maybe, he thought, it wasn't about grand gestures or chasing clients around to write insurance policies. Maybe success—personal and professional—came down to small acts of kindness. Generosity and compassion for the sole purpose of being a decent human being.

"Sold those five policies, yet?" Stan asked, elbowing him out of his thoughts. "You snooze, you lose," he added, shooting Rebecca an amused look. She shook her head and turned back to the fax machine.

"You're in a chipper mood today," Brodie said, looking into the adjacent conference room to see the typical early arrivals. The caustic odor was now undeniable. "Is something burning?"

In the narrow kitchen, the glass carafe warming on the coffee maker was smoking. Someone had failed to turn it off after pouring the last cup.

"Becca," Stan said, "the coffee pot."

"Are you serious?" Brodie said and rolled his eyes. It took three measly steps to reach the coffeemaker, press the red button, and set the pot in the sink on top of a mishmash of crusty coffee mugs, spoons, and Tupperware.

Inside the meeting room, Vlad Petrov stood, slightly hunched over, talking to two of his European friends. He hadn't noticed Brodie yet, and Brodie hoped to stay off his radar today. He wasn't in the mood for one of Vlad's monologues. Seated together in the second row was the Holy Trinity. Three impeccably coiffed agents, two blondes and one brunette. They rarely bothered to acknowledge him or any of the other agents. Instead, they tapped their manicured nails on their phones, checked their Rolexes every two seconds, and exchanged glances with each other at overheard conversations.

Betty and her cronies were seated in the back. She'd changed her wig color from light brown to red, from curly to straight. She looked over, and Brodie waved. She smiled in return. He slid two slices of pepperoni pizza onto a paper plate as Stan shoulder-checked him, nearly toppling the slices.

"Thanks," he said, taking the plate from Brodie.

"Really?" Brodie shook his head and grabbed another plate. They stood together looking around the room. "Is Betty done with the chemo?"

Stan shrugged. "No clue. She's a pain in my ass. Did you read my email?"

"You're heartless, and no, I haven't gotten to your email. Anything of interest?"

"Just the usual," he said, donning a self-satisfied grin as pepperoni grease glistened on his lips. Something was up, but Brodie didn't care enough to pry it out of him. And if it was anything worth knowing, Betty would fill him in.

Stan, Betty, and Brodie went through the company's agency training program together in North Carolina. They shared an office suite when first starting out. Every Friday evening, after a long week of cold calls, hundreds of rejections, and a few wins, they headed to the pub on First Street to drink beer and play pool. Whoever sold the most policies that week bought the first round. Stan weighed one hundred pounds less than he did today. He had a full crown of coal black hair, drove an old Mercedes convertible, and claimed he could "talk the coat off an Eskimo." He thought he was quite the man. Stan the Man. He loved slapping down the first twenty for drinks. He'd pile quarters on the edge of the table and begin flirting with Betty. Once he graduated from a nice buzz to slurring inebriation, his aggressive, desperate side oozed out. Betty had tolerated his flirtation months longer than Brodie had expected. One Friday night, though, Stan had just made a huge sale and insisted they drink scotch to celebrate. He handed the waitress a credit card and told her to keep their glasses full. After the fifth round, Betty and Brodie turned their glasses face down, but Stan continued drinking alone.

"Hey, Betty, you like this?" Stan moved the cue in and out of his circled fingers. Back then, pour him a few drinks and he behaved worse than a twelve-year-old who'd just discovered his penis. "Nice and smooth, like this . . . or maybe you like it harder—"

"That's enough," Brodie said. When the waitress circled back, he made a cutting motion across his neck to indicate no more tonight. Betty had been a good sport up to this point, but when Stan claimed she had chalk on her sweater and brushed his hand across her breasts, she cold-cocked him. And what did Brodie do? He met Betty for coffee the next day and talked her out of filing a grievance with the company. He convinced her to let it go by reminding her Stan was just a stupid ass, and making trouble for him might hinder her career. For some reason, neither he nor Betty could understand, Stan was well liked, or more likely, feared by the District office. They tended to overlook infractions for agents whom they favored or feared. Whenever Brodie thought back to those days, he felt like a coward. It wasn't as if Betty had threatened to turn him in for inappropriate behavior. It was the fear of finding himself on opposite sides from Stan. Then, as well as now.

Brodie folded his first slice in half and took a large bite. He thought about how, in the end, Betty had abandoned her plans to complain about Stan to the district manager. She did, however, immediately break her lease and find another shared office space. Once she left, Brodie bailed as well, figuring it was time to go out on his own.

Now he grabbed a diet soda and headed over to sit with Betty. Before he could dodge Vlad, Brodie found the man's beefy hand on his shoulder.

"Hey, Marshall," he said, in his thick accent. His dark eyes, half-hidden under bushy black brows, were level with Brodie's arm pits. "Are you in the market for a car? Your daughter must be . . . what eighteen now? My friend from the Rotary Club just got a lead on these pristine used cars."

"That's great." He couldn't afford a second-hand Schwinn much less a pristine used car.

"See, I was buying flowers for my wife," he said, lowering his head as if addressing the carpet. "No occasion. I just like to surprise her now and then with a bouquet. Keeps her happy. Tell you a secret. Safeway. You can't beat their prices on red roses, except on Valentine's and Mother's Day when everyone tries to stick it to the little guy."

Brodie nodded and looked over at Betty, who was shaking her head and grinning.

"You know, Marshall, I can fix anything." He looked up and squeezed Brodie's arm. "Give me a screwdriver and wrench and set me loose on any appliance in your house, but damn if I can figure a way out of this economy. I've got family in Russia, hell, they're doing better than me. Imagine that! This is America. My cousin, he's in banking and—"

"Hang on, Vlad." Brodie stepped aside to let another agent pass. "Looks as if we're about to start."

"Better eat before it gets cold." He pointed his chin at the pizza. "Don't forget to call me if you need a good, reliable car. My neighbor just picked up a Lincoln Town Car. Guess what he paid?" Vlad's eyebrows shot up as he waited for Brodie's response.

"Great talking to you, Vlad. Catch you later." The guy was as harmless as a daisy but as annoying as a seed stuck between your teeth. Still, Brodie hoped word never got back to him that Stan coined the phrase "Pulling a

Vlad." The moniker had become quite popular among the younger agents after hearing Stan use it during a meeting which Vlad hadn't attended.

Betty was talking to the agents from the Concord area when he approached. She pointed to an empty chair. He'd been introduced enough times by now that it was too awkward to admit he couldn't recall their names. What he remembered about the woman on the right was that her husband had been an early investor in Apple. Even after the market crash, he was still sitting on a shitload of stock. Retired at forty-five, lucky man. Betty said the man's wife kept working despite not needing the extra income. Brodie couldn't imagine not hoofing it right out the door. The other woman had self-published nearly a dozen romance novels on Amazon. Apparently, the romance novel industry was booming. She was considering closing her agency to write full-time. She'd told him once that avid romance readers often devoured two or three books a day. In response, he'd said, "Damn. That's a lot of bodice-ripping." She'd laughed, not with him, but at him. She told him he shouldn't believe the stereotypes. Her readers weren't all a bunch of lonely, uneducated, southern women.

"Ladies, how are you?" he said, hugging Betty and shaking hands with the other two agents. He smiled at the author and wished he hadn't been so condescending at their first introduction. It would have been interesting to learn more about her writing and publishing. Since his stupid remark, she'd obligingly shaken his hand but had shown no interest in getting to know him. The other agent, simply put, intimidated him.

"Have you returned to the office?" he asked Betty.

"Part-time. Like me as a redhead?" She shook her head from side to side so that her bobbed wig swung back and forth like a hula skirt. Her eyebrows had not grown back but were drawn into place with a brownish-red pencil.

He nodded and Betty squeezed his hand. "I've missed all of you, except for Idiot over there. He's a pain in my ass," she said, echoing Stan's earlier comment about her.

As he ate his now cold pizza, he thought about his mom's cancer. She was diagnosed with breast cancer in the fall of his freshman year in high school. Two months after diagnosis, he and Keith said goodbye to the hospice nurses and entered the foster care system. He never figured out why, in the warped design of the universe, his mother couldn't have been one of the lucky ones to celebrate her five years cured. Hell, he would have been grateful for one year, or even six months.

"Alright, let's start," Stan said, clapping his hands to get the attention of the thirty plus agents he managed. The PowerPoint slide depicted a funeral setting—wife and children—sitting in front of a closed casket. The caption above the casket read:

Life Insurance Policies
2011 Goal
40 Policies per Agent

Two recent graduates of the company's training program sat at the back table wearing cheap suits and wrinkled shirts, trying to look the part of the young professional. Their ill-fitting jackets reminded Brodie of the Sears suit he wore daily for the first eight months of cold calling. When he finally could afford a second suit, Karen, in a preemptive strike, cut off the legs and arms of his old suit even though he'd insisted it was good for another few wears. Now, he rarely wore anything other than a company-branded Polo shirt and slacks.

Watching these young guys play on their laptops, nudging each other to check out something on their screen, he wondered how long they'd last under Stan's reign if they didn't pull their heads out of their electronics and start networking to bring in business. They didn't seem to care. They probably had fallback positions available to them—moms and dads willing and able to offer room and board, or maybe girlfriends with better-paying jobs. Besides, selling insurance was typically a first job out of college—it wasn't meant to last forever. Like the proverbial starter marriage, just something to cut your teeth on.

Stan's next slide listed the agents and their life policies sold to date. Marty Clayton's name appeared first in bold green letters with sixty-six policies. He'd earned his ten-thousand-dollar bonus and a free trip to Fiji.

Despite how high the company raised the bar each year, Marty exceeded the targets and often met the quota within the first two months. As usual, he wasn't here today. He didn't bother with mandatory meetings. As the district's biggest producer with the second-largest book of business in California, he could do what he pleased. And as long as Stan got his bonus, his happy ending, he loosened the leash on dear ol' Marty.

An email message popped up on Stan's screen. Before he could delete it, the entire room erupted into laughter. The message was from luvtofuk@800girls.com.

"Call me! I'm wet thinking about you."

"Getting some action there, Stan," called out one of the old-timers.

"That's disgusting," said the woman seated next to the jokester. When the hilarity and comments quieted, Stan's scowl faded.

The Excel chart listed the agents' names (green or red) and life insurance policies sold to date. Green meant you'd met your goal. Red indicated you were short and most likely not going to receive a bonus. Brodie's name, as everyone probably expected, was in red. Five policies short of target. Betty was texting on her phone and didn't look up at the slide to see that she was eighteen policies shy of earning her bonus. The punks in the back glanced up from their laptops and snickered when they saw they'd sold a whopping three policies between the two of them. Lillian, the agent who transferred from Los Angeles, kept Marty company at the top with an impressive fifty-two policies. Didn't hurt that Lillian had the cleavage and looks of a mid-career Ann Margaret. In truth, he knew she was damn sharp and involved in nearly every local cause. She was constantly being courted for non-profit board positions.

"It's the eleventh hour, folks. Better write those policies today or say adios to ten thousand dollars. I don't know about you, Betty—" She looked up from her phone to find Stan staring at her while nearly everyone else, Brodie noticed, looked away. "But, I sure could use ten grand." He folded his arms and glared at her. Another instant message popped up. This one was from mike@hiddenoaksjaguar.com. "New car is polished and ready. Let me know where you want it delivered."

Betty whispered in Brodie's ear, "Yeah, hookers and new Jags don't come cheap." She looked straight at Stan to let him know he was the butt of the joke. Brodie offered a conspiratorial smile, yet shifted in his chair a few degrees and checked his phone. *How in the world could Stan afford to buy a new car, and for fuck's sake, a Jaguar?* he wondered.

"The client's medical exam can be scheduled for a later date," Stan said, "but you've got to collect all signed applications and premiums by midnight tonight. You snooze, you lose."

Brodie's phone showed fourteen new emails and two texts, none from Keith.

"Questions?" asked Stan. He looked around for hands but found none. "Alright, then." A new slide appeared. The bar chart compared Stan's district to the next district's cancellation and non-renewal rates. Several heads looked up from their phones to see that their district was fifteen percent lower than District Seven.

"What's happening here, folks?" Stan set his hands on his hips. The equivalent flesh of two plump turkeys hung over his belt. Brodie noticed he no longer chewed his nails as he had when he first met him. There was a sheen. This guy had time and money for manicures.

"You want to know what's happening?" asked Walter, a newer agent who had switched from selling stocks to insurance after the crash. "The company keeps returning our client's premiums with cancellation notices. We work our ass off to land a client, and the clients get a goddamn, excuse me, ladies, a goddamn letter saying their trees are too close to the roof."

"Get this," Betty chimed in. "They canceled a policy because there were steps missing off the master slider. The owners were in the middle of landscaping and building a new deck. No warning. Just adios, here's your money back. If that doesn't instill goodwill."

Vlad nodded. "You want to see a pissed-off client? Wait till they get a threatening letter from their lender saying they're in violation of their mortgage. Then it's kiss goodbye to the auto, the umbrella, the health, everything."

Disgruntled agents spiked stories back and forth. Abrupt cancellations due to unsigned documents, neighborhoods deemed too risky, hillsides too steep. Brodie had his own stories—a client out in Brentwood:

four-bedroom house, a week into the policy, coverage canceled—no warning. The premium was refunded with a form letter. Alright, maybe this one wasn't the company's fault. Turned out every room and closet in this guy's house was jammed with stolen electronics, custom bikes, art, even gravestone figurines. The client had been in such a hurry to set up his fencing shop, he didn't realize he'd checked off the box on the application authorizing a thorough home inspection for an additional discount. And Brodie had been in such a hurry to record the premium that he checked off the box indicating he'd done the agent inspection when, in fact, he had only looked online at aerial and street views to see that the property appeared insurable.

When it happened, he had expected to be ripped a new asshole by Stan for exposing the company to potential losses. And maybe even, given the company's skittishness of late, kicked to the curb. But it turned out Stan was only concerned about his financial future. He didn't want Brodie's sloppy work ethic to reflect poorly on him as the district manager. A letter of reprimand arrived with a warning that if he ignored company and industry protocol again, he was out of a job.

"And now after Katrina," Vlad shouted over the other voices. "Every damn bank insists on flood insurance. Of course, to the client we're the bad guys, but all we're doing is passing along FEMA's insane rates. Half the houses I look at are nowhere near a creek, maybe one tiny corner of their property lies in a flood zone. But one chance in a million of a hundred years' flood, get ready to fork over the big bucks."

Feeling smug, Brodie was thankful not to be standing in front of this firing squad. Stan had lost control of the meeting.

"Okay, already," he yelled over Vlad and the others. "Let's move on to the next item." The room quieted. "I've got good news and bad news. Marty Clayton, after fifty years with the company, has just announced his retirement."

A rumble of "What . . . when?" roared through the room.

"There will be a company dinner with a no-host bar on June twelfth," Stan said over the competing chatter. "Save the date."

"How is the company going to split Marty's book of business?" Vlad asked. The murmur stopped. Everyone's gaze fell on Stan. Even the two youngsters in the back looked up from their laptops. Stan slipped his hands in his pockets.

"I'm thrilled to announce I'm reopening my agency. The company and I feel that Marty's clients would be best served by my agency and—"

Betty slammed her phone on the table. She stood and yelled, "You greedy bastard."

"I think you should calm down," Stan said, putting out a hand as if to stop an oncoming train.

"I think you should go screw a lawnmower," she said and looked around the room. "Why should this unethical asshole get a million-dollar book of business handed to him? Have you forgotten his famous flyers? How many clients called us demanding to know why this Stan guy is offering home insurance at half the rate? He and his bullshit quotes made the rest of us look like shysters." Her eyes moved from table to table. No one would meet her stare. Rebecca stood at the door with her arms crossed and stared with hatred at her boss.

"Am I the only person here who thinks this is wrong?" Betty's voice cracked. She scratched her neck that had broken out in reddish welts. "Seriously?" Her voice rose. "No one is going to say anything?"

An uneasy quiet swept through the room. Betty shrieked and Brodie nearly jumped out of his seat. Her hand flew up. She yanked off her wig. Her face and bald scalp glistened. She flung her wig across the room toward Stan, the red strands fanning out in all directions as it soared over the tables. Brodie's mouth hung open. The wig fell short of its target and landed on the Pine Crest agents' table with a whisper. No one moved. Brodie and the others knew Stan was one of the industry's biggest assholes, but for now he was still the district manager, and as such could make the life of an agent hell. At this moment, Brodie was faced with a decision: protect his own interests by remaining neutral, as he always did, or step out on the cracked ice to defend his friend.

"He stole my clients and has badmouthed me to all of you," said Betty. "And you want to know why? Do you?"

The former Los Angeles agent, seated in front, drew her shoulders in and hunched over her chair. Vlad sat there nodding, quietly. Betty shook her bald head. The welts that began at her neck had risen past her ears. Brodie's heart sank for his friend. There might have been great sympathy for her in the room, but the consensus seemed to remain neutral. He doubted that anyone wanted to know the details. They all just wanted to cover their balls, so to speak, and hobble out of the room.

"He couldn't accept No. No, as in I won't sleep with you. No, you can't grab my ass or feel up my breasts. Not that there's anything left to feel up."

Oh, Betty, don't go there, Brodie thought. He reached for her hand and whispered, "It's okay. Sit down." She threw off his hand. He didn't blame her. Her head dropped and her shoulders trembled. He heard footsteps. Rebecca walked over to the Pine Crest agents' table, picked up the wig, and wove between the tables toward Betty.

"Here you go, sweetheart," she said, placing her arm around Betty and leading her from the room.

Hookers. A new Jaguar. A million-dollar book of business. There was greed and there was unfathomable greed. Stan was right up there with the greediest of bastards. Brodie picked up Betty's purse and followed Rebecca and her from the conference room. As he tossed his soda and paper plate into the garbage can, Stan walked up from behind. He was smiling, but the creases in his forehead betrayed him.

"I hope I can count on your support," he said, gripping Brodie's shoulder.

In his mind, Brodie said, "Count on this." Then he'd pop him soundly on the nose. He shrugged off the man's hand and turned as the women's bathroom door opened. At the sink, Rebecca stood next to Betty, combing the tangled red wig with her nails. She glanced at Stan, then at Brodie, and rolled her eyes. He cringed at the thought that she might suspect he was in cahoots with her asshole boss. Before the bathroom door closed, Betty looked over and locked eyes with Brodie. The look on her face summed it up. You lame ass coward. Will you ever take a stand? She cocked her head. He swallowed and lifted her purse. She turned away, and he was left holding the bag.

He walked next door to the coffee shop. A large dose of caffeine was desperately needed. He held the door open for a disheveled, sun-weathered woman who reeked of urine, cigarettes, and filth. He tried not to stare as she shuffled to the register. A table of college kids looked up from their laptops to gawk at the sight. The crotch of her black leggings hung down to her knees. One could see daylight through the threadbare cotton and make out the silhouette of her thin legs. Her sweater was inside out. The tag hung by a thread. Oddly, though, she was wearing new Nike tennis shoes. He imagined a kinder world where some young family saw a woman in need and did what they could to help her out. Karen would have given the shoes off her feet if she saw someone in need. Me? Brodie wondered. Probably not. He couldn't get past the worry that one day he would be this homeless person.

At the register, he stood behind the woman, leaving ample space between them as she stank. He imagined lice and other bugs crawling around in the matted hair tucked inside her A's baseball cap. Bugs gave him the heebie-jeebies. The smaller they were, the worse his fears. He remembered their housekeeper, Graciela, coming to work in a dither. Her son's preschool had sent a kid home with lice, and the others were given notes asking parents to check their kids thoroughly before returning them to school. She'd referred to them as animals, pronouncing it, on-ee-moles. At first, he and Karen couldn't figure out what she was saying. Then she pantomimed bugs crawling in her hair, and they both recoiled. She kept her son out of school for the rest of that week. She didn't want him or her clients and their children to be invaded by on-ee-moles.

"We're all just one mishap away from living on the street," the phrase one heard so often it had become a tired observation. Acute fear of the bag lady, that was what he had. He'd seen too many clients and friends living the lifestyle of their dreams one minute. The next a quick succession of unforeseen events, or sometimes one large financial investment gone sideways, then they were screening their calls to avoid aggressive collection agencies, couch surfing from friends to family, and visiting real estate brokers' open houses for a free lunch. Brodie knew he was not strong enough to live like one of these people.

When you're a kid and your mom dies of cancer, when your father, estranged by years of womanizing and drinking, is not the sort of man to step back into the role of dad if you even knew how to locate him, when there aren't grandparents, aunts or uncles with a spare bed for two teenage kids, then the state must care for you. They can't simply toss you in an abandoned field as, sadly, some might an unwanted pet. Once you've aged out of foster care, however, you're on your own. It was the most frightening, vulnerable feeling Brodie had ever experienced. He'd sworn never to find himself in that position again. Yet, here he was leading himself by his shriveled balls to that end.

Stan entered the coffee shop, grinning to himself as if he'd just walked away from a heist unmarked. The homeless woman grabbed her cup of coffee, her hands, sun-freckled and filthy. Brodie noticed the pretty cashier didn't charge her for the drink, and the woman didn't make an overture to fish some change from the tote she carried on her shoulder. How far must you fall before Starbucks starts doling out free coffee? Another barista announced a blended coffee drink in the clipped language that every kid over six seemed to be fluent in. Brodie placed his order and watched the homeless woman shuffle toward the condiments station. Stan glanced her way and had yet to acknowledge Brodie. He figured his old friend would take the widest path around the woman to avoid possible contamination, but Stan pulled out his silver money clip and peeled off a bill. The woman held the sugar jar over her steaming coffee and swayed as the stream of white crystals flowed freely into the cup. She reached for a stirrer, but Stan appeared at the ready. He drew one for her and also slipped the money into her palm. She looked at the folded bill, then up at Stan, almost amused by the gesture.

Who in the hell is he pretending to be? Brodie wondered. A man with a heart?

Stan cut in front of the guy behind Brodie and said, "Hey, let me buy you a cup of coffee." Mister Million Dollar Book of Business was all grins and high spirits, and full of goodwill. Goodwill, my ass, Brodie thought. May he rot in hell. "I can buy my own," he said, handing the cashier the last three dollars in his wallet.

jenny

EVEN BEFORE THE ELEVATOR pinged and opened onto the first floor, Jenny was greeted by the aroma of chocolate and vanilla. It was teatime at Creekside. Time also for Jenny to sneak out before the well-wishes for a fun and safe vacation. She grabbed her purse, looked around her office one final time, and bent over to tickle Herman's ears. He nipped her hand. She smiled at her feisty friend.

Squinting in the early afternoon sun, she walked to her van and thought about how sometimes the most incongruous events set plans into motion. For Jenny's birthday in March, Rhonda had invited Jerrod and her for a celebratory dinner at the posh Portside Grill. They drank three bottles of Perrier-Jouet. By the time coffee arrived, Jenny was feeling giddy and alive. She caught a flicker of light coming from the swinging kitchen door.

"I said no cake or fuss," she whispered to Jerrod. He nodded toward Rhonda. "You try stopping her."

"Nonsense. We must all eat cake on our birthdays. And gifts are a must."

Rhonda pulled a slender, paisley-wrapped box from her purse. The waiter set a slice of cheesecake, decorated with chocolate shavings and fresh raspberries before her. A half-melted pink candle flickered.

"Make a wish, dear."

Jenny considered several possibilities. She looked at Jerrod. He'd removed his necktie sometime during the dinner and looked more relaxed than she'd seen him in months. His beautiful eyes glistened as he waited for her to blow out the candle. She couldn't remember when she'd last felt happy, not even a tinge of happy. *I wish that this feeling would last*, she said to herself. *Please let me not wake up tomorrow feeling guilty.* With one quick blow, she extinguished the flame and grabbed her spoon.

"Me first!" She carved off a corner of the cake. "Mmmm!"

As they took turns whittling away at the cake, Jenny opened her gift, hoping Jerrod wouldn't be embarrassed for not getting her anything. She peeled back the tissue and gasped.

"This is beautiful."

She carefully unfolded an exquisite orange, silk scarf and studied the floral design. "Oh my god . . . it's so soft." She held it against her neck and cooed. "Feel it," she said, pressing the fabric against Jerrod's face. He stiffened at her touch. "Nice. Right?"

"I picked that up in Thailand last year," Rhonda said. She rubbed one of her arthritic knuckles. Every year her fingers seemed to bend in new, painful directions. "Thought it would look beautiful on you."

Jenny stood up and hugged her. "I absolutely love it. Thank you!"

"One more gift," Rhonda said, leaning an envelope against Jenny's water glass. "This is the main event!"

Inside was a hand-drawn card with three stick figures standing on the deck of a ship, waving goodbye under a shower of streamers and confetti. A banner above the figures read, "Bon Voyage. We're off to Alaska."

"What?" Jenny asked. "Is that us?" she pointed to the stick figures.

"Yes, indeed." She grabbed Jerrod and Jenny's hands. "I've always wanted to see Alaska. I figured I'd take my favorite son and my most favorite daughter-in-law." She loved to refer to Jerrod as her favorite son, even though he had no siblings. "Let me know when you can both take a week off of work, and I'll book the tickets."

"That was a fun evening," Jerrod said later as they stood side-by-side in the bathroom, brushing and flossing their teeth. He climbed into bed first, threw off the comforter, and peeled off his sweatpants. Jenny found a short t-shirt in their closet, hoping she'd give off that sexy, college-girl vibe. Jerrod turned off the bedside light. Jenny held her breath in anticipation as he leaned toward her. He kissed her on the nose. "Good night."

She lay on her back thinking, *That can't be it. Maybe he's scared.* She inched closer to him, pressed her body against his so that the warmth of his body infused with hers. She kissed his neck. "Do you want to make love?" she whispered. He scooted closer to the edge of the bed and said, "I'm beat."

As she lay there quietly crying, she knew by his breathing that he wasn't sleeping. Before the accident, there was never a time he was too tired to make love. Once again, the rejection felt like the worst kind of betrayal. The worst kind of loneliness. *How was it possible to be so lonely and yet within an arm's reach of someone?* It was then that she made up her mind. She just needed the right opportunity.

Schedules were coordinated. The Alaskan cruise was booked. Five days before Jenny, Jerrod, and Rhonda were set to sail out of San Francisco, she realized there was no way in hell she'd spend an entire week confined in narrow quarters with someone who seemed to despise the very existence of her. When Jerrod announced on Tuesday evening after they'd shared a pizza that he'd scheduled a deposition requiring him to travel on Friday, she froze. She stared at him as he grabbed another beer from the refrigerator. He must have misread the look on her face because he quickly said, "Don't worry. I'll catch a flight back on Saturday. I haven't forgotten about the cruise."

She'd mumbled, "Okay," but secretly knew she'd just found her opportunity. Here was her chance to find the courage to do what she needed to do.

The night before the deposition, Jerrod had sat down at his piano with a tall tumbler of scotch. Jenny deposited herself at her kitchen table, staring down at the printout of the cruise itinerary that Rhonda had emailed her. Antsy for some distraction, she went to the junk drawer and rooted around until her fingers found what she was searching for. The beginning notes of Chopin's funeral march made her nearly scream. She hated this melody—so heavy and oppressive. How could it not depress him to play that song? She tossed the box cutter from one hand to another, enjoying its surprising heft. With the press of a button, the blade slid open. Open. Close. Open. She liked the clicking sound it made. She grabbed the new phone book that Jerrod had dutifully picked up from the driveway, brought inside, and set next to the house phone. She ran the box cutter blade diagonally across the plastic shrink wrap and removed the book. She flipped through the pages—the flutter of thin pages casting a slight breeze and whisper—and stopped on the "M's." When she came to their name and phone number, she saw no address listed. Growing up, everyone used the phonebook; every family listed their address. That was how you knew where to drop off your kids for parties. Nowadays, people didn't bother installing land lines. Schools printed out directories and parents could opt-in or out. Numbers and addresses were withheld. When was the last time their home phone rang? She couldn't remember the last time she gave that number out to someone.

Pressing the blade firmly against the phone book cover, she carved out a large rectangle and removed the cutout. Starting at one corner, she dug the blade in again, deeper, tracing the cutout. She cut layer after layer until she'd scored the counter's surface, then she tested the blade against her palm to see if she'd dulled it beyond usefulness.

"What are you doing?" asked Jerrod. She jumped and turned, now realizing the music had stopped. "You're bleeding." A dotted line of garnet red blood beaded across her palm.

"I was just testing the blade. I was thinking about taking down the fort. In the dining room." She moved past him to grab a dishtowel. He eyed the blade, and with it in sight, followed her movements.

Suddenly, boldly, he reached for the knife. "Not today." He tossed the box cutter into the kitchen drawer. She stood there mutely, replaying his words, *Not today.*

"Not today what?" she yelled. Take down the fort? Kill myself? Say what you fucking mean!

As if he'd heard her thoughts, he said, "We need to figure out a way past this."

"This? What exactly is THIS thing we need to get past?"

"THIS! THIS! ALL OF THIS!" He flapped his arms as if he were a pelican stuck in an oil spill, unable to free himself from the mess.

"THIS . . . as in the fact that you still blame me. You can't even look at me, can you? I'm the person who killed your son. Well, fuck you!"

She swept past him. He sighed and went back to his piano. With her heart on fire, she grabbed some paper and a pen from their shared office.

Hi Brodie,

It's me again. I'm sure by now you recognize the handwriting. I hope, even as I write this, that you throw out my letters without reading them. And yet, a part of me hopes you do read them—

Jenny managed to leave the office without having to say goodbye to anyone. She started her van with the intention of going directly home but changed her mind. The short drive to the BART station was deliriously quiet. She parked and purchased a ticket. Forty minutes later, she was in San Francisco. She exited the Civic Center station and hailed a cab.

"Where to?" asked the driver.

"Sutter at Baker."

She gazed out of the window. A gaggle of tourists stood near the Civic Center, their cameras aimed at the UN Plaza and the impressive dome of San Francisco's City Hall. Traffic stalled. The driver nearly clipped a pedestrian. They drove past the San Francisco Library. She remembered chaperoning a busload of Creekside residents to hear the city's Poet Laureate read before they had dinner at Max's Opera Café. The big city outing had been a logistical nightmare, a comedy of errors they'd all somehow survived. She had felt insecure in her new job, early on, always trying to prove herself to her colleagues. Now she didn't give a damn, which she knew wasn't fair to the residents and their families. The cab headed down Geary and they made their way to Lower Pacific Heights.

"Where exactly?" the driver asked, turning onto Sutter from Baker.

"A few houses down on the right. Okay, stop here."

She scooted to the edge of the seat, not making an overture to pay the driver nor depart the cab. "Do you mind if we sit here a bit? You can restart the meter."

The driver cracked his window and picked up his phone.

"I used to live in that house."

Her heart thumped as if she were, once again, trespassing on the lives of another intact family, a family not yet broken. The Victorian was now painted caterpillar-green. Its bay window, the door, and the smaller second-story windows were all trimmed in white. The tempered glass panes were outlined in black. Gone were the howling purple, hot magenta, and glowing green colors chosen by the landlord for his terminally ill partner. Even the front steps, once done up in purple, had been sanded and stained to complement the subdued color scheme.

The air in the cab was humid and musty—too many fast-food meals eaten on the road, too many dirty shoes, too many people coming and going. She looked back at the house. In her mind's eye, she could see herself pushing the stroller toward the front gate. She could hear her breathing, heavy and labored, after descending the last hill. Home after another morning spent exploring a new part of the city. The moment her son spied the purple stairs, he'd begin bouncing in the stroller.

In the increasingly warm cab, she felt as if she was suffocating in a burlap sack drawn tight around her neck. She peeled away a long-sleeved silk shirt, leaving a camisole. The driver glanced back at her through the mirror. She'd been nothing but cold and numb these last months. Now she was on fire, burning from the inside out. It wasn't inconceivable that at thirty-six she might be entering an early menopause. Her mother was post-menopausal by forty. Yet, unlike her mother, she had never intended to bear only one child.

"You seen enough?" the driver asked.

"Do you mind rolling down my window? And a couple more minutes, please."

He lowered her window a few inches. A cool breeze tickled her nose. Fanning the hem of her skirt helped dry her damp legs as she stared at the house. Balloon curtains now adorned the bay window. Gone were the landlord's beet-dyed curtains. Gone were the McDonald's plastic toys that, once upon a time, lined the windowsill. Early in their marriage, Jerrod had worked constantly. He was always gone. Sacrificing so much to prove himself to the firm's partners. Home enough, however, that she managed to get pregnant. They had moved from LA—the city where Jenny was born and raised—to San Francisco, trading warm, sandy beaches for tacky Fisherman's Wharf and cold, windy Ocean Beach. Alone with a two-year-old in an unfamiliar city, not a friend outside of a few acquaintances from yoga, she and her son were left to acclimate to this new life.

In the first year, they learned the transit system and the neighborhoods of the city probably better than most Bay Area natives. Every morning after breakfast, they headed out. Her son, strapped into his stroller, held the map in his lap with the destination circled and pretended to lead them on an adventure. To commemorate the discovery of a new neighborhood— the Marina, the Sunset, Cow Hollow, South of Market, the Castro, the Haight—they'd find a nearby McDonald's and buy a Happy Meal. Daniel never ate more than a few fries. It was the prize they sought. They'd give the bag of food to a homeless person, and once back at the purple house, they'd set the toy in the window beside the other prizes. At bedtime or mornings, when Jerrod slogged home, the boy dragged his dad to the window to show off his newest toy. Even though you could smell the odor of exhaustion on Jerrod and his suit, he'd listen, feigning rapt attention as their son replayed the day's adventure. She had loved her husband completely in those days and in the years preceding their son.

As much as she had grown to enjoy the city, she had had enough of being vigilant against the potential dangers of urban life. After inheriting a modest sum from her aunt, her mother's only sibling, she lured Jerrod to the suburbs with the promise of a grand piano and enough distance between houses that he could play at odd hours without bothering the neighbors. What happened to all those racing cars, Disney themed dolls, finger puppets, and Ninja turtles, she wondered. Had they left them behind? The move had been chaotic. A chore that fell, largely, on her shoulders.

"Pardon?" The driver stared at her through the rearview mirror. Had she mused aloud?

"Will you take me to the Exploratorium?" she asked. "The science museum at the Palace of Fine Arts." This was one of her son's favorite destinations.

After driving around the city that afternoon and tipping the driver fifty dollars on top of the fare, she had boarded the train. A filthy man sat across the aisle from her on BART. Wearing ratty, smelly clothes, he fingered his matted beard. She watched him and thought about how she would have ushered her son to a different car. She had wanted to protect him from all the potential evils and sufferings in life. She didn't think, however, to protect him from herself. She glanced at the homeless man as he continued to bother his beard. Their eyes locked. "Cunt," he said, sharp as a sword cutting the air between them.

Aghast, she laughed nervously.

"You cunt," he said, now looking everywhere but at her.

She refused to look away, daring him to turn back toward her. *Try to hurt me,* she thought. *You can't. Your words can't begin to describe my unworthiness.*

Over the PA system, her stop was announced. She stepped onto the platform, accosted by a cold wind as commuters pushed past her. She stood for a moment, facing the tracks, watching cars zoom by on Highway 24, drivers on their way to Oakland or San Francisco. The far hill was covered in white crosses, installed to honor the U.S. soldiers killed in the Iraq war, planted into the soil to express, in many cases, opposition to the war. After the doors shut, the train pulled past in a roar as loud as the ocean. She looked again at the crosses. Thousands of lives sacrificed for nothing other than civic duty and lies. If Daniel had lived, had come of age during the invasion, had decided to join the fight, she would have begged him to reconsider. The vibration of the platform shook her body like an empty vase during an earthquake. It wouldn't take much to reach the tilting point and shatter. She looked at the third rail in the tracks, imagined the deadly electrical current coursing through her body, and wondered if she had the courage to jump.

brodie

JUST AS BRODIE arrived back at his office, Mimi Balfour pulled up in her white Mercedes. The gold lettering on her car advertised M. Balfour Interiors. Damn. Interior designers could be such Type A control freaks. When the last agent retired, and her book of business was split among the district, he got Mimi and Tim Balfour's account as well as two dozen others. He held the door open for Mimi and waited as she approached the office with the confidence of a woman who knew she had an incredibly scorching body. Her peach-colored suit obediently followed every curve. Silver-heeled pumps created the perfect exclamation point.

"Mr. Marshall," she said, shaking his hand firmly. "I recognize you from your newsletters."

"Pleasure to meet you. Please come in."

She followed him past Andrea's desk, and once seated in his office, said, "I'd like to know why you doubled the rate on my Mercedes." All civilities were gone. They were down to business.

"Let me bring up your account."

He typed Mimi Balfour into the Customer Search field and scrolled past a renter's policy, a Camry policy, and clicked on the Mercedes policy. He read the household history and scanned the renewal offer. Indeed, her rate had doubled. Discounts unchanged. No accidents. Oddly, though, the estimated annual mileage had increased from seven thousand to eighteen thousand. He drilled down into the policy change and skimmed the underwriter's notes made two weeks before the renewal processed.

"It appears the increase is based on your annual mileage readings over the last twelve months."

"What?"

She clicked her lacquered peach nails on his desk. She picked up his stapler, opened and closed it several times like a compulsive gunman checking his revolver.

"In April, your odometer reading was one hundred and twenty-six thousand and change. Earlier in January, one hundred twenty-one thousand. September . . . one hundred and—"

"Hang on. How did you get my odometer readings?"

The hair on Brodie's neck rose from her shrill tone. He rolled his chair away from the desk. "Perhaps we should reschedule this meeting for a time when your husband is available."

"Don't be condescending," she said. "Just tell me how the company gets their hands on my odometer readings."

"The typical way would be the Mileage and Usage Declaration forms we mail out to clients every year."

"I never received one."

"Then there are databases that keep records of VINS and odometer readings. For instance, when you have your oil changed, the shop enters these numbers into their computer so they can send you those reminder cards. The company can access this information to help us audit—"

"I don't know what sick big brother game you're playing, but there's no way I drive eighteen thousand miles a year. I work from home. I see clients maybe once a week."

"What about Mr. Balfour?" he asked. "Perhaps he's put some extra miles on the Mercedes this year?"

"Well, he has driven it a few times for work, but he has his own car."

When would people learn to quit lying to their insurance agent? he wondered. Agents were like dogs when it came to sniffing out bullshit.

"His car, the Camry, is it running?"

"Yes," she said emphatically. He waited. "Well, it needed a new transmission. We didn't have the money to fix it, so it was parked in the garage for a few months. But it's running now."

"Given Mr. Balfour works in sales and he was sharing your car, is it safe to assume that he ran up the odometer more than usual?"

"Yes. But we can't pay another seven hundred—"

"Hang on, Mimi. We'll get the premium adjusted."

He printed a Mileage and Usage Declaration form. She went out to the car to write down the odometer number. When she returned, he noticed perspiration stains had darkened the fabric under her arms and could smell the fatigue radiating from her skin. He couldn't bring himself to feel any ill regard for her personally, or for her trying to cheat the company because he knew the majority of people out there were just trying to survive. They were all hoping their financial ruin wouldn't become gossip served up at dinner tables.

"Indicate seven thousand miles," he said, pointing to the correct line. "Then write here that you work from home and your household has a second car."

While she completed the form, he selected the Change Request tab on the company dashboard and typed a request that they adjust the annual mileage. She watched him scan the document and attach the file to the change form.

"I should hear back from the company by Wednesday."

She slumped.

"Wednesday? But the premium is due today."

He wanted to roll his eyes like Sasha was always doing, but he restrained himself.

"Let me call underwriting to see if I can . . ." He stopped there. She wasn't interested in knowing the process, only that her rate would be cut.

"Underwriting. Neal Crawford."

Shit, Neal. Even though what Brodie was about to request should have been a no-brainer, he knew that this guy would find some reason to reject the request or insist on a hundred more documents before waving his magic pen.

"Hey, Neal, Brodie Marshall. Trying to find the link on the company dashboard for the, uh, home fire alarm discount. Where would that be?" Mimi frowned, and he put up his hand as if to say, "I'll explain later."

"Mr. Marshall, I work on the auto side. Besides, you must know that Underwriting doesn't handle those inquiries. Please refer to your agent handbook or call the help desk because we're not here to—"

"You're right. Take care." He dialed again and whispered, "Guy's a jerk."

"Underwriting, Melanie Nelsen speaking."

Not his first choice, but she would do. The company figured out long ago not to give out the direct numbers to underwriters. Otherwise, he imagined the Neal Crawfords of the world would be picking their noses all day with no one to talk down to.

"Hi, Melanie. Brodie Marshall. How are you today?"

They exchanged pleasantries for a minute before he said, "I've got a client in my office." He gave her the name and policy number. "If you look in the image center, you'll find a new Annual Mileage form I just scanned in. My client is requesting that her mileage be set back to seven thousand as it was before the renewal."

"I can't make that change retroactive unless we've made some error."

"Today's date is fine, Melanie."

"Hang on. I see the document."

He heard her typing. In the background were the sounds of the other men and women talking and working on their keyboards. One gigantic floor of the company headquarters housed the underwriting department. Underwriters were omnipotent. They had the power to make your job easier or harder. He looked at his watch while the underwriter typed. Two-thirty. Not much time before David Knight arrived.

"Do you know what the new premium—"

"Hold on." Finally, one loud tap on her keyboard. "Done. You can open her policy now and you'll see the new premium."

And there it was. He turned the screen toward Mimi and pointed to the number. Her shoulders dropped inches as she set down the stapler.

"Anything else, Mr. Marshall?"

He cupped the receiver and said to Mimi, "Just need to discuss one other quick matter." Mimi nodded and began fiddling with the magnetic paperclips on his desk. "Yes, but it's a home coverage matter."

"That's okay. I work both auto and home lines. What do you have?"

"One of my clients." He swiveled his chair around so that his back was facing Mimi and lowered his voice. "We had him insured for a renter's policy. Turns out, he notified us several months ago that he'd bought the house he was renting and wanted to change his coverage from a renter's to homeowner's. I don't know how it happened. We were undergoing some staffing changes." How many lies was that today? "But his policy was never converted."

"You can't convert a renter's policy to a homeowner's. You would have to—"

"I know, write a whole new policy. That, I'm afraid, is where the ball got dropped. So now he called me today to say his house burned down. He's coming in this afternoon."

"Whew," Mimi said. He swiveled back around. She signed her check and ripped it from the book with great flourish before tossing it to him. "Glad that's not me."

"Hang on, Melanie." He covered the receiver. "This might take a while. Is there anything else I can help you with? Perhaps some life insurance?"

"Nope, not today." She stood and picked up her purse. "Good luck. I'll let myself out."

"Sorry about that, Melanie. So what do I tell this man?"

"Do you have documentation that he requested a homeowner's policy?"

"There's an envelope in his folder with my former office manager's notes to convert, I mean, write a homeowner's policy."

"And he never thought to review his paperwork? Never questioned that his premium hadn't changed?"

"No, but how many people look closely at all the paperwork they receive from us? And I don't get too many phone calls asking why their rates are so low."

"Good point. But it's his business to read the policy and declarations. I don't know what to tell you, Mr. Marshall."

Brodie picked his thumbnail.

"Do you think the company might pay out?"

"I know, for a fact, they won't." She cleared her throat. "Had a similar situation last month and they wouldn't budge. You've always got your E & O insurance. That may be your client's only recourse."

He looked at the stack of bills and knew that somewhere in the growing collection of unopened envelopes was a past due notice on his Errors and Omissions policy. It was becoming painfully apparent that even if he did write life policies for Keith and his family and received his bonus, ten thousand dollars wasn't going to keep this boat from capsizing.

"Thanks," he said, his chest constricting. The pain radiated to the tips of his extremities so that it felt as if he was wearing a wet suit three sizes too small. He half hoped it was the onset of a heart attack so he wouldn't have to deal with David Knight today. Karen and Sasha would collect on his life insurance, and after paying out on David Knight's eventual lawsuit, they'd still have money for their anger-bereavement classes.

"Any other policies or questions?"

"No. You've been great. Thanks."

Brodie slumped in his chair and dialed Karen to try to catch her before she mailed out the graduation checks they'd written for a half dozen of their friends' children, many of whom Sasha had known since preschool. Even at fifty a pop, the least amount they could give without coming off as cheapskates, the checks still totaled three hundred dollars—probably three hundred dollars more than they had in their checking account currently. When Karen didn't pick up, he slammed his fist on the armrest. It was a mystery why she even carried her phone.

"Hey, Karen. Did you mail the graduation checks? If you haven't, let's hold off a bit longer. Call me, please."

jenny

JENNY'S MINIVAN IDLED at a red light before a busy intersection. The whoosh of another BART train entering the station could still be heard from blocks away. She thrummed her fingers on the steering wheel, waiting for the green light. What would happen if she gunned the engine? Drove right into the cement barrier? Besides the obvious honking of horns, screeching of brakes, crunching of metal, tearing of bumpers, shattering of glass, screaming, blood, broken bones, would the damage be enough to kill her? If she unclicked her seatbelt right now, lifted her foot off the brake and punched the accelerator, would the impact be enough to throw her through the windshield or crumple her into a ball like a piece of tinfoil? Even if she could gather the courage, the aftermath and collateral damage that flashed in her mind put the fantasy to rest.

The light switched. The little green man on the pedestrian traffic sign appeared. The first time her son noticed the green man, he shrieked with excitement. "Mom, look a green man." She'd scanned the sidewalk for some odd guy wearing green makeup, but realized he was talking about the *walk* symbol. There were so many wonders he had yet to discover. She exhaled until it felt as if her lungs had collapsed and she was suffocating. Proceeding through the intersection slowly, she half-hoped for a red-light runner in a military-grade Hummer. She wanted to be mowed down like a bowling pin. It wasn't a perfect analogy, she knew, because bowling pins got knocked down and righted again, whereas, for some people, that wasn't true. Sometimes one's inner workings broke down permanently, from one or repeated collisions, and there was no more righting the situation.

She wasn't ready to go home yet to an empty house. In the past, when Jerrod was traveling for business, she might have called one of her girlfriends to meet for coffee or a glass of wine before picking up her son from daycare. Her friends, though, had long since quit calling, and it would have felt awkward to reach out to them now. Even her yoga friends had stopped trying to entice her back to the studio. She never made any real connections at the support group she had attended for a brief time.

Her stomach growled and she realized she was hungry. Approaching the onramp to South 680, she thought pancakes, whipped cream, and blueberries. Bacon. The comfort food of her childhood. She had passed a Denny's earlier, but in her mind, she saw herself sitting in a restaurant, the waitress acting extra friendly and accommodating to this customer eating all alone on a Friday night. To hell with that. She'd stop at the grocery store and fix her own pancakes.

Since her son's accident, she never got past the uneasiness of running into someone from her past. Someone who knew her as a wife *and* a mother, say a parent or child from her son's preschool, a former yoga pal, or someone from the swim club, the dinner club, or the book club. She found the risk of coming cart to cart with someone whom she couldn't avoid acknowledging nearly debilitating at times. Both sides pretending Jenny hadn't ignored their early phone calls, texts, and emails. Both sides pretending Jenny didn't see how they downplayed the updates on their children when she'd inquired. Both sides pretending not to notice how truncated their answers were. "Tim is playing Little League." versus "Tim is killing it at shortstop. He and his dad spend every weekend at the batting cages." Or "Jackie is still Jackie. She keeps busy." versus "OMG. Jackie has so many afterschool activities, we need a spreadsheet just to keep up with her schedule, and with all the birthday parties. We're washing her uniforms and gear 24/7."

The few times she turned the corner of a grocery aisle and came face to face with a former book club member, neither mentioned the current book selection nor asked if the other had read anything remarkable lately. Similarly, the men and women from Jerrod and her dinner club, if she happened upon them in the organic produce section, never lingered long beside the sweet minty smell of basil to recap a recent feast they'd prepared. Everyone played their role, careful not to cross the margins of the set boundaries. Her yoga friends had really tried. As recently as January, the studio sent a postcard with a handwritten note: "Thinking about you. We would love to see you."

Jenny had managed, as best as possible, to avoid these potential situations as one might avoid slamming the car door on their fingers. She started shopping in the late evenings. She brought yogurt and sandwiches to the office to avoid cafes or restaurants. But tonight, it was still early. Rather than risk shopping at her neighborhood Safeway, she bypassed the upcoming onramp and headed to the store off North Main.

In the grocery store, she stood in the express checkout line and glanced at the display racks of impulse items—sweets and carbs, food substitutes that didn't belong in a child's diet. She had read a study that claimed nearly a third of children born after 1999 would develop diabetes during their lifetime. She thought about the Creekside resident from 206, whose body was now cold and stiff. A photo of his misshapen feet, the missing toes should be hung above this crap that was being pushed on children. She held her handbasket, waiting for the man ahead of her to unload his cart and step aside. When he did, as he stepped around to pay, she saw the baby sitting in the cart. She backed up abruptly, colliding with a woman who had apparently just joined the queue. She turned away from the baby, apologized to the other shopper, then stared at the latest edition of *Sunset Magazine*. She could pretend to have forgotten something and wave the woman ahead of her. No. She wanted to get home.

Out of the corner of her eye, she saw the cart move forward. She drew a sharp breath and slowly removed her groceries. Pancake mix. Syrup. Butter. Eggs. Oil. Bacon. Blueberries. Whipped crème. A bottle of wine. Nine items. She looked right and left, up and down—she scanned racks of chewing gum, mints, hard candies, and chocolate bars. There were Slim Jim's. Duracell batteries. Reader's Digest with their annual issue of fast and easy BBQ ideas for the summer. She allowed her eyes to finally settle on the baby, a beautiful boy with a crown of curly black hair. His head control was strong for a baby of six or seven months. He sat in a padded, shopping cart cover—the fabric a swirl of avocado green and milk chocolate. She watched him suck mechanically on a pacifier. When the dad reached below the cart for a case of bottled water, she ran her fingers over the baby's dimpled hand, wondering if the customer behind her would notice and alert the father.

She hadn't wanted to look at any baby, much less touch one these past two years, but now she craved to bend over and smell this baby boy, to kiss his soft black curls. But she restrained herself. No one likes a crazy lady in the grocery store who slobbers all over a stranger's child. The baby smiled at Jenny, losing his hold on the pacifier. The rubber nipple fell to the linoleum floor. She waited to see if he would cry. The first bottom tooth had broken through the gum. A slow river of drool trickled down his chin. She closed her eyes against an upsurge of pain. She retrieved the pacifier from the floor, the wet nib now speckled with dirt and lint, and said to the father, "Excuse me. He dropped this."

The baby's eyes tracked her hand as she reached across the basket. He began to whimper, his little paw reaching out for the pacifier.

"Hang on there, Buddy," said the father. He wiped the nipple on his sweater before introducing it back into the baby's mouth. He noticed the grimace on Jenny's face. "A few germs won't kill him," he said and smiled.

Why take the risk? she thought and turned toward the magazine rack to quiet her thoughts.

brodie

AFTER HANGING UP with the underwriter, he entered Mimi Balfour's payment information into the computer. In her signature, she had drawn a smiley face in the "B" of Balfour. She had actually lifted her pen after the "r" and gone back to the "B" to add two dots and a half circle to complete her signature. What adult still does that? He printed the receipt and wrote on the bottom: *Thank you for your business. Best regards, Brodie Marshall.* He wondered if she would notice the smiley face he'd added to the B in Brodie, and if so, what her reaction would be. It was childish, but he laughed anyway.

"Andrea," he called out. "Will you come in for a sec?"

"What's going on with this?" he asked, pointing to her cleats. "Did you sleep here last night? And where is your car?"

She started to say something, but the bell on the front door rang.

"Looking for a signature," Luke called out. Even if the U.P.S. delivery guy hadn't announced himself, Brodie would have recognized his heavy gait. "Permission to enter," the driver said in his former Marine's voice, bowing slightly to clear the door frame. He was an inch taller than Brodie and built like a solid, dark redwood that had lost its flora. He handed Andrea his electronic clipboard and set the box of company brochures on the conference table.

"Did you catch that collision at the plate?" he asked Brodie. "Man, I saw Buster Posey go down, and I thought, that's not good, not good at all."

The driver shook his head and crossed his muscular arms. His stance widened as he waited for Brodie to take the bait. Any other day, he'd happily engage in local sports news, but now, Brodie found himself praying that the guy's radio would go off.

"What a shame," Brodie finally said. "Won't be the same season."

"Hear Scott Cousins has been getting death threats. You think they're going to change the rules?"

"No clue," Brodie said, looking at Andrea with wide, beseeching eyes. She held the clipboard out for the driver, but he didn't seem to notice it.

"Shit, if that was me at the plate," he said, leaning against the table. "I would have clocked him."

"Yeah." Brodie glanced at his watch, hoping the guy would get the hint that they were pressed for time. He looked at Andrea again. This time the driver followed his gaze.

"Well, guess I'd better get to my truck." He took the clipboard from Andrea and typed in her name. Brodie smiled and said nothing. Given even the slightest opening, the guy would pounce, and there'd be another five minutes lost. The driver turned and stopped to point to a framed photo of Sasha with her first-place medal at North Coast Champions last year.

"Your daughter was in the paper again. Is it true she's heading to Stanford?"

Brodie nodded. "In fact, she's got a meet today. Trying to finish up here so I can watch her throw a new dive."

"Sweet!" He just stood there, grinning like a big kid craving attention. Brodie opened his desk and picked up the top folder, which happened to be the CANCELLATION folder, and started flipping through the pages. He was surprised to see the name of Sasha's orthodontist added to the list and wondered if he should call him.

"Have a good one," said the driver as he ducked under the doorframe. He peeked in the crib. Thank heaven, Maria was sleeping, or he'd ask to hold the baby. Andrea and Brodie watched as he headed to his truck—his shoulders taking turns moving up down, up down in time with his bobbing head.

"David Knight should be here soon," Andrea said. "I'll get out of here so you can finish preparing."

"Not so fast. What's going on?"

"Just had a big fight with Ron last night. Jerk went out with his friends, and he totaled my car. I don't even have a car seat for Maria anymore. And no, I didn't sleep at the office. I slept at a friend's apartment, and she drove me to work. We didn't have time to drop by my place for a change of clothes."

As she closed the door, Brodie thought about Stan taking over Marty's book of business. How had he finagled that? The guy was set for life, assuming he didn't do something stupid. Of all the people Brodie knew, Stan was the person least deserving of this good fortune. How would he even service his clients? Stan hated dealing with the public. Brodie figured the bastard would hire a staff of assistants to create a barrier between himself and his clients.

Before the days of "Do Not Call" lists, the company had organized mandatory monthly call-a-thons. An agent pretty much had to have a dying grandmother to get out of these sales call marathons. Betty, Stan, and Brodie were still sharing an office. Stan, in his special way, managed to make these evenings even worse. Betty and Brodie would be working the phones, trying to keep prospective customers on the line and listening to each other's pitches when Stan would walk over and flip the light switch on his way to the bathroom or kitchen. He'd chortled like a fool, leaving them in the dark to fumble with their pen and paper. Usually, they lost the sale, because the minute they became flustered and started apologizing, asking the person to hang on for a second (while they turned the lights back on), the potential client found the perfect out: we're busy, we're not interested, we just renewed . . .

Stan was a prick. No denying that. Brodie shook his head and started composing a text to Betty: *I'm so sorry about today. I hope you're feeling better* . . . but he was too ashamed to hit send. Hopefully, by next week she wouldn't hate him as much as she surely did right now.

He had no idea what to do about David Knight and his loss. The whole situation made his throat constrict. It felt as if he was trying to dislodge a goldfish. His mind was reeling, unable to hold a thought more than a second. Is this what a panic attack feels like? he wondered. He straightened his posture, breathed in deeply, and exhaled, just as he and Karen had practiced during Lamaze classes. His breathing relaxed. He unfolded his stalker's letter and started again at the top with *Dear Brodie.*

Once he got to the place where he'd left off, he read more slowly.

My son had always slept so soundly. He was such an easy-going baby, the envy of other parents. I'd have to wake him to nurse, and he always preferred his own bed. I never imagined he'd wake up that night and leave the tent.

We were gone about an hour. By then, the munchies had set in and the guys decided to raid the food we'd bear-bagged after dinner. While they jumped up and down trying to grab hold of the rope to untie the bag, I checked on my son. One minute life is great, you're laughing at the spectacle of your stoned husband and his friends trying to lift one another up to the overhead bag without throwing out a back and the next minute you've unzipped the tent to find it empty. I turned over all the sleeping bags and pillows again and again. Nothing. He was gone. That's when I knew we'd failed him.

My husband found him just before dawn hanging by his binocular strap from a limb of a fallen tree. I remember the tree well because my son had always feared it. He would say, "Mommy, run fast or the tree will get us." We had all fanned out in search for him. Then my husband screamed. I'll never forget that scream. When I came around the bend, he was leaning over our son. At first, I thought maybe it was just a badly broken leg, at worst a bone poking through the skin. My husband was a guy who can have a tooth drilled without pain medication, yet he was now clearly freaked out. He yelled for me to get back. I came closer and saw the strap of the binoculars twisted around our son's neck. He just fell over Daniel and cried.

Brodie didn't want to find out what happened next. He couldn't handle knowing right now. David Knight would arrive soon to learn he was screwed. Then he'd have to rush to make Sasha's dive meet—the final high school dual meet before the North Coast Championships. She'd give Brodie the silent treatment for days if he missed her reverse one-and-a-half somersault.

He texted Karen. *No need to stop by the office. Details after the meet.* He searched Google Images for a photo of Maureen York—a potential new client. On the top row of results were three identical headshots in different sizes of the same close-cropped brunette wearing a red sweater with black and white trim around the collar. The first photo linked to her Facebook page, the second to her Twitter, and the third was to her LinkedIn. Following Maureen's headshot were rows of seemingly unrelated images, including a photo of George Washington and several gravestones that shared the surname, York. There were a few random cartoon sketches, and of course, the obligatory soft-porn shots that seemed to find their way into every Google Image lineup regardless of the subject searched. He dialed the number written on the back of Keith's business card.

"Hello, Maureen York?"

"Yes," said the woman who stared back at him from his computer. "Who is this?"

"Brodie Marshall. You know my sister-in-law, Emma Marshall. I believe your daughters are in the same kindergarten class. She mentioned you and your family just moved to California and that you might be interested in getting some insurance quotes. I'd love to—"

"Now's not a good time." He heard a child crying in the background. "Hang on." Then a young voice said, "She's sitting too close to me. Make her move."

One of the images at the bottom of the Google results page was that of an ill-kept man with beady eyes who looked like a serial rapist. This character shared a page with Maureen York, who, at this moment, was mediating an argument over a toy. If Six Degrees of Separation wasn't complete bullshit, then Maureen York, Karen, Sasha, and every other female were only six steps away from this serial-rapist-looking fellow. What a frightening thought.

"Sorry about that. Who is calling?"

"Brodie Marshall. It sounds as if you're busy. Is it possible to set up a better time—"

"There's never a good time around here. So Emma's your sister?"

"Sister-in-law. She said your daughters—"

"Scoot over and give her some space. What did I just say? Hang on."

There was metal clanking as if someone upturned a drawer of silver-ware, then the sound of a door slamming.

"I'm back. What were you saying?" Her voice now sounded far away and muffled. "Ow. Blasted hangers."

"Are you okay?"

"Yeah," she whispered. "I'm hiding in the hall closet, hoping they won't find me. I just need a few minutes of peace. Do you have kids?"

"One daughter. Eighteen. Are your kids okay?"

"They're fine. It's me you should worry about. I'm about to lose my effing mind—"

A tiny voice called out, "Mommy, why are you in the closet?"

"Shit. I've been found. Does your daughter babysit?"

Brodie looked at the composed woman on the computer and couldn't reconcile her to this crazy person hiding from her children in a hall closet. When he didn't answer quickly enough, she asked more emphatically, "Your daughter, does she babysit?" There was pounding on the unseen door.

"Whatever. Bring your wife and daughter for dinner tomorrow night. Your daughter can watch the girls while we discuss insurance. Also, mind picking up a bottle of wine and maybe dessert? Something simple. Not ice cream, though. My husband is lactose-intolerant."

"Pardon?"

"Whatever you bring will be fine."

"MOMMY."

Perhaps you'll invite us to clean your kitchen afterwards and maybe fold a few loads of laundry, he wanted to say.

"Your address?"

When they hung up, he searched the internet for a 2011 Full Moon Calendar. Generally skeptical about urban legends and superstitions, he would have loved to find something—perhaps a gravitational pull—to blame for all the erratic behavior he'd encountered today, but May 17th had come and gone. Christ Fucking Almighty! Burying his face in his hands, he laughed at the dreadful notion that this could be his life for another twenty years.

jenny

JENNY SAT IN HER VAN in the grocery store parking lot and watched the father from the checkout line buckle his baby into his car seat. The first time Jerrod had ventured out alone with Daniel, he was so nervous. What if he becomes fussy or hungry? Should I bring a bottle? What if he does one of those monster poops? Should I bring the diaper bag? It was if they were headed out for a long mission to outer space rather than a simple run to the grocery store.

A smile bubbled up from her chest.

"You'll be fine," she had said, trying to sound confident. In truth, she was scared he'd take his eye off their son for a second and someone would steal him right out of the cart. "The first time is always the scariest."

She watched the man jog the emptied cart over to the cart corral. Jerrod and Daniel had returned to the house a half-hour later—Jenny pacing until she heard his car pull into the driveway. Baby and father had returned, unscathed. Jerrod's confidence as a new father had been bolstered by that first adventure. Jenny also relaxed and allowed him to play a bigger role in caring for their son. She realized she didn't need to rush in and take charge of every whimper or meal or bath time. She and Jerrod were a team—it was okay to say, "Tag, you're it."

Rhonda had visited them in the hospital the morning following Daniel's birth. She'd generously stocked the refrigerator with ready gourmet meals, dairy products, and fresh produce. They wouldn't need to shop for a week, she said, as she reached out her arms to hold her grandson. His eyes were open and taking in everything around him. She touched the tiny tip of his Roman nose and smiled at Jerrod.

"He has your nose. He's going to be smart like his daddy."

"Thank god," Jenny teased, "wouldn't want him to be dumb like his mommy."

"My dear, you are anything but dumb." She rubbed Jenny's hand. "If Daniel has one-fifth of your compassion, your integrity, your courage . . . he will be well-equipped to handle whatever life brings him."

Courage, as in giving up on life, Jenny now thought. Integrity, as in lying to everyone, including her husband. Compassion, as in disregarding the feelings of everyone she cared about. She wiped away a tear and picked up her phone.

"Hey, this is a surprise," Rhonda said. Jenny detected the happy hour slur. She looked at the clock and figured her mother-in-law was just starting a second glass of wine. "I was just thinking about you."

"And what were you thinking?"

"I have a few formal dresses from my San Francisco Black and White Ball days. Do you want me to send you some photos? You're about the size I was back then."

Jenny imagined beautiful, timeless gowns hanging inside Saks Fifth Avenue and Neiman Marcus garment bags. "You are so sweet. I think I've got what I need; I can't possibly squeeze another dress in my suitcase."

Rhonda yelled at Mickey to leave Elsie alone. The dogs' barking was drowned out by Rhonda's coughing fit. Jenny held the phone at a distance.

"Sorry about that. This damn cough."

"Do you think Jerrod blames me for Daniel's death?" Jenny asked. The question had been on her mind since the accident, but she'd never had the courage to ask Rhonda. She feared the answer wouldn't be what she most wanted to hear.

"Oh, darling. No. No. No. It was a terrible accident. No one is to blame."

"I know neither of us meant for it to happen," Jenny said, picking at a loose thread in the hem of her shirt. "I just feel like he's never forgiven me. That had I not been in such a rush to get to yoga, I wouldn't have—"

"Stop that. You were a good mother who loved your son with every atom in your body. The sad fact is that sometimes God's plan isn't clear to us."

Jenny's eyes blurred with tears. She didn't share what she was thinking about God and his plans. Why would any loving person or being *plan* to take an innocent child's life? It didn't make sense. Rhonda's faith held no solace for Jenny.

"I've read up on these back over accidents," Rhonda said. "The devastation it brings to the families. So many horrible stories. You know there is a term . . . the Bye-Bye Syndrome, when a child goes outside to say goodbye. I'm not saying . . . I'm not sure what my point . . . I know that simply reading about other people's experiences doesn't make me an expert."

Rhonda started coughing again. "We can only be so careful. Nowadays they have cameras on cars and that's great. Have you spoken to Jerrod about your feelings?"

"I've tried. He just shuts me out." She yanked out the loose thread and laid it on the dashboard. "The night of the funeral, after the reception, Jerrod and I went straight to bed. Neither of us had said more than a couple of words to each other all day. I felt so lonely. I just wanted to turn off my mind. I nuzzled up to him. I needed something physical to distract me. To blot out everything that was swirling in my head. I wanted to feel the weight of something other than heartache. It wasn't that I was horny or anything."

Jenny heard Rhonda take a large swallow of wine. This wasn't the type of intimate conversation she generally had with her mother-in-law.

"I made an overture, and he pushed me away. He said, 'How can you even think about sex? We just buried our son.'" Tears rolled down Jenny's cheeks. "He pulled the covers up to his chin—I remember he'd nicked himself shaving that morning—and simply turned toward the other wall. Away from me. Away from the person he probably hated more than anyone else. I'd never felt so filthy and ashamed, so lonely."

"Oh, my dear," Rhonda said softly. "I'm so sorry."

"I've only made one other attempt, but he claimed he was too tired. Whenever we accidentally brush against each other in the bathroom or the kitchen, we move away quickly. Never a comment. Never apology. Just two strangers, coexisting."

"Maybe this cruise will provide some healing."

"That's very optimistic," Jenny said. "As much as he hates and blames me, I've had to struggle not to hate and blame him. I mean . . . he was supposed to be watching Daniel."

"That won't help either of you," Rhonda said. "I think . . . hell, I don't know what I think."

"I know it's not his fault." Jenny sighed. "You're right. It was just life shitting on us. You know what . . . I've got a few groceries in the car and I'm exhausted. I appreciate you listening. Let's talk tomorrow. Love you."

"I love you, too." She started to say something else, but Jenny ended the call. She blew the thread off the dashboard and headed home.

brodie

HE HEARD THE BELL on the front door ring. Andrea had taken Maria out for their daily walk. Every afternoon, weather permitting, Andrea pushed Maria in her stroller a few blocks up Main Street to the convenience store to buy chips or a chocolate bar.

"David, nice to meet you," he said, greeting his client at the front door. David's hand was rougher and stronger than he'd expected.

"Rather it be under different circumstances," he mumbled. His mouth settled into an upside-down U, bracketed by deeply carved wrinkles.

"Shall we?" Brodie nodded toward his office. The man stood at the display of miniature chairs, picked up one, studied it from various angles before inspecting a couple more.

"My wife," Brodie said.

They sat opposite each other at the conference table.

"I'm glad no one was hurt. Have you found a place to stay?"

"A motel that allows cats," the man said so softly, swallowing the last couple of words, that Brodie found himself leaning forward to hear. "It has a little kitchenette. I'll get by."

"Do you know how the fire started?" Before he arrived, Brodie had looked up the property on Redfin. It was a 1920's nine hundred square foot rancher with shake siding and a shake roof. Add to that an original fireplace, which likely had a few cracks, surround it with massive oak trees and you had yourself a box of kindling. It was a moot point now, but that house wouldn't pass the company's underwriting today.

"Some talk about the wiring in the garage." He yawned so that every silver filling in his cramped teeth was visible. "Look, Brodie, I know you're trying to be nice, but I haven't slept properly in two days. What I want to know is, how do I start the claim to get my house rebuilt? I can't live in a motel forever. I need the quiet. I need a place to set up my equipment. I need . . ." His words trailed off.

"What is it that you do for a living?"

"I'm a potter. I lost everything—my wheel, my kiln, all my glazes, and tools. What am I supposed to do now?"

What are any of us to do now? Brodie wondered. The man could couch-surf at Brodie's house until the bank served up their foreclosure papers. He imagined the introduction to Karen could go something like: "Hi sweetheart, meet David Knight. I screwed up on his insurance and now he has nowhere else to go. And, heads up, it won't be long till we're fucked ourselves financially. I've let things slip. It's not as bad as Enron or Lehman Brothers, though. Can you still love me?"

He looked at David Knight and wanted so badly to let his head fall onto the table.

"Was your studio in the garage?"

Brodie pictured some shoddy, ungrounded wiring feeding an energy-sucking appliance in a poorly ventilated space and a bunch of dry rot in the flooring. Poof! This guy was lucky he and his cats got out alive. He opened his folder. The PG&E envelope sat on top of his paperwork with his scribbled notes.

"There's a slight problem. Turns out, we never switched your renter's policy to a homeowner's policy."

"That doesn't sound so slight," David said so emphatically that Brodie's eyebrows shot up.

"It isn't, really. What it means is that the company is contractually obligated to pay for your temporary living arrangements for up to two years and will cover your lost personal property up to twenty-five thousand with certain limits."

"Such as?" He rubbed his thin lips and squinted at Brodie like a crusty actor in an old western.

"Limits on electronics, jewelry, and furs, for instance."

"Ain't got none of that. What about my kiln? A new one is going to run me about twenty-two hundred. Who's paying for that?"

"My guess is a kiln would be capped at a thousand unless you took out a separate endorsement, which you didn't."

The man's chest was starting to rise and fall at a quicker pace. Brodie began to worry that he might lunge across the table and snap Brodie's neck like a breadstick.

"David, I'm going to be honest with you. I pride myself on being thorough, making sure my clients are properly covered, and providing excellent service. However, sometimes I mess up." He showed him the PG&E envelope and nervously tapped it on the desk. "I have no idea how it happened, but we dropped the ball on this one. It's obvious you spoke with my previous office manager because she took down these notes. My guess is that after you hung up, she got interrupted and somehow forgot to convert your policy."

David's Adam apple rode up and down. He gripped the edge of the chair. Brodie pulled in a long breath and thought, if I wanted to be a prick, I could point out that he should have realized he never signed the paperwork on a new policy or received a bill for the higher premium. But he was willing to roll solo under the bus.

The man chuckled. Brodie cocked his head.

"I sold an eight-hundred-dollar vase at the Marin Art and Wine Festival last summer and forgot to ship it. Two months later, the buyer calls, accusing me of scamming her, threatening to contact the Better Business Bureau, the Festival organizers, and every Bay Area newspaper. I convinced her I wasn't trying to rip her off. I'd just accidentally packed her vase with my booth displays." He stared at the miniature chairs for a minute, then turned back to me. "So what do we do now? You need to make this right."

"Absolutely," he said. "I've got Errors and Omissions insurance for unintentional mistakes such as this one." He didn't mention that he hadn't paid the premiums. "I'll help you open a claim against me. Once we start the paperwork, a claims adjuster will contact you. In the meantime, let's open a claim on your renter's policy to cover lodging and other necessities. We can request an advance to help with your motel bill and to buy some additional clothes. May I bring a company check by tomorrow?"

The man's weathered hands settled flat on the table. "God bless you." He sighed and cracked his neck so loudly that Brodie grimaced. He wrote down the name of his motel and the room number and stood up. "Don't like to admit it, but I figured you'd be one of the sleazy insurance guys. You know, trying to blame me and weasel out of this. But you seem like a decent fellow."

He shook Brodie's hand.

"I have a few of my pieces in the car I picked up from a gallery this morning. They were held on consignment, but with the economy, there's been little interest. Figured it'd be nice to have them in the motel to keep me company. Would you like to see my work?"

"Yes, sure."

Brodie glanced at his watch. The meet had started.

"Absolutely," he said, trying to sound genuine.

He pictured the judges taking their seats and heard the emcee's voice announcing the order of the divers. Sasha was going to be angry, but surely he could give this man the courtesy of two or three minutes. He followed David to an old, dented Volvo station wagon. David was one of those political/environmental/peace-loving sticker people. The back of his wagon was stacked with old newspapers, rolls of packing tape, and two banker's boxes with KNIGHT printed on the lids and sides. From one box, he removed an object the size of a basketball, covered in blankets of recycled bubble wrap.

Brodie prepared his "Oh, my, that's wonderful," smile that, as a parent of an artistically-challenged daughter, had helped disguise his "What in the hell is that supposed to be?" reactions, when confronted with an unrecognizable object of art brought home from school.

The smile fell from his face. He was honestly stunned. In a positive way.

"That . . . that's incredible."

The man held a round, yellow vase with a narrow gold-painted opening about the size of a half-dollar. Sealed under the cracked yellow glaze were random bursts of mint green that looked like iridescent moth wings dipped and fanned out in mother-of-pearl.

"May I touch it?" Brodie asked. He ran his fingers over the vase expecting a bumpy finish. "This is incredible." The glaze was as smooth as a candied apple.

"Uranium oxide," David said. "And nickel. That's what makes the crystals green."

"Is working with uranium a bit risky?" Brodie pictured radioactive men glowing in Russian mines.

"For me, but not for the end-user. The uranium is trapped under the glaze. Check this one out." He pulled another bundle from the second box and peeled away the bubble wrap to reveal a taller yellow vase with a wider mouth. "See here." He handed Brodie the vase and pointed to a faint streak of blue that ran down the sides, highlighting the edges of the crystals. "Used cobalt blue. See how these crystals are darker? I threw in silver nitrate."

"No wonder your house burnt down," he said before he could filter the thought.

David turned away and began repacking the first box. Like an idiot, he'd insulted him with his insensitive joke.

"Do you have more?" he asked, turning the vase around. He wanted to blow into the small opening to see if it would make a sound similar to the ocean, but he figured he might think him even more of an imbecile.

"I've got to run," David said as he took the yellow vase from Brodie's hands. "Another time, perhaps."

"Your work is impressive."

"Well, Brodie, thank you for your time."

"I'll stop by tomorrow with a check. And, if it's not a great imposition, may I bring along my wife? She goes to art festivals all over the Bay Area."

David jingled his keys. "Be pleased to meet her," he said in the tired voice Brodie first heard earlier on the phone. He could see the man was impatient to go.

"Will you be okay at that motel?" Brodie said, digging his hands into his pockets. "That area can be sketchy at night."

David Knight snickered. "I grew up in one of those sketchy areas. Think I'll be fine."

Andrea came into view. She dropped her phone into the stroller's cup holder and pushed Maria past the Volvo. David backed out, waving.

There was a sticker on his back window that read, "I'd rather be at my OTHER wheel."

Brodie imagined him hunched over, sitting at his potter's wheel, hands wet and gooey. The entire world and all its complications and worries drowned out by the steady hum of the motor. He envied this ability to take a dense, lifeless lump of clay and push and pull and dig until he'd created a beautiful vessel—something greater than himself.

"I've got an idea," he said to Andrea. "Let's bring in the welcome mat. You and Maria come with me to Sasha's dive meet. Maybe one of the parents will have an extra car seat to loan you."

While Andrea gathered Maria's diaper bag and shut down her computer, Brodie retrieved his keys. Just before he turned off the office lights, he slipped the letter from his stalker in its envelope and stuffed it into his briefcase to finish reading tonight.

jenny

JENNY PULLED INTO the driveway and waited as the garage door opened. She glanced at her neighbor's house. Every window was lit up as if it were Christmas Eve. She felt guilty for being so rude earlier that morning. What was Emma going to ask her about Jerrod? Why does her husband play music like an insane man? Jenny shook her head. It didn't matter now.

She looked in the rearview mirror. A car slowed as it approached her house. The glare of the sun made it difficult to see whether it was someone she knew. She hoped not. When the driver pulled up behind her and Jenny saw it was Jerrod, her shoulders collapsed. What was he doing home? He was supposed to be in Dallas tonight. No, no, no. . . .

"Did you work late?" he asked, climbing out of his car.

"You're home?" she asked, as if, possibly, he was only a mirage.

"Wow, you sound disappointed." He sighed and removed his luggage from the trunk.

"I'm just surprised you're home early."

"They postponed the depositions. I have to go back week after next."

Biting her tongue until she couldn't stand the pain, she thought, please God, I can't wait another week.

"I was thinking, perhaps," he said, clearing his throat, "we could do something tonight. Maybe dinner out. It's our anniversary."

Why now this sudden interest? She shook her head like a belligerent child. The hope on his face was waylaid by defeat. She ran into the house, dropped the bag of groceries by the kitchen door, and locked herself in their bedroom. A few minutes later, the first sharp note of the piano, to be undoubtedly followed by hours more, elicited a downpour of silent screams as she paced the room, trying to figure out an alternative move. Her cell phone pinged. She grabbed her purse and plopped down on the bed. The text was from Beth.

"Have fun on the cruise," Beth wrote. "Sure I can't come along?"

Feeling trapped in her room, she fell back against the pillow. In her mind, she composed a letter.

Dear Brodie,

My husband came home unexpectedly tonight. It's our anniversary. I had hoped it would slip his mind. Now I'm lying in bed wondering how I'm going to kill myself without him interfering. He can tune out the world once he starts banging away on his piano.

I bet if I were to look inside my husband's suitcase, I'd find a stash of miniature soaps, shampoos, conditioners, and lotions from the hotel. Even now, he still brings them home. The vanity in the guest bathroom is crammed full of them.

In his early days of non-stop traveling for work, my husband would bring home these hotel souvenirs for our son. He'd tell him that the toiletries were actually adult-sized, but he'd put them through a special shrinking machine at the airport so they'd all fit in his suitcase. How can I hate a man who brought so much happiness to our son?

The letter I left for you today wasn't completely honest. It's true that my son is dead. But it wasn't a camping accident. Hopefully, you and your family have realized I've meant no harm with these letters. I know it must be a bit disconcerting having a stranger write. Not understanding the motive—

Enough, Jenny thought, squeezing her fists until her hands shook. She got up from the bed and went to the bathroom to collect the prescriptions she had stashed under the sink. She opened the cabinet and dug out the floral makeup bag she'd hidden behind the Charmin. Another cosmetic bag caught her attention. She locked the door and sat on the floor. She removed a clear plastic cylinder. Eight inches long, curved on one end and flat on the other. In her mind, she saw Daniel and Jerrod coming home from an ice cream outing and calling out her name.

"What's going on here?" she had asked, finding Jerrod and Daniel sitting in the living room sporting enormous grins. Daniel, as usual, was bouncing up and down on the sofa cushions. His chubby hands were swinging excitedly, holding a pink polka-dotted bag. Sticky trails of chocolate ice cream ran across his cheeks.

"Mommy, we got you a present."

"What's the occasion?"

Jerrod winked at her and said, "Oh, just a little something."

Before she could take the bag from her son, he'd reached inside and pulled out a phallic-shaped object filled with pastel-colored flakes. The flat end of the container had a screw cap.

"It's bubble bath," he said, holding it up proudly. "Can we take a bath with it 'night?"

"Wow." Jenny plucked the container from his hand and inspected the design. A knowing look was exchanged between her and Jerrod.

"It's quite large. A dream for any girl. Who picked out this nice gift?"

"I did," Daniel said, grabbing it from his mom. Jerrod pulled her into a hug. "Look, you turn the cap here and shake."

Colored flakes rained down from the tube's opening and onto the coffee table. Jenny swept them into her hand and smelled the chips. Lavender.

"Maybe daddy and mommy will also take a bubble bath," Jerrod said, winking again.

That evening, after Daniel was asleep, they lay against each other in a warm bubble bath. She held up the empty tube and asked Jerrod, "So what else can we do with this?"

Now, sitting on the cold bathroom floor, she tapped the tip of the phallic-shaped container against the cabinet door to check that it hadn't become too brittle for use. Satisfied it was still structurally sound, she lowered her underwear. It took a while of rubbing back and forth to coax some feeling back into that region of her body. Eventually, her breathing quickened and her body shuddered. Her eyes squeezed shut. As soon as the spasms ceased, her body folded inward like a clover at night. Sadness and guilt seeped in as she cried quietly, hugging her knees. Finally, she tossed the container into the trashcan, visible for Jerrod to notice tonight when he stood at the toilet.

brodie

STILL TRYING TO PROCESS everything that had happened so far during this weird, screwed up day, Brodie couldn't believe his luck. A truck pulled out of a parking spot near the aquatics center just as they entered the high school lot. His phone pinged with a text and he ignored it. Whoever it was, even Keith, would have to wait. Maybe he wouldn't be too late to see Sasha's reverse dive.

He held the gate open for Andrea. Maria, half-asleep and cradled in her arms, startled at the rumble of applause coming from the spectator's stand. Wow. There were more people here than he'd ever seen at any of the other league championship meets.

They entered the deck area. Sasha's head popped up from the water as scores were read: "Eight, eight, seven and a half." She looked around first to the bleachers, then to the scoring table, to the bathroom/changing area, and again to the bleachers. He started to wave, hoping to catch her attention. He wanted to let her know that he was here for her, but she ducked under the water and swam to the ladder. Shit, he had missed what was, apparently, a damn good dive.

They approached the scoring table where four parents were passing divers' score sheets around in a circle. Karen sat in the third chair, armed with a pencil, ruler, and calculator. Ginger immediately stood up. She barked at Brodie, her tail wagging excitedly as she pulled and bit on her leash. She yanked hard and the table jerked forward; papers went flying. She apparently thought she was going to be saved from the boredom of being tethered to the scoring table. One of the nearby parents popped out of his chair and gathered the score sheets before they were blown into the pool. Why in the hell would Karen bring Ginger to the meet? Brodie thought, shaking his head. That dog was a maniac.

Petting Ginger and telling her to calm down, he gave Karen a look:

169

Really? You couldn't leave her home? She ignored his frown and said, "Sash was worried you weren't coming. I never got around to calling you back." She looked from him to Andrea. "Is everything okay?"

Some guy behind them said, "Hey, Brodie, I can't see through you."

"Yeah. We'll talk after."

He motioned for Andrea to follow him to the bleachers. Two divers ran past, whipping towels at each other's legs, and nearly knocking Andrea into the pool.

"Settle down, guys," Brodie called out.

"Sorry, Mr. Marshall," the boys answered in unison, dodging the sharp bite of the other's towel. The taller boy, a year behind Sasha, turned back to check out Andrea. A smile formed on his face, and Brodie thought, even though the kid is too young for her, he'd be a huge improvement over Ron. But then he recalled how last season he kept seeing the kid at meets with bruises all over his neck, chest, and back. He didn't want to become tangled in a domestic situation, but he couldn't ignore the bruises. When he finally gathered the courage to ask him about the marks, the kid said they were from paintball, and Brodie believed him. He had played once at a bachelors' party. Those gumball-colored balls had left gnarly bruises. Then one afternoon, he heard another teammate teasing the kid, saying the girlfriend needed to find a hobby besides sucking on his body. They were hickeys! How could Brodie have been so naïve?

Sasha's principal stood to the right of the bleachers in her suit and pumps. Sasha was probably stunned that she'd shown up. Hopefully, the principal wasn't going to interrogate them further about the forged forms. He didn't think he could reproduce the lie.

"Mr. Marshall, you just missed a great dive," she said.

He watched her gaze shift to Maria, then to Andrea as he helped Andrea climb the bleachers. She looked at Andrea's cleats, and again at the baby, and back at Brodie as if he owed her an explanation. Let her imagine the worst, he thought, glancing around for Sasha. She was kneeling at her coach's chair and nodding as he demonstrated with his hand the sharp pike-out he expected to see in her next dive.

Standing on the board now was Sasha's archrival from another high school, Holly Kurtz. Holly adjusted the board's fulcrum. She ran a tie-dyed towel up and down her legs before slamming the towel on the concrete, creating a loud smack. The emcee called out her second dive. Brodie had missed only the first round. They must have gotten a late start. Sasha finally noticed her dad. She gave him an exaggerated, insincere smile, all teeth and gums, and then turned away. He'd disappointed her again. Holly lifted off the board. She threw her arms hard, and grabbed her ankles tight for a front double somersault. She came out too late, landed on her face and chest. Ginger barked at the huge splash. Brodie shuddered at what had to be a painful smack. Holly emerged from the water, gasping for breath. The scores were read—two, two and a half, and three. He expected to see a slight grin on his daughter's face, but she looked bored.

"She blew it," he heard Eric Kurtz say from a few rows behind. Holly's father was on his cell phone, as usual, recapping the dive for Mrs. Kurtz, who traveled all over the world for Apple and rarely made a meet. The men exchanged nods. As Brodie turned back to face the pool and search for his daughter, he saw Holly mouth, "Sorry," to her father. Poor kid. Sasha glanced his way again and noticed Andrea and Maria. She clapped her hands and skipped over to say hello. She smiled at the principal before glaring at Brodie.

"You're late," she said. "But I'll forgive you because you brought my two favorite people." She threw her tanned arms around Andrea, enveloping Maria as well, getting them both wet. "You're coming for dinner, right?"

Andrea looked at Brodie.

"Certainly, they're invited." He had no idea how they would pay for three, much less four. He wanted to add, "Don't think I've forgotten about our talk tonight," but now wasn't the time or place.

"You must be getting excited about Stanford," Andrea said while Sasha played with Maria's chubby toes.

"Oh. My. God! I can't wait. High school can't end soon enough." Where did that animated Valley Girl voice come from? Brodie wondered. All he ever got these days was sarcasm or disdain.

Andrea nodded. "I remember feeling that way."

Sasha pointed at Andrea's feet. "I like this new fashion. The girl jock look." They were spared having to explain the cleats when Sasha's name and dive were called.

"Crap," Sasha said, hurrying to the board, nearly tripping over one of the judge's feet. Her red swimsuit, stamped on the rear with the school's logo, had risen up her ass. Brodie wanted to yell, "Pull your suit out of your crack." Every season, the suits seemed to get teenier and teenier. At times, it felt awkward standing next to these half-naked girls and engaging them in conversation.

Sasha stood on the edge of the board, arms by her side, shoulders relaxed, and every muscle of her lower body squeezed tight. She was so focused as she primed the board and lifted off. Reaching behind her head, she threw into a deep pike position. Her beautiful entry produced a tiny splash. Brodie let out an ear-piercing whistle. As Maria started crying, Andrea frowned at him and bounced her daughter in her arms, cooing to calm her. Ginger barked and lunged toward the pool. This time Karen was ready and gripped the leash firmly.

When Sasha looked over at Brodie, he gave her a thumbs-up. The scores from her back one-and-a-half pike somersault—a dive she had never performed consistently well—put her that much more ahead of Holly. When a meet was close and Karen was working the scoring table, all he had to do was look over and read Karen's body language, look for the cautious smile on her face. He'd always dodged the job of helping at the table, but Karen enjoyed it because she liked being one of the first to know who had won the meet.

Holly's father sighed. "Damn. Nailed it. Yeah, she's got a lot of points to make up now."

Brodie imagined Mrs. Kurtz sitting in an important meeting, holding up her finger to stop the conversation for these updates.

By six-thirty, the divers were on their ninth round. The emcee announced Holly's next optional, a full-twisting front one-and-a-half somersault. Her approach was lousy, but she managed to hold it together. Even with the rip entry, her scores—eights and nines—were generous.

"Yes, yes," Holly's father yelled. Brodie turned around. "Nice job."

The man beamed as he dialed his wife.

The next girl, Megan, a new member of the high school dive team, was a former elite gymnast. Her dive was announced. Andrea said, "Holy, crap. What's the degree of difficulty on that?" Brodie shrugged. Karen had memorized the entire dive chart, including all the numerical identifications for each dive and corresponding letters for each position. Yet, after years of hearing dives called out, season after season of listening to Sasha and her teammates talk about their dives in these alpha-numeric codes, he knew the difference between a 101B and a 201B: a front dive pike versus a back dive pike, but that was it.

Megan's hurdle was clunky, yet she threw a tight front-two-and-a-half somersault and kicked out above board level. The crowd roared. A group of her peers drummed their feet on the bleachers. Over the noise, he heard Kurtz say, "Maybe we should all get divorced so the coaches will give our kids extra attention."

Andrea leaned over and whispered to Brodie, "I think he's got *assholitis*."

They both sniggered. Despite the applause and the solid entry, the judges' scores were stingy: fours and fives. Next year, with a summer to work on her form, there was no doubt Megan would make nationals and probably push Holly Kurtz, a senior by then, aside to take first at North Coast Sections. And that fact, which had certainly not escaped Mr. and Mrs. Kurtz's notice, gave Sasha and her dad great pleasure.

Sasha's final dive was her dreaded reverse one-and-a-half somersault pike. There were simultaneous shouts from her teammates as well as her opponents. "You got this, Sasha. You can do it. Just like practice!" Coach gave her a reassuring nod. She had her game face as she ran the towel over her legs one final time and threw it down hard. She opened and closed her palms, five times, always five times. Maria babbled beside in Andrea's arms.

"Come on," Brodie whispered, filled with awe at Sasha's strength and courage. Once, he had asked her if it was difficult to make yourself throw a new dive that you'd only seen others perform or watched coach model on deck. "Of course, it's scary," she said and rolled her eyes. "Otherwise,

I would have done it a million times already. But just because I've never done it, doesn't mean I won't be able to." Her confidence, luckily, reflected more of Karen's gene pool than his own. He watched her take her first step on the board and thought about how improved his own life would be if he committed himself like his daughter. If he committed to being a better parent, a better husband, a better salesman, a better human being. That kind of dedication, he felt, would require enormous effort.

Two steps into her approach, Sasha stumbled. Andrea grabbed his arm. They watched as Sasha composed herself and walked with mummy-like concentration down the board. A strong, upright hurdle and she was in the air demonstrating expert distance—closer to the board than looked safe.

"Come on, come on . . . come on, you got . . ." Her ankles, or ankle, Brodie couldn't quite tell, hit the board, and he sprang to his feet.

"Judges, please hold your score cards," called the emcee as the coach and the principal shoved their way past the gawking divers to the ladder. Sasha wasn't crying. There were no ribbons of blood in the water. Luckily, it wasn't her head that struck the board. Brodie stayed back to let her coach help her out of the pool and assess her injuries. The minute she stood on deck, she was greeted with hearty applause. Her right ankle was now bleeding. She held it up and hopped a few steps before gingerly setting it down. The coach and the principal both said something to her. Sasha grinned. Karen stood at the scoring table, restraining Ginger and trying to calm her down. She watched Sasha limp over to Brodie. Coach yelled to one of her teammates to get the first aid kit.

"Did you see that?" Sasha said. "I hit the frickin' board."

He hugged her. "Yes . . . and you scored fours for scaring the crap out of the judges and audience, not to mention your mom and dad."

She buried her face in his shirt, her body trembling. He waved to Karen to let her know Sasha was fine. She held up one finger, which he interpreted to mean that even if Holly received a perfect score on the next dive, Sasha still had first place wrapped up.

While Holly adjusted the fulcrum on the board, Sasha leaned closer and said, "Know what the principal said to me? 'That's why I don't attend these meets. I don't have the stomach for the sport.'"

174

"It takes courage." He hugged her tighter. "And you've certainly got it in spades."

The emcee called out Holly's final dive, a fifty-two thirty-three, free position. Mr. Hickeys jogged over, carrying Sasha's favorite 101 Dalmatians towel and a yellow toolbox.

"You okay?" he asked. "There's Band-Aids and shit in here."

Sasha thanked him and wrapped herself in spotted dogs. Her voice quivered as she said, "Can we sit down?"

"Shall I bandage you up first?" Brodie asked.

She shook her head and plopped down in his lap as she used to do when she was a little girl. He held her close and inhaled the potpourri of chlorine, fruity shampoo, and suntan lotion. In his mind, he saw her at age two standing at the edge of the bathtub twirling around and around as he wrapped her in her favorite towel until she resembled a giant burrito. He'd throw her over his shoulder and carry her across the hall to her room to dress her for bed. She would be all giggles and squeals. The thought that they had one summer left and then she was off to college filled him with regret. How many times had he wished he could advance time? Push forward the hands of the clock to high school graduation? He'd played out the scene often: pulling away from the dorm curb and waving goodbye, assuring Karen and himself that Sasha would be fine, then the second honeymoon. He had been so focused on what he saw as the payoff for all those years of complete, hands-on parenting: extended alone-time with his wife. He hadn't considered how bittersweet the day might be. Stanford was just an hour's drive, he realized, but it meant no more sitting down for dinner in the evenings as a family, not knowing for certain she was safe when he went to bed, not getting to meet her friends and dates before she left the house. On the flip side, there would be fewer teenage mood swings, dirty dishes, and laundry in the house. No driving her to school every morning and hearing, "Could you just not talk?"

She leaned into Brodie, her body still shaking, as they watched Holly's impressive back one-and-a-half somersault with one-and-a-half twists. Behind Brodie, Eric Kurtz said to his wife, "She nailed it, hon. No matter though. Might as well as have saved it for North Coast."

Sasha shifted in her dad's lap and whispered in his ear. "I'm glad you don't act like them." He thumped her gently on the head. She slapped his hand, saying in a dramatic voice, "Dad, you're supposed to be nice to me. I'm injured."

The PA system cut out several times as the coach announced the District 3 Championship winners, starting with the girls. Brodie squeezed in around the one-meter boards with the other parents and classmates, applauding the divers, whistling for those who qualified for NCS. Karen gave out the medals and hugs to those who placed seventh and higher while one of the dads and a local newspaper photographer took photos. When the coach called out Holly's name for second place, Brodie clapped heartedly. Everyone looked around the pool area for Holly. Finally, one of her teammates said something to Karen. In turn, Karen said something to the coach. Holly had already headed to the locker room to change. Brodie spotted Mr. Kurtz standing by the gate, keys in hand.

"And last, but not least," Coach announced. "In first place, is our own Sasha Marshall. Scoring 342.25 and heading to NCS and then Stanford." Sasha hobbled dramatically over to Karen and lowered her head for the ribbon. She shook Coach's hand, and he pulled her into a tight hug. After the boys' medals were given out and the kids headed to the locker rooms, Coach congratulated Karen and Brodie on a great finish to Sasha's high school dive career.

"I'll miss her," he said. "One of my hardest working kids. Ever." He looked at Ginger and scratched her head. "I'll even miss you, ol' girl. Even though you can't stay out of my pool."

Ginger whined. She was certainly a rascal. Someone called Brodie's name and he turned to see who it was. Ernie Waldman. The dad of one of the divers, and unfortunately, a new client. One of Brodie's least favorite people.

"I'll help put away the chairs," Karen said, pinching him on the arm. She smirked mischievously as if to say, "One day you'll learn to run while you've got the chance." Coach sighed as the men exchanged looks of dread.

Ernie Waldman stormed over, his hands clenched. He was one of those rare macho guys who wore rubber bracelets supporting various popular causes. He nodded hello to the coach and stepped right up to Brodie. Judging by the stench of alcohol, it was clear he had already slammed back a few bourbons.

"Coach . . . a word with Brodie, please."

"Sure." Coach gave Brodie a sympathetic nod and shook his hand.

"How are you?" Brodie asked, realizing Ernie's newest girlfriend hadn't attended any of the meets since just after the start of the season.

"You have fucked me over."

"Please, watch your language."

Brodie looked around to see if anyone had turned their way. The kids pulling on the faded blue pool covers hadn't glanced over.

"Telling me to go with a thousand-dollar deductible. I'm screwed because of you. I just got into an accident and called the help desk. The woman told me the first thousand is out of my pocket."

Brodie's immediate thought was DUI. Now wouldn't that be a nasty surprise at renewal, he thought, almost laughing. Although, he'd seen this guy at parties drink a considerable amount of alcohol and remain steady enough to walk a line.

"Any injuries?"

"Don't pretend to care. Where in the hell am I supposed to get a thousand dollars to fix my car?"

"Perhaps we can meet tomorrow to—"

"Screw that! I didn't even want to raise the deductible, but you—"

He started to jab his finger in Brodie's chest but must have realized he would look idiotic standing on his toes to reach. It took a lot of self-restraint for Brodie not to laugh.

"Let's make this absolutely clear," Brodie said. "I didn't force you to do anything. You came to me looking to save money. Of the options we considered, increasing your deductible was the one you said you felt most comfortable choosing."

The client rolled his blood-shot eyes and blew out an exasperated breath. Brodie nearly fell over. "Don't you dare try to pin this on me. I'll make it my mission to tell everyone in the entire East Bay that you're a crook."

Brodie wanted to punch him in the throat. He knew it wasn't worth the risk to him personally or professionally. But how he would have loved to cock his fist back and knock the hot air right out of the fool. This was a person he had defended on numerous occasions when other parents had gossiped about his obvious issues with alcohol and the constant stream of new girlfriends.

Ernie smirked and then belched. He looked so self-satisfied, as if he had Brodie's balls in his hands.

"You know, Ernie, by the smell of the alcohol screaming out of your pores, you should be counting your blessings that you're not sitting in the Martinez jail right now. You might think about getting some help. Rehab, AA? I really believe the accident might be a wake-up call."

The man's eyes widened. His jaw fell open. For once, Ernie Waldman was speechless.

Brodie laid his hand on the man's shoulder in a fatherly fashion. "Seriously, Ernie. Get some help. My brother had a serious drinking problem, and AA was a game-changer for him."

jenny

JENNY STOOD IN THE KITCHEN facing the dusty window box. She leaned against the sink and counted three dead flies and one shriveled spider. The potted herbs and flowers had long since withered. While she had been in her bedroom figuring out her next move, Jerrod had unpacked the groceries. Everything except the pancake mix and syrup had been put in the refrigerator.

The explosive sounds of music charged in from the other room—no match, however, for the lonely silence closing in around her. Under the spell of desperation, she paced from one corner of the small kitchen to the other. Finally, she went to their shared office. Sitting at her desk, she wondered, Now what? She opened her laptop and searched Brodie Marshall Insurance. She clicked on the link to his agency. Before the site fully opened, she heard a man's voice and jumped.

"Looking for insurance in Hidden Oaks . . ." In the top left corner of her screen, under a green banner, stood Brodie wearing an ill-fitted suit and tie. His posture was unnaturally erect. God, he was tall. His spiel ended with an awkward, forced smile. With another click, she brought him back to life. "Looking for insurance in Hidden Oaks? I'm your local all-lines agent. Contact me, Brodie Marshall, to learn more."

She hit the play arrow again and again. Each time she heard Brodie's voice, she startled. At the bottom of the homepage was a photo of a blonde boy hugging a golden retriever. The caption read, *Term Life Insurance: The simplest form of Life coverage. Contact me to learn how to affordably provide for your family's future and well-being.*

Her chest felt scorched. She looked around the office and noticed that, as if by some unspoken agreement, Jerrod had removed all the photos of their son. She hit the play button again. And twice more. "Looking for insurance in Hidden Oaks? I'm your local all-lines agent.

179

Contact me, Brodie Marshall—"

"What is that noise?"

She looked up. Jerrod stood at the office door with his arms crossed. She hadn't heard the door open. She laughed to herself. Her husband could tolerate his own piano playing for hours on end, yet *this* noise had disturbed him. She slammed the laptop shut and stared back at him. He shook his head and left the office. Coward, she thought.

brodie

"I DON'T KNOW what you said to that man back there," Andrea said as she fastened her seat belt. "But there was smoke blowing out his ears."

Brodie shook his head and handed Maria to her. The parking lot was loud and chaotic—swimming, diving, and baseball athletes and their families all trying to merge and squeeze their way through before the next red light. It was dinnertime, each man for himself. All civilities were gone. Karen had somehow managed to get to the front of the line. She was driving separately to pick up a car seat from one of the mom's and drop Ginger off at the house.

"Was he drunk again?" Sasha asked from the backseat.

"Why would you ask that?" he asked, glancing in the rearview mirror at his daughter's sunburnt face.

"Everybody knows he's a boozer. Last week he came to watch practice totally wonkered. Couldn't even walk straight. He called Trevor a faggot in front of everyone. Told him to grow a pair 'cause he refused to throw an inward one-and-a-half. He told him to get his ass on the board right now or forget about coming home."

"Someone needs to call CPS," Andrea said.

What parent says such a thing to his child? Brodie wondered. Humiliating him in front of his coach and peers? The world was full of idiots.

"I didn't see his son at the meet today," he said, waving to Holly's dad to go ahead of him in the long line of cars.

Sasha shrugged. "He hasn't been at school either." She unzipped her swim bag and fumbled around for something. Brodie thought about the spiked Gatorade and wondered if she would have drunk it by now if he hadn't intercepted it this morning. Would her injury this afternoon have been worse than a mere scraped leg?

She shoved her bag aside, apparently not finding what she wanted.

Brodie had suggested the Pasta Patch in the mall. One of Sasha's favorites. The food was mediocre, but it was affordable and reliable. The girls loved the all-you-can-eat salad bar and garlic breadsticks. Karen and Brodie could each enjoy a glass of house wine.

Andrea prepared a bottle for Maria while they waited in the car for Karen to pull into the parking lot. When she arrived, Brodie greeted her with a kiss.

"Did you get my message about not mailing the graduation checks?"

She wrinkled her nose and said, "Sorry. I haven't looked at my phone."

He closed his eyes and allowed himself to entertain one resentful thought: Couldn't she carve out a few minutes between her Pilates classes, her volunteer work, and Sasha's senior ball decoration committee meetings to read his texts and answer his calls? He shook his head miserably. This must be how his clients felt when he avoided their calls and emails.

"You okay?" she asked.

"Not really. We need to talk."

She took his hand and squeezed it as they approached the hostess. Brodie looked at the woman's hair, decorated with iridescent green streaks and feathers. *Did she wake up one day and decide she wanted to look like a mallard?* he wondered. Their group was seated at a booth near a large group of middle-school girls in matching softball uniforms. At the adults' table sat their coaches and families sharing three carafes of wine. Brodie smiled at their lively conversation.

Their orders were taken by a native of Nebraska (as stated on her name tag). Sasha slouched in the booth next to Andrea. They both looked exhausted, each for different reasons. Physically, they were opposites— Sasha with her copper-red hair and freckly, normally snowy skin versus Andrea with her curly black hair and mocha complexion. Yet if Brodie focused on their eyes, he saw a similarity, not in the shape or color (Sasha's blue eyes were wide-set and prominent; Andrea's brown eyes were smaller and hooded), rather in the shared look of gloom.

The waitress approached with two glasses of wine. Thank you, god! Brodie thought. He'd never understood his brother's addiction. Sure, alcoholism was a real thing that destroyed the lives of people, families, and communities. But for Brodie, alcohol was always something he could take or leave. He wasn't one of the drinkers who looked at a half-empty glass of wine left on a table and wondered how in the hell someone walked away from an unfinished drink, something Kevin once mentioned after he'd quit drinking. Tonight, however, Brodie wished he could get wasted, smashed out of his mind to numb the anxiety and stress that had plagued him all day. He knew that the likelihood of connecting with Keith tonight was nil.

The waitress delivered the salads and breadsticks. "Another glass of wine?" she asked.

"Darn, dad. Bit thirsty, were you?"

Brodie felt his face redden. Karen's glass was still nearly full.

"Just water, thanks."

"Let me hold Maria while you eat," Karen said, reaching out for her. She pressed her nose against Maria's. "You are such a sweet, beautiful baby. I could eat you all up."

Brodie felt a familiar sting of jealousy, jealousy he had felt eighteen years ago when all Karen's attention was taken from him and given to their newborn. It was pathetic, he knew, resenting a tiny creature for the love you want to be all yours, and yours only, as if there was a scant supply to go around. A few years ago, Brodie and Keith had met up for drinks and appetizers after work. They both kept glancing at a family in the adjacent booth. The wife was fawning over a baby while the husband sat ignored, playing on his phone. It struck Brodie then that he and his brother had watched this scene play out over and over throughout their high school years in foster care. Their foster parents, already grandparents by their grown biological children, usually took in babies. But when a case worker had difficulty finding a family to take in two teenage boys, she talked this older couple into taking the Marshall boys both so they could stay together. Mom and Dad, as they insisted the boys call them, were loving enough, provided them with decent meals and clothes, even chipped in for their prom tuxedos, but the boys always felt a sense of dreaded anticipation when the doorbell rang. How many times had they answered the door to find case workers holding another infant carrier?

Mom would get a call, or they'd suspect she had because overnight she'd be transformed into a maniac. Everything had to be dusted, wiped down, vacuumed, and scrubbed. Anything that posed a choking hazard—coins, batteries, matches, bottle caps—had to be picked up even though it was rare for her to set down a baby long enough for them to put any of these found treasures into their drooling mouths. Brodie spent too many of his high school years expecting to come home and be told there was no longer room for Keith and him.

The waitress appeared at the table holding, the dessert menus as Brodie pulled out his credit card. "I hope you've saved room for our signature chocolate, Kahlua mousse," she said.

Sasha popped another piece of bread into her mouth and reached for a menu. He noticed she had eaten both of the humungous meatballs, all of the spaghetti, and the steamed vegetables on her plate. She had the appetite of a beast after being in the pool. At least they didn't have to deal with eating issues, like some parents.

"Not tonight," Brodie said, holding out his VISA card. "Just the check."

"Dad, you don't have to be so rude," Sasha said as she scanned the dessert photos.

Softening his tone, he said, "Thank you, but we'll try it next time. We've got ice cream at home."

Moments later, the waitress returned. She leaned toward Brodie and whispered, "Your card was declined. I tried running it twice. Do you have a different card?"

Oh, fuckity fuck fuck! Humiliated, he sat there, his thoughts a montage of self-abuse. "Dad, give her another card."

He laughed. Here, take my whole goddamn wallet and good luck, he wanted to say. The waitress shifted from one foot to the next. How many times in a week did she have to face this awkward situation? Were the parents at the next table staring at him?

"I'll swing back around in a minute."

She walked over to the hostess stand giving Brodie time to figure out how he was going to pay for their meal. The two hostesses leaned into each other, whispering and looking his way. He felt he deserved the prize for the biggest loser in the world.

"Brodie, you okay?" Karen whispered. "Surely you've got—"

Out of the corner of his eye, he saw Andrea dig a card out of her wallet. "No way." He gently knocked her hand down before the waitress could come over to grab the card.

"Stop," she said. "This is nothing compared to all the meals that you and Karen have bought for me. Please let me."

Brodie closed his eyes. "Thank you. But I'm going to write you a check tomorrow." He turned to Karen. "Did you use the card today? I could have sworn—"

"Darn," said Andrea, sliding her card to the edge of the table and nodding at the waitress. "Your Errors and Omission insurance was set to cancel for non-pay, so I used your card to pay the premium. I meant to tell you."

"Oh my god! I love you. I love you. I love you."

He threw his arms around Andrea and rocked her back and forth.

"Dad, get a room, why don't you."

"You don't understand," he said, laughing. "I thought the policy had lapsed. I thought I was going to . . . to have . . . you see, this client's house burned down. Never mind. It's just . . . I so needed this break." Keith hadn't come through for him, but at least he still had professional liability insurance that would cover David Knight's eventual claim.

Brodie led them from the restaurant, shivering when struck by the cool evening air. Sasha was about to pass through the door he was holding open. She paused and held up her phone. He squinted at the screen. It held a picture that Karen had taken of Sasha last year at Nationals. Her eyes were crossed so that the pupils nearly disappeared into the tear ducts. Her thumbs were stuck in her ears, fingers splayed. Her entire face was scrunched up and distorted. Brodie started to ad-lib a sarcastic response, wanting to build on her levity, but he feared he'd say the wrong thing again. Instead, he whispered, "I love you. You rocked today at the pool."

"I'll take Andrea and Maria to their apartment," Karen said, "and meet you both back at the house."

"I want to go with you, mom," Sasha said.

"Fine, fine. Go with your mom. Andrea, do you need a ride in the morning?"

"I'll ask my friend."

"If you need anything," Brodie said, and he let that hang in the air for a moment, "you'll call us. Right?" He was certain she understood he was referring to Ron.

He waved goodbye and smiled to himself. If Sasha thought she was getting out of having a talk later, she was sadly mistaken. He enjoyed a peaceful drive home and sang along to the radio as if all of his troubles had magically disappeared.

jenny

JENNY SAT ON THE COLD, hard edge of the bathtub. She'd emptied all of the vials onto a towel that lay across her lap and admired the colorful mound of pills. She took a large drink of the wine she'd poured into an old jelly jar and stirred the pills with her fingers as if they were pebbles found on a beach. She thought about how every day for the past two years had begun and ended with lies. A bone-crushing accumulation of lies. Starting with Rhonda's 7 AM calls and their practiced script of "Good morning, how are you?" Lies to Beth and her colleagues. "Oh, I'd love to, but Jerrod is taking me to Napa for the weekend . . ." Lies to her gynecologist, to her primary care doctor, the therapist she'd seen a few times after the accident. "It's been hard, but we're managing. We've turned the corner. Yes, I've forgiven myself. I know it was simply an . . ."

After the early weeks of endless grief, she realized it was easier for everyone to tell people what they wanted to hear. "I'm fine. I'm so thankful that Jerrod has been there for me." Despite their skepticism, they gratefully accepted her assurances. She masked her despair with resilience and faith. "It was God's will . . . Daniel is in a peaceful place," and other bullshit like that. She spared them the discomfort of those awkward early encounters where they undoubtedly braced themselves for the onslaught of grief. She spared them the need to prepare thoughtful words that wouldn't sound like a cliché. Now, ending her life offered enormous relief. No more lies. No more pain. She could drop the facade.

Jenny turned the faucet to scalding hot. She dipped a toe in and jerked it out. After another gulp of wine, she tried again, this time tolerating the searing pain for a couple of seconds. Then another gulp. Finally, she submerged both feet into the hot water, grimacing until the pain was unbearable. She placed her steaming, red feet back on the tightly woven bathmat and panted through the pain. This should be so easy, she thought. The final leg of the journey. She looked at the pills and said aloud to herself, "You've thought about this all day. Do it. Don't chicken out now."

She stifled a cry and stared at the grout around the tub, cracked and gray like her heart. If they continued to ignore the damage, moisture would seep into the cracks, and soon, the tiles would loosen, and mold would grow, leading to more costly repairs. As the water drained, she thought about Rhonda's suggestion that the accident might have been *God's plan*. She personally refused to believe that Daniel's death had been part of some grand design. Why would God purposely orchestrate all the suffering and cruelty that man inflicted upon each other and endured? Why create beautiful flowers and music and love only to ruin it with disease and destruction and betrayal? Was the goal to teach us compassion and forgiveness? she wondered. Compassion both for ourselves and others? She'd read in one of the grief books that all parents could do was to try their best in every given moment, and know that even while doing their best, sometimes bad things happened. Neither she nor Jerrod had anticipated that Daniel would go outside to say another goodbye. Neither of them had foreseen their son being backed over by her car. If they had, they certainly would have behaved differently. But did that really change anything? The accident still happened.

She breathed deeply. Why are you doing this to yourself and those who love you? she asked herself. What will you really gain? You're not the first person in the world to lose a child. She tried to envision what it would feel like to forgive herself, to forgive Jerrod. Did she have the courage to let go of the grief and anger? Could she accept the fact that it wasn't her time yet to be with her son? He wouldn't want this for her. She felt her shoulders drop as she grabbed a handful of the pills and tossed them into the water. Plink, plink, plink, like pebbles, they fell to the bottom of the tub. She scooped up another handful but changed her mind. She would save them for an emergency.

She sucked in a breath as she stood at the piano in her bathrobe. Jerrod's defeated body slouched over the piano as he played the notes from memory. The pain was visibly etched on his face.

"It hurts so much," she said. He didn't look up. "I'm trying to move on. I don't know if I can—"

His hands stilled and came together in his lap. "Then let's try together." His beautiful green eyes met hers. "Let's just start over."

"Start over?" His casual tone infuriated her. "There's no starting over. It's not like a game of LIFE. Oh, let's clear the board and place our little pink and blue cars on this big journey of life, and this time—" She shook her head and started to walk away.

"For Christ's sake, stop."

"What's the point?" She looked at the foyer table near the front door. Abandoned on the table were the blueprints for their renovation. Jenny leaned against the piano and looked around the living room. When they first bought the house, they'd sit on the sofa, drink wine, and nibble on cheese and olives after their son had gone to bed, and sketch basic layouts for the remodel. They discussed the aesthetics of hardwood versus tile versus carpeting. The house had so much potential like their marriage once had.

"I'm willing to try counseling. Maybe even talk about having another—"

"Now you're going to gang up on me with your mother?" she yelled. "And how in the hell am I supposed to get pregnant if you won't even touch me?"

She saw the rabid look of anger and hurt on his face. He vigorously scratched his forehead, tears forming in his eyes. Telling herself that she'd done her best as a mother, forgiving herself for killing their son with her carelessness, neither of these things would change the fact that she'd crushed the man who at one time meant everything to her.

brodie

HE HAD COACHED HIMSELF on the drive home from the Pasta Patch, telling himself to be patient and calm. If they put Sasha on the defensive, she would clam up and their talk would stall without any meaningful resolution or insight into what was behind her recent behavior. He would never admit this to anyone, not even Karen, but he feared learning something distressing about his daughter—something he could not later simply choose to forget or ignore. Something that would need to be addressed now.

While he waited for Karen and Sasha to return, he opened the slider off the kitchen to let Ginger out. "Go do your business, girl." She ran three circles around the yard as if she had been cooped up for a week rather than a couple of hours. He watched her dig her nose in a few shrubs, barking at whatever, her tail wagging happily. Finally, she settled down and chose a spot to empty her bladder.

He filled the kettle and turned on the stove in case Karen wanted tea. He was hoping to redeem himself after the credit card humiliation. The water was starting to boil when his phone buzzed, a text from Keith. He looked at his watch and shook his head. It was nine o'clock and his brother was just getting back to him.

"Hey, Bro. So sorry. Can't do insurance tonight. Talk later. K"

He started to text, "No worries," but then thought, screw him. He was not going to suck it up once again. He typed, "You're some piece of work. I have been waiting on you all day, and now you don't have time. Well, fuck—" He sighed and deleted the text. "I was counting on you," he typed. He wanted to add something clever, maybe, "I'm drowning here, dude," but that sounded lame. He didn't have the energy to be pissed or creative. He deleted the text. "OK," he wrote and hit send—Adios bonus.

He skimmed the recent email in his agency inbox. One from the company read, "On a clear day in the Southwest Pacific, from your hammock you'll gaze upon the Kingdom of Tonga. Don't miss this All Expenses Paid Vacation for you and your family. FOUR hours remain." Might as well have been four days. Or four hundred.

Karen and Sasha entered the kitchen from the garage. Ginger greeted them at the door, nearly knocking them down like a bowling ball hitting a spare.

"Someone is happy you're home," Brodie teased. "I turned the kettle on for you."

Karen smiled and led Sasha into the living room; they sat next to each other on the sofa. Ginger jumped up and rested her head in Sasha's lap. This was how it was going to be: three against one, Brodie thought.

"So what's up with forging my name?" he asked, plopping down on the oversized, leather ottoman. "And the vodka?"

"I don't know," Sasha mumbled, separating the hairs in a section of Ginger's matted coat to detangle burrs and stickers from the dog's fur.

"Let's not start with this 'I don't know' crap. Were you planning on ditching school to go drinking with friends?"

Brodie watched her create a discard pile of stickers on the glass coffee table. She was more interested in grooming the dog than in participating in this conversation. Why were they even bothering?

"Brodie," Karen said, reaching over to slap his hands. "You're picking your nails again."

He rested his hands on his knees to help him avoid his nervous habit. "I'm serious. Fuck this, 'I don't know' crap." He lifted his hands to start picking again but stopped himself.

Karen turned toward him. "That's not helpful." After a beat, she looked sternly at Sasha. "Tell us what's going on."

"What do you want me to say?" she asked Karen as if she was the only concerned parent.

Despite his pep talk to himself earlier, Brodie's impatience was growing. He had had a shitty day and now this. Just as he started to launch into a speech, he caught himself. He sat back quietly and waited.

"It's like . . . like . . . this idiot in my AP Stat class was bragging that he'd gotten his parents to sign the form; they didn't even bother to read it or ask what they were consenting to. The next week, he signed himself out of school twice. I guess I wanted to feel excited about something."

"You're going to Stanford," Brodie said. "Isn't that enough excitement? Do you realize what you've risked today? There is no way I can give you that kind of education. You lose your Stanford scholarship and it's hello community college."

Sasha shrugged.

"What does that mean?" He closed his eyes in fury.

"I don't know. I don't know if I want to go to Stanford." She leaned against her mom and said, "I don't even know if I want to keep diving."

Brodie looked at Karen and Sasha. "That's what this is about?"

She pulled her shoulders up as if bracing for an attack. Karen stroked Sasha's arm while they waited for an answer.

"Everyone keeps saying how lucky I am to get a full ride. That I better not waste the spot the team's given me and not someone else."

"Idiots," Karen said. "Sasha, you earned that scholarship. But you always have the right to say thanks, but no thanks. Sure, I think you would be giving up a huge opportunity and you'd probably regret it. But you get the final say in deciding what—"

"Hang on a minute," Brodie said, waving his hand in front of Karen to stop her. "I'm not going to sit here and pretend I don't give a rat's ass if you go to Stanford or the University of Timbuktu. Or tell you that your mom and I just want you to be happy. That's bullshit. You cannot pass up this opportunity. I can't buy you a better education."

"It's always about the money," Sasha spat. "What if something happens and I can't dive anymore? How will I finish at Stanford?"

"Let's cross that bridge if, and when, we come to it," he said. He dropped his head. When he looked up, Sasha's shoulders were slumped. She had that distant, unreachable look in her blue eyes. "For now, let's figure out how to improve communications around here. Starting with you telling us what you were doing with the vodka-flavored Gatorade?"

"I wasn't planning on drinking it before the meet."

"What a relief," he said, with the sarcastic inflection his foster mom had been so fond of using in reaction to one of Keith's transparent lies. "When were you going to drink it?"

"I don't know."

"Damn it, Sasha," Karen said, surprising Brodie. "Answer the question. Quit this 'I don't know' routine."

Score one for dad's team, he thought, pleased to have Karen, for once, stand by him.

Sasha's eyes filled with tears. She whined, "Can we please, please talk about this tomorrow? I'm so tired. All I want to do is go to bed. Please."

She buried her face in Karen's chest. Ginger whined and jumped off the sofa. It appeared the dog was just as frustrated with this conversation as Brodie was.

Brodie looked at Sasha, clinging to her mom as if she were at risk of drowning. When had she become this unhappy, clingy child? Was she gaming them for sympathy? A part of him suspected they had put a shit-load of pressure on their daughter, and that she was indeed exhausted—physically and mentally. Part of him, ever cynical, figured Sasha was trying to manipulate them to get out of this talk. He started to tell her to knock off the drama when he realized she had not seemed truly happy since last summer after attending a dive camp with the Stanford coaches. She had come home so energetic, so happy, so confident. She was bouncing in the car, full of pride after they picked her up from camp, telling them how she had pushed past her comfort zone to learn new dives. Her competitive club and high school coaches were thrilled. She had dived with some of the Stanford athletes as well as kids recruited by Berkeley and UCLA. She had asked them if they would drive her to Santa Clara and Stanford on weekends for platform clinics.

In a gentle tone, Brodie asked, "How long have you been drinking and to what extent?"

"I'm not an alcoholic or something."

"Well, that's good to hear," he said. She obviously didn't give a rat's ass that he cared about her safety. He had had about all the shit he could handle in one day. His heart was pumping fast. He looked at his daughter and wife, and suddenly he felt ashamed. So that was how it was going to be, Brodie? he asked himself. You hit a bump and take a detour? Ignore the possibility that the bump is there for a purpose, to make you slow down and see what's happening right in front of you?

Sasha had seemed genuinely happy after the dive camp. And just like that, it was gone. For weeks after camp, they had made the hour-long trek to those dive clinics until he decided she was long overdue for getting her learner's permit. She needed to learn to drive. Yet she kept finding excuses not to practice or apply for her permit. It came to a head the night her friends invited her downtown for frozen yogurt. They were going to hang out in front of the cinema to do some "peep watching." She had stood at their bedside. Karen was reading. Brodie was watching some stupid sitcom. He couldn't even recall which one, but probably one he'd seen during the regular season.

She had stood in his view, snapping her fingers with a silly grin, saying, "Some funds, daddy-o and a ride." If he had not had such a shitty day, been so frustrated by yet another ridiculous underwriting decision or some irritating client, he would have laughed at her Ginger Rogers' tap dance steps. But there she was, blocking his view, her long red hair wild and tangled from diving all afternoon, her pale skin a cancer-causing red from refusing, once again, to heed their advice to use sunblock.

"Get your license," he had snapped. That was all it took. Her feet quieted. The dance stopped, the smile slid away, and her arms fell to her side.

"Yeah, whatever," she said, moving aside to allow him full view of the television screen. "Don't trouble yourself. I can ride my bike."

Karen had sighed. He could not look at her because he had felt so ashamed. A sitcom. How many teenage girls didn't mind being seen with their dad?

"Wait a sec," Karen said, giving him a hard look. "I'll drive you."

"I got this one, Mom," she had said. "No worries."

She walked out. He turned off the television and looked at Karen. She stared at him in disappointment. They both flinched as Sasha slammed her bedroom door.

"Don't bother. I'm a jerk."

Sasha did not meet up with her friends that night. That was the last time he could recall that she had mentioned hanging out with friends. After that, she quit attending the Stanford practices. He was such a selfish prick, he thought.

"Sasha, I want to help," he said. "You can't keep refusing to talk to us."

"Why not?" Her chin shook.

"Because if you don't talk to us, we'll have to take you to someone who can help us figure out what's wrong," he said. "Would you prefer that?" Her head moved violently back and forth. "Okay, then. What is going on? Why suddenly all these destructive behavior, the note from school, the booze?"

"Sasha," Karen said, "You've got to trust us. We give you our word that we won't punish you for telling us the truth."

Let's not make promises here, Brodie wanted to say. Karen looked at him as if she had read his mind.

"Focus, Brodie. And QUIT PICKING YOUR NAILS, GOD DAMN IT!"

Sasha giggled at Karen's unexpected outburst so hard that she farted. Her eyes opened wide. They all began laughing. Sasha's laughter grew hysterical, almost manic until she was overcome with hiccups. Each time a hiccup escaped her mouth, carrying with the stench of tomatoes, garlic, and meatballs, Karen and Brodie flinched and ducked.

"Are you doing any drugs?" he asked when her hiccups subsided.

"No, Dad," she said, emphatically. "However, if I were so inclined, which I am not, I want you to know that Hidden Oaks is Pharmacopeia, USA. You can get blow from some kid bagging groceries at Safeway or your best friend's older brother. Half the parents in this neighborhood are so oblivious they don't even know they're supplying their children and their children's friends with pills. And if you're really desperate, then Craigslist. You can find anything there. Even meth."

"You're exaggerating," Karen said.

"What do you think kids bring to parties? A veggie tray?"

Karen frowned. "Have you done—"

"No. I'm not stupid. That's why I quit hanging around with those idiots."

Brodie breathed in deeply and thanked God, or the universe, for giving him such a smart child. He took the spot on the sofa vacated by Ginger and sandwiched Sasha's hand between his. "Please don't take chances that could permanently obliterate your future."

"That's redundant," Sasha said. "Obliterate is usually permanent."

"Yeah, well, I didn't get a near-perfect score on my SAT." He tugged playfully on her ear, making her smile. She stuck out her tongue and crossed her eyes.

"I think someone is ready for bed," he said, smiling. "I know I'm done for the night."

Sasha untangled herself from Karen. She stood with her head dipped, stepped around his knees, then suddenly turned and threw her arms around his shoulders with such force he nearly toppled over. He fought back tears. There was an intensity to her hug that reminded him of her first day of kindergarten when she refused to let him go; refused to follow the teacher into the classroom; refused to stop crying. It took three attempts—three mornings of making sure every moment leading up to their arrival at school was executed without a hint of conflict—to get her to take the teacher's hand to be led away from him to the morning circle. Now she clung to him with this same fierce desperation, as if once she let go, he would disappear. Or, perhaps, she would.

jenny

JENNY KNELT in her son's closet over a basket of dirty clothes and held one article at a time to her nose. His T-shirts, his shorts, his little Superman briefs, his mismatched socks, she inhaled deeply. The scent of her son was gone. She picked up his beloved stuffed bear and hugged the furry animal greedily, hoping for a magical squeeze in return.

One of her son's favorite books was a story about a lonely, spoiled English teddy bear who bullied his friends and family whenever he didn't get his way. Every day the young bear would return from school angry and hurt after being excluded from games and activities. None of the bears wanted to play with him. No one would share their pot of honey with him because he hoarded his own. Once home, he would pound his paws on the kitchen table and demand his tea.

"I want my crumpets and jam!" Jenny mumbled the remembered line from the book.

One day, the bear came home to find his mother sitting quietly at the kitchen table. He sniffed the air. Was there nothing baking? There was no mouth-watering scent of cinnamon and honey coming from the oven. Where were his crumpets? He turned to his mom, ready to start demanding his snacks when suddenly she pounded her paws on the table.

"I want my crumpets and jam," the mother bear said in a childish voice, over and over, imitating him. No one liked to be teased. He became angry and pouted. But as he watched his mother pretend to be him, he saw how silly he must have looked to her and his friends. When she finally stopped banging on the table and demanding treats, they both began laughing.

Jenny had read the book dozens of times while her son squealed and kicked his feet in delight. He loved it when she adopted a thick English accent. He would hug his bear and ask if he wished really hard, might the bear become real? His large brown eyes filled with such hope and innocence. She held the bear's arms now and danced him around. "I want my crumpets and jam," she sang. "I want my crumpets and jam. I want my crumpets and jam, oh yes!"

"Having fun?" Jerrod stood at the bedroom door. His work shirt and slacks were wrinkled as if he had slept in them for days now. He nervously picked at the chipped paint on the door frame. Once upon a time, they had argued over hiring a handyman to repair the chipped paint. Jerrod wanted to wait. They would renovate the whole house at once when the plans and permits had been approved. He refused to entertain the notion that it was lead-based, and thereby, if ingested, potentially brain-damaging.

"You worry too much," he had said when she argued for repainting now versus later.

"You don't worry enough," she'd said, releasing some pent-up resentment she hadn't realized she harbored. "Not about anything other than your job and your piano."

Now feeling foolish at being caught dancing a stuffed animal around in her son's closet, Jenny tossed the bear in with the dirty clothes. She stood and stared at her husband.

"Let's do something," Jerrod said. "Go somewhere. Whatever, wherever you want. You bought pancake mix. How about we make pancakes? I'm going nuts. Every time I enter a room, I'm so scared I'll find you—" His chin started to tremble. He pounded his fist on the chipping door frame. "Then I'll have no one," he said, tears welling in his eyes. "Just my fucking piano and mom."

Witnessing her husband cry was rare and painful. She wanted to throw her arms around him and comfort him. But what if he rejected her again? She stared at the carpet and thought about the first time he had broken down in front of her. He had failed the bar exam and lost the job awaiting him. He claimed he was a failure. He refuted Jenny's assurances that he wasn't the first intelligent person to fail the exam and that there was no shame in trying again.

The second time was at the funeral home. He had pulled out his wallet to pay for the coffin and found that he couldn't pry the credit card out from among the others. He stood there fumbling, his hands suddenly ineffective and incapable of doing something so simple. The funeral director sat rigid and quiet. Jenny watched the man and waited for a reaction. What a shitty job he faced, day in and day out. "Sadly, I've seen it all," she imaged him telling a friend at a cocktail party. Jerrod gave up, dropped his wallet on the table, and collapsed into his chair and into loud, convulsive sobs.

Now, as he stood before her crying, she wanted to offer him some hope, but she had nothing to give him or anyone. Nothing to offer that would save either of them. He sighed and turned to leave their son's room.

"I just want so badly to be with Daniel," she said. "To hold him again. Smell him. I can't imagine living the rest of my life without him."

"How do you think I feel?"

"I don't know! Of course, I know you miss him. But what else? I'm sure you hate me. Blame me."

"I don't blame you."

"Maybe not blame exactly, but I caused the accident. If I hadn't—"

"I was supposed to watch him. I fucking dropped the ball. If I hadn't been—"

"No." She shook her head firmly and moved to sit on the edge of her son's bed. "We were good parents."

"Yes . . . we were good parents . . . we're human. It was just a horrible accident. I have told myself those words a million times. They don't provide much reassurance." He walked over and sat next to her. "I was so angry after the accident. At you. At the world."

Jenny stiffened. Here it was. She knew he had blamed her.

"I was angry that you didn't look behind the car . . . that you didn't drag me away from the piano before you left."

He laughed and Jenny was shocked that he thought this was funny.

"And then I realized," he said, "that it wasn't your fault. You would have never intentionally hurt our son. I was the parent in charge at that moment. All the anger I felt toward you, I shifted to myself. What kind of bastard would believe for even one moment that you were to blame?"

She pulled him into an embrace, and thankfully, he did not shrug her off. She had missed the comfort and security of his arms.

"I think we owe it to him to try to move on," she finally said. "We owe it to ourselves. I love you. I don't want to lose you too."

"I feel like I've lost you already." He cleared his throat and wiped his eyes.

"I'm here. I'm not going anywhere."

"What now? Pancakes and bacon?"

"Well," she said, "that's a start." She smiled and kissed him on his nose. "I'll be right there."

He took her hands and held them in his own. "I love you so much. I really do."

When he left the room, she opened their son's closet and looked at the toys, board games, clean and dirty clothes, and costumes. So much *stuff* for one child. He had worn his Power Ranger, Batman, and Superman costumes until the frayed pant legs practically reached his knees and the backs no longer closed properly. She pulled a pair of cowboy boots from the top shelf. He had been over the moon when they came in the mail from Rhonda. For months, he wore them day and night. Refused to wear anything else or trade them for a new pair even when they started to stink worse than sour milk. She hugged the boots and whispered, "Mommy loves you so much. I miss you every day. Please forgive me for everything."

brodie

WHEN HE ENTERED their bedroom, Karen was wearing one of his old T-shirts and the frayed hem was hiked up so that he caught a glimpse of her lacy white underwear. He felt an optimistic stirring below. Setting the glass down on the nightstand, he stripped down to his briefs and fell into bed. Karen's mug of tea, balanced in her lap, nearly toppled. She dipped her fingers into the mug, then flicked drops at his face.

"Better put that mug down because you're about to get the tickle torture treatment," he said. She took a gulp, squeezed her eyes shut.

"Ready?"

She kicked her Pilates-firmed legs as he straddled her and started dancing his fingertips over her belly, working his way up to her armpits. She squirmed and squealed. Both laughed until they could barely breathe.

"Shush. Sasha is going to wonder what we're doing in here."

He let her rest but squeezed her boney hips between his knees and pinned her wrists to the pillow. He licked her forehead, eyelids, ears as if he were an over-affectionate puppy while she tried to buck him off.

"Easy on the family jewels, Bronco Betty."

The metal bed frame squeaked with each kick, and he imagined the screws unwinding themselves, falling loose and taking the frame, box spring, mattress, and them down with them.

"Stop," she cried. "I give. I give."

Collapsing beside her, he blew a wet kiss on her neck, and in return, got a sharp bite to his shoulder.

"Ow, you wicked woman." They rolled around, and he trapped her in a wrestler's hold. "Can I trust you to behave if I let you go?" She nodded, her bangs falling over her eyes. "You sure? There will be dire consequences . . ."

He felt her body relax and trusted she had had enough for the night.

They settled into their usual spots on the bed and rolled onto their sides to face each other. She walked her fingers across the mattress between their bodies to tousle the graying, thinning hair on his chest.

"So how was your day?" She sniggered at the absurdity of her question.

"On a scale of one to ten . . . a two. At best. You?"

"Nine point five."

"Not bad. I'm envious." He felt the smile leave his face.

"No luck with Keith?"

"I was counting on the bonus."

He traced her hips with his hand. She shivered.

"Without it, money will be extremely tight these next few months. Maybe longer if business doesn't pick up. I don't want to end up in foreclosure like the Franks and the Burnetts and so many of the families we know."

She weaved her fingers with his and said, "We've got the home equity loan."

"Tapped out."

"When? How did that happen?"

He felt her body tense.

"Let's not go into it tonight. Please."

"I think you need to clue me in on what's happening." She rolled onto her back. The bed screws whined. "You couldn't even pay for dinner tonight. There's something going on, and it sounds like money is more than just a *little* tight."

"Well, I did say *extremely* tight, not a little."

He stared at their wedding photo. It sat above the bureau across their twice-remodeled bedroom. The first time they blew out the back wall and added a master closet. The second time they added French doors and a private cobble-stone patio. He looked at the young couple posed in front of a three-tier red velvet cake. He was certain his most pressing concern nineteen years ago wasn't whether or not they'd find themselves in midlife facing the possibility of financial failure. He rolled over to his back to avoid the disappointment in Karen's eyes. Their home, larger than they had ever needed, was still one of the smallest on the street. He had always figured, until this real estate implosion, it was a safe investment. A secure place to park their money for later, though now with the first and second mortgages, they were, as they say, underwater without a paddle or life jacket. How could he complain when he had used their house like an ATM? And yes, he had vetoed Karen's many offers to bring in a second income. He always wanted her home for Sasha and, he supposed, he took pride in that she hadn't been forced to work. She could take her Pilates classes, volunteer at the school, meet her girlfriends for coffee. Unlike Keith and Emma, who both worked like fiends and put the children in daycare five days a week, his goal had always been a balanced life for his wife and daughter.

"I got another letter from my stalker," he said, wanting to shift her attention from their troubles. Karen sat up against the headboard and picked up her mug.

"I thought she quit writing you."

"Yeah, well, I received one or two recently. I sort of had forgotten about them, but this one is different."

He didn't know why he hadn't mentioned the last few letters. He supposed it was nice having something that was all his own. Something that just fell in his lap and did not require anything of him.

"Be right back," he said, throwing on a robe.

Sasha's light was still on. He tapped on her door and entered. She was sitting in her favorite Hello Kitty pajamas, crossed-legged, in the middle of her bed.

"Are you studying?" he asked. She looked at the stack of unopened books and iPad on her nightstand and rolled her eyes. Duh, dad.

"You still have that pillow," he said, pointing to a square pillow embroidered with the word "LOVE" on the front.

"Yep. Home Ec. Seventh grade. Mom thought it would be a useful class. So if Stanford is a bust, I can always make pillows."

There was a resonance of defeat in her half-hearted attempt at humor. He kissed her forehead and wished he could encircle her in the safety of a bubble so that all harm simply bounced off her shell. But then, wasn't it the kids who were never allowed to roll around in the mud or play with the shared toys at daycare that had such fragile immune systems? Had no defense against outside forces?

"Alright then, lights out at eleven."

"Right, dad. I'm not two."

He paused at their bedroom door, praying Karen would not bring up their finances again. She was sitting in bed with a hardback novel propped up on her knees—the latest New York Times bestseller. She grabbed a subscription card that had fallen out of one of the many magazines stacked next to her nightstand and marked the page, which, not so surprisingly, was now closer to the back cover than the front even though it had only just arrived from Amazon.

They slid under the cool sheets. Karen nuzzled close as he unfolded the stalker's letter. "Your feet are freezing," he said. She rubbed them together.

"Better?"

He nodded and started at the beginning.

Hi Brodie,

It's me again. I'm sure by now you recognize the handwriting. I hope, even as I write this, that you throw out my letters without reading them. And yet, a part of me hopes you do read them.

I had a son. I've mentioned him briefly in a few of my letters. His name was Daniel. He died two years ago, ironically the same day I found your wallet.

Karen shivered and looked up at the ceiling fan. It felt as if the temperature in their bedroom had dropped ten degrees. He picked up the remote control and turned off the fan then continued reading.

We were gone about an hour.

When he got to the part about the camping trip, she sighed loudly.

"Morons."

Brodie squeezed her knee.

By then the munchies had set in and the guys decided to raid the food we'd bear-bagged after dinner. One minute life is great, you're laughing at the spectacle of your stoned husband and his friends trying to lift one another up to the bag without throwing a back out and the next minute you've unzipped your tent to find it empty. I turned over all the sleeping bags and pillows, again and again. Nothing. He was gone. That's when I knew we'd failed him.

"Duh, lady," said Karen. "Stupid idiot."

My husband found him just before dawn hanging by his binocular strap from a limb of a fallen tree. I remember the tree well because my son had always feared it. He would say, "Mommy, run fast or the tree will get us."

Karen crossed her arms tightly over her chest and shut her eyes.

"I'm not sure if I want to hear anymore."

"Shall I stop?"

She grabbed his hands so he'd stop picking his thumbnail. He folded the letter. She swallowed.

"Might as well finish it," she said, pulling the covers to her chin.

We'd all fanned out in search for him. Then my husband screamed. I'll never forget that scream. When I came around the bend, he was leaning over our son. At first, I thought maybe it was just a badly broken leg, at worst a bone poking through the skin. My husband is a guy who can have a tooth drilled without pain medication, yet he was now clearly freaked out. He yelled for me to get back. I came closer and saw the strap of the binoculars twisted around our son's neck. He just fell over Daniel and cried.

Daniel had begged us to buy those damn binoculars for his birthday. He wore them night and day. I know I removed them when I kissed him goodnight. He must have put them back on before leaving the tent. The sheriff figured he'd slipped down the embankment and the strap caught on a branch.

People often say they have no idea how they'd survive the loss of a child. I'd say your darkest imaginings can't compare to the ugly, and I mean UGLY truth of it, especially if it's your fault.

My husband and I pretend not to notice each other. These last couple of weeks, as our son's birthday approaches, he sits at his piano for hours playing Mozart's 20th Concerto and Prokofiev's Piano Sonata No. 7. The same dark songs, over and over and over, until I want to scream. I can't do this anymore. I want to find a bat and bash in my husband's skull, as if that would help somehow.

"Good god, lady."

He's going to Dallas for a deposition, so I'm going to take advantage of having the house to myself. I've done some research on the internet. Hanging would be quick. It would provide some symmetry, a sense of justice. I want to feel what my son must have felt when his breathing was cut off. I want to know the panicked attempt at tugging and pulling on a cord to no avail.

"Shit . . ." Brodie and Karen said in unison.

Yet, I know I'm too much of a coward to tie a rope around my neck. Pills it will be. They are handy and, I'm hoping, painless.

Christ, Brodie thought. Had this woman been waiting all day for him to read this letter, hoping that somehow he would save her?

It's cruel to leave behind my body for my husband to deal with. But I have a suspicion that he'll be relieved not to feel me lying next to him in bed, not to feel the bed shift every time I adjust to a position more likely to induce sleep. He won't have to listen to my sobs when I wake up after dreaming about our son.

It's strange. Now that I've made the decision, I feel at peace. I'm not a religious person, but I hope, I truly, truly hope that there is something else, that I'll be reunited with my son. Then we'll just wait for my husband to join us.

I wish you well. If you have read to this point, please know that having someone to write to these past two years has largely been what's gotten me through the day.

Regards. J.M.

Karen slapped Brodie's shoulder, and he nearly fell off the bed.

"Jesus, woman."

"Wait a minute. The piano playing. Don't you recall Keith mentioning something about his neighbor who plays the piano nonstop? Same neighbors, I'm almost sure, who had lost a child. It's got to be them."

None of it sounded familiar to Brodie. But then again, his memory had been shit this past couple of years. Stress, according to articles he had read.

"What should we do?"

Karen raised her eyebrows. "Call 9-1-1?"

"And say what? It could be just a cry for attention."

"Seriously?" She rolled her eyes. "I think we should go over there. Talk her off the ledge, so to speak."

A reel of possible scenarios, all unpleasant, ran through his mind.

"What if it's the wrong house? The wrong family?" He folded the letter and set it on the nightstand. "Besides, it's really none of our business."

"Excuse me? That's it? It's none of our business?" Karen grabbed the letter and climbed out of bed. "I'll drive."

"Wait, aren't we still discussing this?"

"Discussion over. Come on."

She threw on jeans and a hoodie. Brodie slipped on his slacks, and to stall, he pretended to consider his options of sweaters. If this suicide prevention mission turned into a miscalculation in either their timing or the woman's intent, there was a strong probability they would find themselves facing a disturbing, or at a minimum, awkward situation.

"Good lord, Brodie. Throw on a shirt and let's go."

She knocked on Sasha's door.

"Hey, sweetie. We're going to Safeway. Are you okay being home alone?"

"Mom, I'm not five years old. I think I can manage."

"We'll be home soon," Brodie added. He hoped so, anyway.

brodie

"SLOW DOWN!"

Brodie grabbed the door handle as Karen drove through a stop sign, barely glancing left or right. The last time he saw her this focused behind the wheel was the time Sasha called while they were having dinner at the Yacht Club to say that Lucy, their now-deceased German Shepherd, a predecessor to Ginger, had gotten into a scuffle with a skunk and was curled up on their bed, whining.

They were doing fifty-five down Mt. Diablo Boulevard, facing a hefty ticket and a spike in their insurance rates if they had the misfortune of encountering a police officer. Pier One Imports, Divorce for Men Only, and the Tile Shop all zipped past his window. It was Friday night, and up ahead, people were coming from and going to restaurants, coffee shops, and the Cineplex.

"Downtown looks busy, you might . . ." he said, clutching the door handle.

She yanked on the steering wheel and pulled a hard right. The wheels screeched over his voice.

"Want to kill us both? This woman might be a total nutcase for all we know. Maybe she just wants attention or to mess with me."

"Unlikely," Karen said, her hands gripping the steering wheel at two and ten.

He looked at the clock, ten forty-five, and wondered how they would announce themselves. "Excuse me, but we're worried that you may have strangled yourself or overdosed."

"What are you going to say?" he asked. Karen shrugged and laid on the horn when the Mini Cooper ahead failed to blast through the intersection the second the light changed to green.

"Come on, asshole, drive already," she said, riding his bumper. Brodie prayed the driver wouldn't stomp on his brakes to tell them to get off his tail.

"When, and if, Sasha ever decides to start driving," he said, his eyes glued to the road, "your services as her instructor will not be required." Although he said it lightheartedly, he was serious. When she didn't laugh or react, he tried another tactic.

"Hey, the woman is either dead, or she isn't. You're starting to scare me." He snapped his fingers to make her look over. She finally glanced at him. "A few minutes, at this point, won't likely make a difference. If she slipped the letter in my mailbox this morning and meant to follow through with her plan, we are probably hours too late. Let's just get there safely."

When they arrived at Keith's street, Brodie saw his brother's Subaru parked in the driveway with his custom plates, "DOTCOM2G." The bastard was home, watching the Giant's game, no doubt, not giving a thought to the fact he had left Brodie in the lurch. He noticed that despite the rollercoaster drive over, the stabbing pain in his back was gone—the only upside to this God-forsaken day.

"What do you think?" asked Karen. "The neighbor to the left or the right of Keith and Emma?"

Two homes bookended Keith's, both sharing similar bones: 1950s L-shape ranchers with street-facing garages, large front porches, wide eaves, and stucco siding. The house on the right was painted a spearmint green while the house on the left a trendy taupe. Both had low-pitched, asphalt shingle roofs that needed replacing. The major difference between the two was the nearly completed addition over the garage of the taupe house.

He pointed to the addition. "Unlikely they've remodeled recently. I'm betting on that one."

"You're right," Karen whispered as if someone might hear them. They looked at the house on the right. Partially visible from the front bay window, through the slightly drawn curtains, was a dark shape that they would soon confirm was a grand piano. They rolled down their windows and listened for the angry music described by his stalker. He heard the rumble of an unseen Harley-Davidson or some other badass bike tearing down a nearby street, and the loud, monotonous chorus of crickets, yet no frightening sounds coming from a tortured piano.

"I don't hear anything. We should go home and chalk this up to a bad idea."

"No way." Karen turned off the engine. She checked her hair in the mirror.

"Really? Is my hair okay? Maybe you have time to give me a trim?"
She punched him in the shoulder.

"Stop punching me. What's the deal with everyone today?"

"On the count of three," she said. "For better or worse, here we go."

From the porch, they could hear music. It was not the morose music he expected to find. This was beautiful and ethereal. He found himself holding his breath and waiting for the notes.

"Ring the bell," she said. He looked at her as if to say, "Okay Sarge." They waited. Nothing.

"Ring it again," Karen said.

A car drove past, and Karen grabbed his arm. The headlights faded into the darkness. Brodie could make out the hum of a BART train rolling through Hidden Oaks toward Pleasant Hill. He pressed the doorbell again. They waited on the porch and watched two moths flit around the one working light bulbs in the sconce.

"Stay here," she said. "I'll tap on the window to get his attention."

"Maybe we should just call the police."

"And say what?" She slapped away a moth. "I'll be right back."

"No, I'll do it."

He climbed through the shrubs, overgrown with weeds. He wished he had taken a piss before leaving the house. He wondered if his shadow was visible through the curtains. If so, he was certain to scare the bejesus out of the guy. He rapped his knuckles on the windowpane. Come on. Nothing. Shit. He knocked louder to the count of eight. How could the guy not hear him knocking when Keith was likely calling the police right now to report a stranger creeping around the neighbor's bushes and banging on their windows?

He climbed back through the weeds to figure out an alternate plan with Karen.

"Let's see if it's unlocked," she suggested.

He shook his head and knocked again. The delicate notes continued unabated.

He tried the knob and found it unlocked. Excessive speeding, trespassing, entering without permission—not bad for a Friday night in the suburbs.

"Hello," he called out as he slowly pushed open the door. "May we come in?"

"Stop!" A woman's voice.

Brodie froze. Karen squeezed his arm and stayed close.

"You're going to make me . . ." The same voice was coming from a room toward the back of the house.

He started to move but stopped as Karen stepped on the heels of his sneakers and he nearly tripped. There was no one sitting at the piano. The music was coming from somewhere else in the house.

"I've got you right where—" said a man.

"No!" cried the woman, followed by provoking laughter. Images, none of them benign, came to Brodie's mind.

"What do we do?" Karen whispered.

Other than the piano, a cardboard fort in the corner of the adjacent room, and a set of architecture drawings left on the foyer table, the house was sparse but tidy. They were here to investigate and prevent a possible suicide, so he expected unopened mail strewn about the entryway, cobwebs and gagging odors, but the house looked as if it was standing ready for inspection, mouth wide open, saying, "Look, I've even flossed those hard to reach areas."

Karen gripped his elbow and urged him forward, her nails digging into his arm. They walked toward the music and voices, and strangely, the aroma of bacon. They crept past a wall of photos—a gallery of a normal, happy family that might have hosted the annual gingerbread decorating party for the neighborhood. A large, black and white picture of a blond boy in swim trunks hung on the wall. He was dripping wet with cartoonish dolphin goggles pressed to his face.

A loud clap of metal sounded. A shattering sound of glass. Brodie flinched. There was a shriek. They rushed into the kitchen to find his stalker—the woman from this morning—perched on the kitchen counter and fighting off a spatula-armed man. Was she being robbed or assaulted? He noticed a glass of champagne sitting on the counter, another in shards on the floor. Next to a crackling cast-iron skillet filled with smoking bacon was a plate of ready pancakes.

This did not appear to be a home invasion.

"What the fuck?" the man asked, stepping protectively in front of the woman. He pulled out a butcher knife from the chopping block, grabbed the purse that sat on the counter, and threw it at Brodie. "Take it. Take what you want and get the hell out of our house."

Our house. If he was her husband, Brodie wondered, was the entire letter a lie? Wasn't the husband at a deposition in Dallas or Houston? Brodie could feel Karen's nail biting into his arm as he stood frozen. The man stepped toward them. His wife's eyes were wild and fearful.

"Stop, Jerrod." Jenny slid off the counter. "I know these people. I . . . I can explain."

Brodie started to fish the envelope from his pocket, when the stalker's husband stepped closer, brandishing the knife. Karen held firmly to the sleeve of Brodie's sweater.

"Hang on. It's just a letter . . . a letter we believe is from your wife. One of many letters I've received from her."

"What is he talking about?" the man asked his wife. She didn't answer. Instead, she stood there hugging herself and looking at the broken glass.

Brodie held out the letter. The man read the first page and turned to his wife.

"What's wrong with you? Why would you do this?" He tossed the knife into the sink and flung the letter onto the counter. He stepped around the broken glass and yanked the cord out of the outlet to shut off the CD player. The house became still and quiet.

"I'm so sorry," she said, reaching out to stop her husband from leaving the kitchen. He shrugged her away. "I didn't mean to hurt you again," she mumbled, her arms falling to her sides.

Brodie could not figure out how her day had gone from planning her suicide to a late-night champagne/pancake romp, but truly, this was one screwed up couple. A door slammed and they all jumped. The bacon on the stove was burning, a caustic smoke rising from the pan.

"Look, we're going to go and let you and your husband sort this out," Karen said. "But the letters have to stop. I am really, really sorry about your son's accident, but please don't contact my husband again or come near our family. It's obvious you need some help."

The woman nodded. Karen tugged on Brodie's sweater and led him out of the kitchen. He turned and said, "Good luck. I am sorry about your son. You might want to turn off the stove to avoid a fire."

jenny

JENNY EMPTIED the remaining champagne into a coffee mug and took a long swallow. Steeling herself, she picked up the letter, stepped around the broken glass, and went to find Jerrod. She opened their bedroom door. He was sitting on their bed with an open suitcase. So far he'd only packed a few briefs and socks.

"Jerrod," she said meekly. He did not turn toward her. He simply stared straight ahead at the maple bureau as if he were in a trance. She sat on the edge of the bed and set the letter down between them. "Please let me explain."

"What in the hell is wrong with you? Who were those people?"

She squeezed her eyes shut and saw herself running from the house. Climbing into the Honda—Jerrod would not likely try to stop her—and driving to the highest point of the Richmond Bridge. At this time of night, with little traffic on the bridge, she would have enough time to stop the car and jump over the rail before anyone tried to intervene. From that height, the desired result was all but guaranteed. It would be so much easier, so much less painful than having to admit to her husband what she had done. To tell him how crazy she really was.

She imagined him answering the door. Inviting the police into the house. Offering them some water or coffee. The humiliation. The hurt. The confusion. If she had not already done so, she would finally destroy him. If there was indeed a hell, the jump and aftermath would certainly buy her a one-way ticket there.

"I'm listening," he said, slipping off his shoes. He threw one across the room. "For Pete's sake, Jenny. Why?"

She gasped as the shoe hit the wall, leaving behind a dent that would be a reminder of this night for years to come. He looked at the letter she held in her hand. She saw herself taking the jump . . . feeling the freedom and the cool, damp, salty air engulf her body . . . hitting the water—hard and cold like cement.

"After Daniel's death, I couldn't talk to you. I could not talk to anyone. I was going crazy. I woke up every day either numb or so angry I wanted to rip off my skin. Or die. Or hurt someone. Even you. And then . . . and then I saw the wallet in my car, the man's wallet I'd found at the foot of the driveway."

Jerrod looked at his hands. She wished so badly that he would put his arms around her and assure her they'd find a way through this. But hadn't she just told him that she wanted to hurt him? He was probably thinking more about having her hauled off to the looney bin than gathering some words of comfort. She described the first anonymous letter.

"Every so often, when I was feeling down, I'd write another letter. He didn't know who I was so I could say, or write, anything." She decided to skip the parts about her parking in front of Brodie's house and stalking him online.

"Then Rhonda came up with the idea for the cruise. I panicked. How are we going to show up for breakfast, lunch, and dinner pretending to be this happy, normal couple? Your mother, I love her, but it's like she can't leave well-enough alone. I'm so scared of what she'll pry out of me."

Jerrod took her hand and rubbed his thumb against her palm. His eyes glistened. "Keep going. I want to hear it all."

"So I decided that your trip to Dallas presented me the opportunity to . . . to check out. I wrote Brodie . . . that's his name . . . a letter telling him about Daniel. I don't know why, but I lied about how he died. I think it was easier than admit I had backed the car over our son. And crushed him."

Jerrod's body trembled as he squeezed her hand. An image appeared in Jenny's mind. She and Jerrod were carrying a newborn to introduce to his big brother. Sitting at Daniel's graveside, telling him how much they missed him, and assuring him that his sister would know what a wonderful boy he had been.

"I want another baby," Jenny said. "I didn't think I could do it again, but I can. We can. Rhonda thinks we can," she said, suppressing a burst of giggles.

"Mom would be over the moon." Jerrod wiped his eyes. "I do like your hair short. I didn't think I would, but it flatters you." He ran his fingers along the base of her neck and said, "Let's just get back to *us* before we take the next step. Agree?"

brodie

THEY STEPPED OUT onto the porch. Karen looked at Brodie. "That was awkward," she said, giggling nervously.

"You think so." He tousled her hair and held her hand as they walked quickly to the car. "We're lucky the guy didn't call the police."

"Or stab us."

"Brodie," Keith called from his front door. "I thought that was your car."

He was holding a beer. Was he drinking again? Is that why he didn't have time today? Keith met them halfway across the lawn.

"I didn't know you knew my neighbors."

Brodie glared at the bottle his brother was holding, but Keith did not seem to notice as he hugged Karen.

"You're shaking, sweetie, come inside."

Emma met them in the foyer, boasting her year-round spa tan and a thread-bare Walk for the Cure T-shirt with her employer, Bristol-Myers Squibb, and their slogan, "Together We Can Prevail."

Yeah, let us all prevail, Brodie thought. He pointed at Keith's beer.

"Drinking again?"

"Not what you think, Bro." He turned the bottle so that Brodie could read the label. It was one of those non-alcoholic beers.

"Sorry. Jumped to the wrong conclusion."

"No problem." Keith kicked off his topsiders and pushed the shoes against the wall.

Brodie looked at his watch. There were still forty minutes to qualify for his bonus, but he was too exhausted to plea for help now.

"Do you have a couple of those to spare?" Brodie pointed to Keith's fake beer. "But the real deal?"

They sat down in the family room, an electronics haven for Keith and the kids. Keith retrieved a couple of beers. Brodie took a long swallow, the Arctic cold liquid burned as it went down. Heaven. He told the story of why they had paid a visit to Keith's neighbors, starting with the letter today.

"But wait," Emma said, "that isn't how the son died. It wasn't a camping trip. She accidentally backed the car over him. The husband was supposed to be watching the boy but didn't notice he'd slipped out the front door to find his mother."

"That's horrible," said Karen. "I recall you mentioning the accident, just not the particulars."

"Why would she make up a story about a camping trip, being stoned, and finding her son strangled by his binoculars?" Keith asked his wife. Her collection of self-help books and a sales job at Bristol-Myers Squibb, presumably, made her the most qualified to speculate.

Emma shrugged. She lifted the lid from a wooden box decorated with an inlaid mother-of-pearl mosaic to reveal a pack of Virginia Slims and Bic lighter.

"Mind?" she asked.

Yes, he did, but Brodie shook his head as did Karen. Emma's first drag on the cigarette burned the paper down about a half inch. She was a seasoned smoker. Her lab test results for the life insurance quote would have made her a standard risk. If she were still on Prozac, she would have been knocked down to substandard. Keith would not have been thrilled about the cost of her policy. Blessed with so much, as were his brother and his wife—three beautiful kids, a house decorated to the hilt, her beauty, his success—why the cigarettes, the antidepressants, the canceled dinners with brief explanations? Sure, they both worked a shitload. They had a son who was pretty damn compulsive about his toys and shoes and food and hair, generally everything in his immediate world, and who held some bizarre fascination with the cat's litter box, claiming he could diagnose Oreo's health problems by touching and sniffing her dried turds. Undoubtedly, the house and all these coordinated Crate and Barrel throw pillows, lamps, sofas, and their other must-have stuff had them in debt up to their expensive haircuts. At the end of the week, though, they still had each other. They had a roof over their heads and enough money to keep the electricity on. That, Brodie thought, was more than enough.

Half listening to Emma, he thought about how life had so often felt like one big struggle. Every single, lousy day of recent months. Emotionally, physically, and mentally. He recalled an eerie painting he once saw at the MOMA of a woman skating alone on shattered glass. Karen and Sasha had moved on to the next gallery, yet he stood there transfixed, looking at the woman as she appeared on the verge of toppling. The artist had depicted utter hopelessness in the woman's face, in her posture, in her dismal surroundings. He could feel her last wish: to lie down and bleed until she finally stopped hurting. In his mind he saw his client, Scott Zabat, take that fatal dive off the overpass. There was his stalker. Betty. Andrea. All hurting. All tired. All just wanting . . . what exactly, he wasn't sure.

"That story makes them sound negligent," Karen said.

Emma craned her neck to blow the smoke behind the sofa. "Maybe she wanted to hide her identity. Anyone with half a brain would have eventually put you and Keith together."

Keith sneezed loudly. He noticed the silver fillings in his brother's molars had been replaced with veneer caps. Keith hadn't made one installment on the money he owed them, and yet he could shell out thousands for cosmetic dental work. *God, where did all this resentment come from?* Brodie wondered. He was getting to the point where he could not even stand himself.

"I've got some news for you, Bro," Keith said. "We're done with that other stuff, right? The neighbors?" He was sitting on the edge of his chair, fists clenched, and knees knocking together in rapid succession.

"The suicidal wife and knife-wielding husband," Brodie said, rolling his eyes at his brother. "I suppose we are. What's up with you? You're grinning as if you just won the Mega Millions."

"Bro, *we* almost did," he said. "*We* were this close . . ." He held up his hand, his thumb and index finger an inch apart: the familiar This Close gesture. "We nearly hit the winning numbers in spades. But still, as of three o'clock this afternoon, CloudFire is now the proud baby of

Google." He double punched the air as if he were a kid striking a piñata with his fist.

Brodie was stunned. Keith had done it. Brodie had done squat with his own life, and here was his little brother—one of the Silicon Valley little guys who had built and sold a business to the internet behemoth. He chugged down the rest of his Heineken and said, "That's great. You can spare another beer then."

"We can do better than that." Keith jumped up from the chair and headed to the kitchen, doing a two-step jig every few steps.

Karen faced Emma. "What does this mean? Rich, really rich, or insanely—"

"Not quite in that latter neighborhood. But enough to fund the kids' college and pay off the creditors and employees AND back Keith's new idea he has about building bomb shelters for the rich." Emma took a drag off her cigarette, extinguished it, and grabbed her lighter. "Supposedly, it's becoming a booming specialized business."

Brodie could hear Keith in the kitchen, opening the fridge, cabinets, and drawers. Glasses clanked. Silverware rattled. He texted Sasha to tell her that they had stopped off at her uncle's house and would be home later. She responded with a thumbs-up emoji.

"Honey, where's the . . . oh, never mind." He snickered and slammed a drawer shut singing, "I feel good, dun nan a nan" in his cute, off-key way.

Hearing how over the moon excited his brother was, Brodie realized he needed to get his head out of his ass and be happy for him. Keith would not have been sitting here, begrudging his brother if the situation were reversed. Say if Brodie had landed the health insurance account for the California Transportation Authority. He went to help Keith in the kitchen as Emma and Karen began debating whether it was even worth surviving a nuclear disaster given that everything—water, food, basically our entire world—would become poisoned.

Keith was at the sink staring at his phone.

"Everything okay?" Brodie asked.

His brother grinned and slipped the phone into his pocket. "Just reading a text from one of the attorneys. Dude's wasted. Hope he doesn't spend his fee in one night buying drinks and hookers."

"I'm proud of you." Brodie slapped Keith on the back. "Must admit I'm envious, but I know you've worked hard, you went for it and look what you've done. Amazing. My brother is now one of those guys who sold a startup to Google."

"Not bad, eh?" Keith peeled the foil off the bottle of Mums.

"Does this mean I'll get my twenty grand back now? I wouldn't bring it up if the need weren't dire."

"Oh, man, I'm sorry. I never got together with you on those insurance policies. This week's been all-nighters. Today it was non-stop with the lawyers and bankers, crossing the t's and dotting i's, and all that bullshit. I didn't mean to string you along." He twisted the cork and aimed the bottle at the far corner of the kitchen. "Bombs away!"

One loud pop and the cork took flight, ricocheting off the ceiling and hitting a frosted globe on the chrome-plated chandelier. The globe crashed to the terracotta tiled floor. The cork landed in a bowl of unshelled peanuts. Fragments of glass danced at their feet.

"Oh, shit." Keith covered his mouth to muffle the giggles. In an instant, they were two scrawny kids, laughing and hiding in the bushes after having just thrown rocks at the streetlamp.

"What's going on in there?" Emma called out. "Are you trying to wake the kids?"

Brodie laughed harder because if the shattered glass did not wake the kids, surely Emma's yelling would. The cat hobbled in on three paws to investigate the noise.

"Hey there, Oreo," Brodie said, scratching him under his chin.

"Just a little collateral damage," Keith called out to Emma. "Looks as if we finally get to replace this hideous light fixture."

"So how much money?" Brodie asked, thinking Keith was the next billionaire.

"After all is said and done, about ten mil. The numbers started higher, but then it turned out they were working on something in-house that made what we were doing somewhat redundant. But still, they must have figured they would get us under one roof. You know what this means though? Next time! I just have a feeling that it's going to keep getting better."

"I hope you're right." Brodie rubbed the tense muscles around his neck. "Nix that. I know you're right. If one of us Marshalls can do it, you're the man!"

They rejoined Emma and Karen in the living room. Brodie noticed there were three cigarette butts in the ashtray and Emma was reaching, again, for the wooden box. He grabbed the box and held it high above his head.

"You need to stop this habit before it kills you, my dear."

"Don't you start, too." She picked up her glass of champagne.

He recalled a comment in one of his stalker's letters, where she mentioned her neighbor constantly yelling at the kids. He looked closer and saw more fatigue than usual in her brown eyes. With the box hidden behind his back, he picked up a glass and listened as Keith offered a toast.

"Here's to family," he said, holding up a bottle of Perrier for himself. "Here's to standing by each other, never saying 'You're wasting your time.'"

"To the moon, my brother," Brodie added, clinking glasses.

After one and a half glasses, he was feeling a mighty buzz. Dinner had long since digested, and his stomach was starting to growl. He hoped that Karen wasn't too drunk to drive, because he sure as hell didn't want to add a DUI to the day's recap. Keith and Emma walked them to the door. They both looked exhausted.

Before he turned to leave, he said to Keith, "Remember how we'd get a can of cashews for birthdays and Christmas."

Keith smiled and slipped his arm around Emma's shoulders.

"At first we thought it was a joke," Brodie told Emma and Karen. "We figured our foster parents were just trying to trick us into believing that was all we were getting, that the real gifts were still hidden in a closet. We never had much money, especially after our dad split, but at least with our mom there were real gifts under the tree. When we realized it wasn't a joke, all we were getting was a can of broken nuts, not even the expensive whole nut variety, it became a contest to see who could put on the best, most convincing face at birthdays and holidays. It's hard, though, to fake excitement about another can of nuts."

"Is that why you hate cashews?" Karen asked.

"They give me gas." Brodie smirked as Emma wrinkled her nose. "But the thing is, they meant well. They may have preferred babies to two sassy teenage boys, but they never made us feel like unwanted guests in their home. And when we both finished high school, they gave us a choice, we could live with them for another six months free, or they would help us with a deposit for an apartment. They didn't have to do that. The state wasn't paying them to keep us longer. But they did and I've never forgotten that."

They all looked at Brodie as if confused by this tangent.

"Fact is, I've been consumed with resentment for months," he said, trying to weave together these thoughts. "Today's been one big pity-party. But there is something inspiring about seeing you so excited about *almost* becoming a billionaire. Celebrating that you got This Close." He mimicked his brother's earlier gesture. "I just need to go out there and make it happen."

"Love you, dude," Keith said. "I'll get that check to you tomorrow for the loan. Next week, we'll sign the paperwork for the life insurance. Promise." He tossed out "Promise" like a feather that would get swept away in the breeze and never land on Brodie's doorstep. His chest swelled with resentment. For all his talk about making it happen on his own, he still wanted Keith to bail him out of this bind.

"But babe," Emma said to Keith. "Didn't he need us to sign today to get his bonus?"

"It's fine." Brodie took Karen's hand. "We're all exhausted here."

Keith cracked his neck. "Oh, man. I'm sorry." He grabbed Brodie's arm. "Let me at least go grab a check for you for the twenty grand. Give me a sec."

brodie

THE MOOD IN THE CAR turned somber the instant their seatbelts clicked into place.

"Are you disappointed about the bonus?" Karen asked, starting the ignition.

He threw his head back and closed his eyes. "Yeah, but it's no one's fault but mine." He rubbed the now slight bump on his head from his morning run. The tenderness had subsided. "At least we got the twenty thousand back from Keith. Next year I'll start pushing the life policies earlier."

Karen nodded and stared at the neighbor's darkened house. Good luck to that unfortunate couple, he thought, wondering if Karen was thinking the same. She pulled away from the curb and said, "The details in her letter were way too specific. It's as if she wanted to write a different story, an alternate ending that had nothing to do with her or her son. Can you imagine if that were Sasha? Seeing her crushed by our car?"

"I'd kill myself."

Karen moved so quickly he didn't have time to duck before she whacked his arm. "Don't ever say that."

"Rewind, please. I would never do that to you."

They wrapped themselves in silence for the remainder of the drive.

It was just after midnight when they arrived home. Brodie felt jacked up. Though it had been at Karen's insistence that they try to save the stalker's life, he felt courageous now for having entered a stranger's house despite not knowing what danger or situation he might face. He had risked arrest, or worse, to help someone else. He turned out the lights in the living room and grabbed his laptop. He wasn't going to put things off any longer. It was time to start taking care of business.

"What are you doing now?" Karen asked as she climbed into bed and saw him typing on his phone.

"I've got two more things to take care of."

Instead of letting the call go to voice mail, as Brodie had hoped, Stan answered on the first ring. Brodie stammered, "Uh, hey Stan. Sorry to call so late."

"No worries. What's up?" Surprisingly, he sounded sober. Brodie thought Stan would have tied a major one on after his news this afternoon.

"I need your help with a claim. One of my client's life insurance claim was denied. Her husband, Scott Zabat, committed suicide. Underwriting is saying the guy didn't fully disclose his absences from work and some bullshit about some mental health issues. You think you could help me get this through underwriting. The widow has creditors barking at her doorstep."

"Sure. How about if I stop by tomorrow morning and we'll review the files. Do you have any notes that might help us?"

"I think so," Brodie lied. "Maybe not. But you can work your ol' Stan Magic."

Stan laughed. He loved flattery. "See you tomorrow about ten."

Brodie set the phone down and grinned. He imagined the email from the underwriter: "In light of this new information, we'll reopen the claim." Next, he pulled up the Zabat's account on his laptop. He clicked on the email icon and started typing.

"Who are you emailing?"

"Hang on. I'm going to . . ." His words trailed off. *Dear Mrs. Zabat, I spoke with the District Manager. We are meeting tomorrow to review your claim. I can't make any promises, but if anyone can sway underwriting, it's him. I will call you tomorrow with an update.*

A few seconds after he hit send, his laptop pinged with a new message.

"Who is that from?" Karen asked.

It was from Mrs. Zabat. *Thank you. You can't imagine what a relief it would be to have them reverse their decision.*

"Do you think you might be giving her false hope?" Karen asked, reading over Brodie's shoulder.

"Maybe. But I'm going to fight for her and see if we can do what the policy was set up to do." He opened a new email. It felt good to take charge instead of simply bemoaning his situation.

Karen frowned. "Who are you writing to now? Obama?" She watched as he started an email, then as he deleted everything and began again.

Dear Betty, I feel like a total shit. A coward, in fact. Our friendship means a lot to me. You have always been there for me. I should have acted like a better friend today. Karen and I would love to have you for dinner next week.

He paused to see if he had Karen's okay. She nodded.

After hitting send, he put away the laptop and took Karen's hands between his.

"Here's a crazy idea . . . what if after Sasha settles into Stanford, we look into downsizing. We don't need this big house. We could get by on a lot less, and still have room for Sasha when she comes homes for holidays and summers."

Karen's eyebrows shot up.

"Could you really give up living next door to Mt. Diablo? You love being able to hike from our back yard."

"Agreed. There'd be some sacrifices."

"It would be nice, though, to have fewer bathrooms and floors to clean. Maybe I could get certified and start teaching some Pilates classes."

Brodie nodded. She would be excellent at teaching. The extra income would help. He blew out a long breath and said, "Seeing Keith's excitement today started me thinking. I want to do something else. I don't know what or how we'd afford for me to give up my agency. But maybe I could put in three to five more years of insurance, work it hard, and then do something that doesn't feel as if it's sucking the life out of me."

"A fresh start," Karen said, smiling.

"Yes, a fresh start."

jenny
2016

THE METAL CAFÉ TABLE wobbled when Jenny set down her coffee cup and purse. She held her daughter Evie tightly in her lap and leaned back in her chair to allow the sun's rays to warm her face. They were waiting outside the Solano Avenue bakery for their Uber. In one hand, her daughter held a chocolate muffin, and in the other, her mother's phone as she watched the animated car on the screen navigate through Albany's streets toward them.

"Finish your muffin before the Uber arrives," Jenny said, brushing a blonde curl from her daughter's hydrangea-blue eyes. Evie pulled away from her mother's hand, giggled, then leaned further into her embrace. Inhaling her daughter's sweet essence, Jenny knew the time would come, likely in the fall when Evie entered Kindergarten when her daughter would begin unwinding herself, little by little, from her parents' tight hold. But for now, on this sunny May morning, Jenny rested her chin on her daughter's head and thanked the universe for giving her this day.

A black Honda Accord matching the description on her phone pulled to the curb. Evie jumped out of Jenny's lap and handed her mother the phone. Under Jenny's watchful eyes, Evie ran to the garbage bin and tossed in her half-eaten muffin. Jenny checked the license plate, as Rhonda was always reminding her to do. She opened the door.

"Your name?" asked the driver.

"Jen," she answered. "And you're Michael?" She held open the door and watched her daughter climb across the back seat.

"Feet off the seat, sweetheart." The beige leather seats and rugs were immaculate.

"Headed to Toyota on Broadway," the driver confirmed, looking back at her through the rearview mirror.

Jenny nodded. Her phone pinged with a text message. "Hey. Have you picked up the RAV yet?"

"On my way," she typed. Evie peered over. "It's daddy," Jenny said. "Want to send him a smiley face?" They scrolled through the emojis until Evie found her favorite. She tapped the face and Jerrod's next message appeared.

"Make sure they replaced the wipers."

"Will do."

"You and Miss Evie want to meet up for lunch?"

Pleased by the suggestion, Jenny said, "Want to meet daddy for lunch? Maybe he'll take us out for sushi." Evie scrunched up her nose. "Pizza, pizza!" she said, bouncing on her seat. For a moment, Jenny was reminded of her son, a brother whom Evie would never know, who loved to bounce on the sofa as he watched his favorite cartoons. She took a deep breath and texted back that they would be there around noon.

acknowledgements

I greatly appreciate the immense support and encouragement I have received during the writing of this novel.

Thank you to Sara Marks Brown, Amy Pennington, Ferrell Jennings, Rosalind Boukis, Sue Bleakley, Peggy Vincent, Derek Douglas, Ruth Rogow, Scott Bailey, Anna-Sophia Pretlow, Patricia Estorge, and the Book In A Year class for your feedback and close readings. A special thank you to Matt Bird. A very special thank you to Angela Dula—an incredible editor. For those friends who read various drafts, I am extremely grateful. Thank you to Debbie Hunter for sharing the story about the found wallet and subsequent anonymous letters.

The title of this book was borrowed from a former colleague, Shanna Campos, who said during a hectic accounting close, "Here we are, in the middle of otherwise." Thank you for this clever remark. For years, Lynne Meade and I walked around the Lafayette Reservoir, and she listened patiently to my frustrations and breakthroughs in writing this novel. I appreciate her constant encouragement.

A special gratitude to David Provolo for designing a beautiful book and to Avery Stratford for taking dozens of photos until we found our favorite. Immense gratitude to Judith Estorge for your unending support and hand-selling.

To my sons, Avery and Burgess Stratford, I am eternally grateful for your unending love and support. You fill my life with joy.

To my readers, thank you for spending time in my imaginary world and with characters I dreamed into being. I appreciate your support.

Marie Estorge is a member of the Squaw Valley Community of Writers. Her essays have appeared in numerous publications, including the *San Francisco Chronicle, East Bay Times*, and *Diablo Magazine*. She has published two memoirs, *Storkbites: A Memoir* and *Confessions of a Bi-Polar Mardi Gras Queen*, under the name Marie Etienne. Marie lives in Northern California with her two sons.